BLOOD STORM

BLOOD STORM

COLIN FORBES

**POCKET
BOOKS**

London · New York · Sydney · Toronto

First published in Great Britain by Simon & Schuster UK Ltd, 2004
This edition first published by Pocket Books, 2005
An imprint of Simon & Schuster UK Ltd
A CBS COMPANY

5 7 9 10 8 6 4

Simon & Schuster UK Ltd
Africa House
64–78 Kingsway
London WC2B 6AH

www.simonsays.co.uk

Simon & Schuster Australia
Sydney

MYS Pbk

A CIP catalogue record for this book is available from
the British Library.

ISBN-10: 0-7434-9584-5
ISBN-13: 978-0-7434-9584-4

Typeset by SX Composing DTP, Rayleigh, Essex
Printed and bound in Great Britain by
Cox & Wyman Ltd, Reading, Berkshire

Author's Note

This novel takes place some time in the near future.

All the characters portrayed are creatures of the author's imagination and bear no relationship or resemblance to any living person.

The same principle of pure invention applies to all buildings, headquarters, residences, hotels, villages, institutions and apartments in Great Britain and France.

For Lydia

BLOOD STORM

Prologue

Tweed was dining with a beautiful and very frightened woman. As he cut into his Dover sole he glanced across their table. Her thick blonde hair fell to her bare shoulders. Only her slim arms were exposed by her expensive close-fitting purple dress. Tweed, picking up his glass of wine, held it without drinking.

'You strike me as a lady in need of protection,' he probed. 'Something – somebody – is disturbing you. I gathered from Bob Newman you wanted to meet me to seek advice.'

'As Deputy Director of the SIS – and once a top detective at Old Scotland Yard – your advice is why we are here. I am very worried about the attentions of a very powerful man.'

'His name?'

'I don't feel I can reveal that yet. I could be wrong.'

'Which gets us nowhere.'

Tweed glanced round Mungano's, the most fashionable restaurant in London, checking on the other diners. The place was almost full; it was an octagon-shaped room overlooking the Thames. Tweed had asked for a quiet table, and they were seated in a corner away from the babble of voices, the clinking of glasses.

Mungano's, named after the proprietor, had only been open for five months, and already you had to be known to secure a table, or book one weeks in advance. Waiters were in the majority, but Mungano had recently brought in waitresses, smartly clad in evening dress. No uniforms.

'I have to think it over,' Viola explained. 'I do hope you don't think I'm wasting your time.'

'Hardly, when I have the pleasure of dining with such a very attractive woman.'

Tweed smiled, raised his glass to hers, studied her as they drank. In her early forties, Viola had an almost perfectly shaped bone structure. Below her blonde eyebrows were large blue eyes, a Roman nose, sensuous lips, a chin which expressed character. Her voice was soft and appealing. Tweed recalled how this meeting had come about that morning, in his office at SIS headquarters on the first floor of an old building in Park Crescent.

'Got a favour to ask you,' Bob Newman, a key member of his SIS team, had suggested the moment

Tweed settled behind his desk.

'It had better be worthwhile,' Tweed said abruptly.

'Someone I know slightly may have information about the Cabal. She's a beauty, Viola Vander-Browne. You may have heard of her.'

'No.'

'She's very well educated. Roedean and all that. But not one of your society types who can't talk about anything but fashion and the latest boyfriend.'

The Cabal. The two words summed up the greatest crisis Tweed had ever faced in his career. Three men, all junior ministers, the driving force behind a new plan to merge the SIS, MI5, the police and the coastguards into one security force – to be known as State Security.

The very words sent shivers down Tweed's spine. He had already expressed his unreserved opposition to the idea. It was a giant step towards turning Britain into a police state.

'How does this Viola Vander-Browne come into the picture?' he demanded.

'I gather she knows one of the Cabal. No idea which one. She wants to talk to you. I couldn't get a word out of her – she insists on seeing the top man. You.'

'I'm not sure this is a good idea,' Tweed responded.

'She's an acquaintance of mine . . .' Newman began.

'His new word for a girlfriend,' teased Paula Grey, who was seated in a corner behind her computer. Paula was Tweed's top assistant and a forceful member of the SIS team. An attractive brunette with dark glossy hair which fell to her shoulders, she was the closest of anyone to Tweed, who admired her brilliance.

Newman, almost six feet tall, with a strong face which appealed to women, was in his early forties. Dark haired, he smiled a lot, and he responded to Paula's remark with a gentle punch to her shoulder. She reacted instantly with a clenched fist which hammered hard into his.

'As I was saying,' Newman went on, addressing Tweed, 'Viola has a flat in Fox Street off Covent Garden. She's well off, with a legacy left her when her parents were killed in a car crash. But sometimes she likes to add to her income.' He paused.

'How?' demanded Tweed.

'Don't get the wrong impression, but occasionally she'll have a wealthy man in her flat for the night. She's so good at the feminine arts she charges her visitor twenty thousand pounds. I gather they're happy to pay.'

'I see,' Paula remarked, 'she's a high-class call girl.'

'She isn't!' Newman snapped, turning on Paula. 'You really are very Victorian.'

'You know I'm not,' Paula snapped back. 'I adapt

to the circumstances. I could throw this computer at you.'

'That's enough, both of you,' Tweed barked. 'Any more data on Viola, Bob? You suspect one of her men friends belongs to the Cabal? Is that it?'

'I'm not sure. But she does want to see you to tell you something. I knew you'd think it was a good idea. I've booked a discreet table for the two of you at Mungano's, your new favourite restaurant.'

'Without consulting me. All right, you had to act on the spur of the moment. What time this evening?'

'Seven o'clock. She likes to get to bed early. I only got the table when I mentioned your name to Mungano himself.'

'All right,' Tweed agreed brusquely.

He had no idea he had committed himself to one of the most horrific episodes of his life.

Newman's data passed through Tweed's mind as he studied Viola over dessert. He became aware she was studying him. She saw a man with horn-rimmed glasses resting on the bridge of a strong nose, blue eyes she felt could see inside her, a firm mouth half-smiling and a determined jaw. He exuded shrewdness and physical vitality. She thought he was beginning to like her.

'Do you know many people – people who count and have power?' he asked.

'If you're talking about celebrities, as they're stupidly called these days, no. I avoid them like the plague. They are nobodies puffed up by the media. The people I know and mix with are intelligent.'

'Any people of power I might know?' he persisted.

A waitress carrying a tray appeared at their table, placed a glass in front of Tweed, another in front of Viola. 'Yours is a margarita,' she told Tweed, 'and Madame's is champagne. Compliments of the management.'

Then she was gone. Tweed had a glimpse of a tall slim woman in a black dress, black hair coiffed close to her head like a dark helmet. He looked at his drink, then at Viola.

'The last time I drank a margarita a thug tried to shove me out of my window in Lübeck on the Baltic. It opened on to an inner courtyard. It ended up with my throwing the thug three storeys down on to solid stone.'

He sipped at the drink slowly, absorbing no more than a fifth of it. Something odd about the taste. Viola reached over with a finger, the nail well trimmed and varnished with a delicate pink. She removed a small amount of the salt round the rim, tasted it.

'Salt!' she remarked with surprise.

'It's part of a proper margarita. Ever tasted one? It's very strong unless you're used to drinking.'

'I would have asked for a sip but I'm driving back

to my flat.' She glanced at her watch. 'If you don't mind I'd better get moving. I do hope you're not annoyed that I haven't said much but I feel I'd better think it over. I could be wrong.'

'Wrong about what is frightening you?'

'I'm OK. I'm always nervous when I'm having dinner with someone new for the first time . . .'

No, you're not, Tweed thought. You have the poise of the devil. Don't push her any more, he warned himself.

By now Tweed was feeling dizzy and unwell. He had to concentrate on signing the bill. He had intended to escort Viola home to her flat but he was wondering whether he was capable of driving his car safely. He made a great effort to stand upright as he followed Viola to the exit.

Arriving at the outside world she pointed to a Rolls-Royce Phantom with a uniformed attendant from Mungano's standing guard beside it. She turned, threw her arms round Tweed's neck and kissed him.

'That was the most delicious evening. The company was even better. Already I feel I've known you ages. When I've had time to think things over can we meet again, please?'

She had a gold-bordered card in her hand which she tucked into the top pocket of his overcoat. 'My private number. But I'll probably call you. Bob gave me the number. I like you . . .'

Her velvet coat swinging, she strode across to her car, tipped the attendant. Another attendant had brought Tweed's Ford to the kerb by the entrance. Unhappily, Tweed watched Viola wave, drive off. He concentrated on climbing behind the wheel. What the hell am I going to do now? I'm not fit to drive back to my flat. Then he remembered an obscure cul-de-sac lined with warehouses only a few yards away. Park there, he thought, until I recover.

With a supreme effort of will he fitted the key into the ignition, started the engine. He looked every-where before moving. No traffic in sight, no sound of it. He had lowered his window and cold March air swept inside. He took deep breaths, felt a little better. He began moving. Slowly.

Arriving at the entrance to the narrow cul-de-sac, he cautiously reversed into it. Once he had the car concealed inside he switched off the engine. It was absolutely silent inside the alcove-like street.

He began to shiver, closed the window, locked all the doors. He was feeling worse now, on the verge of falling asleep. He checked his watch. The illuminated hands showed 10.30 p.m. His last thought was to think about Viola. Was she safely home in Fox Street? Why was he so worried about her? Then he lost consciousness, falling into a deep sleep.

1

Thud . . .
  Brief pause.
  Thud . . .
  Pause.
  Thud . . .
Inside the bedroom of her flat in Fox Street, Viola
lay naked on the floor, a gag tied round her mouth.
She had been attacked the moment she entered the
bedroom and switched on the light. A handkerchief
lightly soaked in chloroform had been pressed over
her face from behind. Her unseen assailant had
carried her half-limp figure to the far side of the bed.
She was dumped on the floor, began to regain consciousness. A latex-covered hand had lifted her head,
slammed it down – not too hard. The towel gag had
been applied to her mouth. She was vaguely aware of
something awful happening to her, then the weight
lifted off her. She opened her eyes.

A weird figure stood over her. Clad in a surgeon's white gown, white cap, white mask over the face, huge goggles clamped over the eyes. She couldn't tell whether it was a man or a woman. Terror gripped her as she saw the gloved hand lift a meat cleaver.

Lifted high, the cleaver descended. Thud . . . It severed her left arm just below the elbow. She almost fainted, but the pain was so excruciating she stayed conscious. The lower arm slid a few inches free of the elbow.

Thud . . .

The cleaver descended again, swiftly and with immense force. It sliced off the right arm below the elbow. So great was the force the blade cut straight through bone and muscle, embedded itself into the floorboard. The wielder of the blade had to wrench it strongly to release it from the wood.

Thud . . .

The left leg was severed cleanly below the knee. Viola's upper body was now shuddering. Her sharp teeth were tearing at the gag, now only a reflex action.

Thud . . .

The right leg below the knee was parted from the rest of the body. A lake of blood slithered over the floor. The figure clad in white also wore outsize thick white canvas covers over its normal shoes.

Viola's teeth ripped open the gag. Her mouth opened wide on the verge of a terrible yell.

Time to complete the exercise.

Thud . . .

The cleaver descended through her neck, separating head from body, just before Viola let out a yell of hell. The blow had severed the carotid arteries. An enormous spurt of blood jetted across the room, splashed all over the frosted-glass window overlooking the street.

The white-clad figure sighed aloud, pulled up a sleeve, checked the time. 11.15 p.m. Time to make the arrangement, then leave quickly.

2

Slumped behind the wheel of his stationary car, Tweed stirred. Where was he? Memory of the dinner with Viola flooded back, then feeling so strange as they left Mungano's. He straightened up, worked his arms, found he felt normal. Almost normal enough to drive. He checked the time: 6 a.m. God!

He could hardly credit it – he'd slept seven and a half hours. He drove very slowly, emerging from the cul-de-sac. The street was empty. He knew he could now drive safely. Even so he crawled back to the mews near his flat where he had hired a garage for a small fortune.

Locking the door, he paused to glance everywhere. No sign of a soul. He felt better. The cold early morning air was welcome. He began to stride quickly across the cobbled mews to the exit. A mistake. He still felt wobbly.

Arriving in Bexford Street, lined with tall old

terraced houses, he climbed the steps to his heavy wooden front door. A street lamp on the deserted pavement provided illumination to find the Banham lock.

As he wrestled his keys from an inner pocket he stared at the lock. There were gouge marks round it. Someone had tried to get inside during the night. He had trouble turning the key. Someone had entered his flat. Twiddling with his key he managed to turn it. He opened the door silently.

Once inside, he closed the door without switching on any lights, stood listening. Not a sound. He moved slowly along the hall, his hand counting the panels in the wall to his right. Reaching number four he paused, pressed his thumb three times against a corner, waited, pressed twice, then three times again. The panel slid back. He reached in, grasped the loaded Walther automatic, closed the coded panel, felt his way past the drawing-room door, began to climb the stairs cautiously. Although it was called a flat he owned the entire four storeys. He avoided stepping on the stair tread which creaked, reached the first floor. His bedroom door was not quite closed. After dressing for his dinner with Viola he had been in a hurry, but he still took precautions. Standing to one side of the door he reached inside, turned on the main light. He went inside quickly, gripping his Walther, stared all round. Nothing. His head was playing tricks on him again. He cursed, closed the door, staggered over to his bed, jerked off the top cover on to the floor. He was on the verge of collapse.

Making a great effort, he pulled off his shoes, threw off his overcoat, slipped the Walther under the pillow. Tearing off his tie, opening his collar, he sank on to the bed, switched off the light, lost consciousness.

Paula, determined to start work early, was driving down the short cut which was Bexford Street. She parked outside Tweed's home. She'd leave him a note through the letterbox to tell him what she was doing.

Climbing the steps, her alert eyes instantly noticed gouge marks round the lock. Someone must have tried to break in while Tweed was dining with Viola. She took out the duplicate key he had given her, had trouble turning it in the lock. Before she entered quietly she hauled out the Browning .32 automatic from the holster beneath her thigh-length raincoat.

She closed the front door carefully, walked noiselessly along the hall. Reaching the living-room door, she listened, then stood to one side as she threw it wide open. Her other hand found the switch and she was inside, swivelling her Browning in all directions. No one. No sign the intruder had been in here.

She mounted the stairs, stepping over the creaking tread. Pressing an ear against Tweed's bedroom door, she heard the sound of loud snoring. He never snored. Extracting her powerful torch from her coat pocket, she opened the door, swept her beam quickly. Tweed was lying on his back, eyes closed, which was not normal. His breathing was regular, which was reassuring. She aimed the beam over the front part of the bedroom, froze. Perched on a side table a silver candlestick lay on its side, resting on a folded duster – which would have cushioned the sound. One drawer of a chest of drawers was not fully closed.

Paula knew that Tweed was fastidiously neat in his housekeeping. He would never have left the candle-stick like that if he had caught it with his arm. He would never have left one of the drawers partially open. She made her way across to the front of the room, turned on a shaded table lamp, turned off her torch, set to work.

Seven drawers, the deepest at the bottom. She began with the top one, opened it, searched carefully through piles of handkerchiefs and scarves. Nothing. The partly closed drawer also contained nothing unusual. It was only when she opened the large drawer at the bottom that she found under a pile of shirts what had been planted.

A large old briefcase, not one of Tweed's, was stuffed full – it bulged. Paula put on latex gloves, lifted out the briefcase, unfastened the catch. She sucked in her breath. Inside was a large transparent envelope containing a meat cleaver, the blade coated with a reddish tinge which she knew was dried blood. Inside a smaller transparent envelope were small pieces of dried flesh, also stained with blood.

She reacted quickly. After re-checking the drawer, she carried the briefcase to the window. She heard a car pull up outside. Scared stiff, she doused the table lamp and peered out. Bob Newman's Range Rover was parked outside. He was half out of the front door, peering up. She grabbed her torch, switched it on, held it under her chin, then flashed it urgently. He was jumping out of the car as she headed for the stairs.

'I was just passing and Tweed is often up early—' Newman began.

'Someone is trying to frame Tweed for some crime I don't like the look of one little bit,' she interrupted him. 'Evidence is inside this thing . . .'

She handed him the briefcase, which he took from her without question. He ran back to his car as she closed the door and hurried upstairs, worried in case Tweed had woken, was wondering what was going on. Arriving back in the bedroom she found Tweed still fast asleep. She hurried to the window in time to see Newman was trapped.

Newman shoved the briefcase under his seat as a dark car came round the corner. Its lights, on full beam, focused on him. It stopped, barring his way. A tall

16

man clad in a long black coat ran up to him. Round the left arm of his coat which he perched on Newman's open window was a wide armlet with two words in white embroidered on it: State Security.

'Out of the car. Now! Hands on your shoulders,' he ordered savagely.

His hat was pulled well down over his face, but not low enough to conceal a hooked nose, a thin grim mouth, a V-shaped chin. His other hand was reaching inside the coat.

'Don't do that,' Newman told him, his Smith & Wesson aimed point-blank at the thug.

Newman ripped off the armlet. Evidence. He thrust the long barrel of the Smith & Wesson through the window and struck the thug hard across the side of the face, probably breaking a cheekbone. The thug screamed, moved back, tripped over the kerb. He fell backwards on to the pavement.

Newman was already backing away from the dark car at speed. He switched to 'drive', rammed his foot down, shot forward. The ram on his vehicle was special steel. It hit the dark car, still stopped partly sideways. The collision was ferocious as the ram smashed into the other car's bonnet, destroying the engine. In his rear-view mirror Newman saw another dark car approaching from behind. He reversed at high speed.

His rear ram, also reinforced steel, hit the new

target when it was half-turning into Bexford Street out of a side street. He had more space to do the job this time, therefore more speed. The impact was so violent the second black car was spun round in a half-circle, clearing the entrance to the side street. Newman turned the wheel, sped off.

'I have to get out of London before traffic builds,' he said to himself.

He had already decided where he would head for.

3

The Cabal was assembled in an obscure building down a side street off Whitehall. It comprised three junior ministers with great influence higher up the power chain. The three men worked well together – most of the time. The fact that they were brothers, the offspring of the brilliant and notorious General Macomber, hero of the Gulf War, helped.

'By now Tweed should be out of the picture, reputation smeared forever. It is the first major step in the merger,' remarked Nelson Macomber.

'We should have a report on the operation,' reported Noel Macomber, known as the Planner. 'The scandal will destroy our major opponent.' His lean grim face expressed his satisfaction at the prospect.

The three brothers were a contrast. Nelson was six feet five tall, heavily built, in his forties, his shoulders wide, his striking head large, clean shaven. His eyes were ice blue beneath thick black hair and thick brows. His strong nose was well shaped and below it his wide mouth and jaw suggested energy and determination.

'We should damned well have had confirmation by now,' said Benton, his voice quiet, his thick fingers tapping the table.

The third brother was also well built but shorter than Nelson. He spoke only occasionally, but his reserved manner appealed to women. He was the most cautious of the brothers, taking nothing for granted until it was achieved.

The three men were seated in tapestry-covered chairs at the peculiar table. It was triangular, to stress that none of the three was in charge. The phone rang. Noel's slim-fingered hand grabbed it, listened.

'Are you sure?' he demanded. 'A slip-up? You mean you botched the job. Get back here immediately, you clumsy fool.' He ended the call, gently replacing the phone.

'You spoke too quickly, Nelson,' he said with malicious satisfaction on his spade-shaped face. There was a certain competitiveness between the three brothers. 'Whatever compromising item was delivered to Tweed has been snatched away from his house.'

'Snatched away?' Nelson rumbled. 'Don't take all year to report what happened.'

'Newman arrived and grabbed a briefcase from the Paula Grey woman.'

'Newman again!' Nelson leaned forward. 'That man has become as dangerous as Tweed. What about the troops you sent in two cars?'

'Newman was in a four-wheel-drive built like a tank. He smashed up both cars then took off . . .'

'They should have pursued him,' Nelson rasped. 'That's what they have been trained for.'

'How could they?' Noel asked with a sneering smile. 'Both cars were put out of action.'

'The war has started, then,' Benton said calmly. 'So what is the next move?'

'When the stick hasn't worked we try the carrot,' Nelson suggested, now as calm as Benton. 'I will visit Tweed and explain the position. I shall ask him to join us in the merger.'

'He'll never agree,' snapped Noel.

'It's all a question of persuasion. I'll explain to him the inevitable and offer him the post of deputy-in-chief. I shall make a point of going to see him this morning. So, you agree, gentlemen?'

'It would be the best tactic at this stage,' Benton commented.

'I do not like moves made on the spur of the moment,' said Noel, the Planner.

'You're not observant either,' Nelson whispered.

He put a finger to his lips, stood up without making

a sound, padded towards the closed door leading to the inner offices. The door wasn't completely shut. Open a few inches. He knew he had closed the door before the meeting had started.

Opening the door slowly, he slipped into the next room, a very large space without any of the comfort of the Cabal's HQ. A slim girl, at least five feet nine tall, was crouched over a computer, neatly dressed in black, as if in uniform. Nelson closed the door behind him silently, padded across to her. She spoke without turning round.

'I don't like men who creep up on me. What's the beef?'

'Did you open the door to our sanctum?'

She straightened up, swivelled round, her brown eyes blazing. She had dark hair, well coiffeured, an attractive face with full lips. She was not smiling.

'Are you accusing me of eavesdropping, you absent swine?'

'No, of course not.'

'When are you taking me out again, while we're on the subject?'

Saying which, she flung her arms round his neck, pulled him close. They began kissing passionately until she pushed him away.

'Well, answer the friggin' question. My patience is running out.'

'Soon . . .'

'Soon? It had better be . . .'

'Miss Partridge,' a voice called from the open door to the room beyond. She called back that she was coming when she'd finished with the computer.

Changing her mind, she closed down the machine. She strode off into the next room without giving Nelson another look. It was then he noticed a small girl seated in a corner looking over some files. Coral Flenton, also in the Civil Service and Partridge's assistant, a red-haired girl with hazel eyes and a nice smile. He decided he'd better have a word and walked over.

'You didn't notice anything happening a moment ago, did you?'

'Mr Macomber . . .' She swung round on her swivel seat. 'Nothing has happened here for hours. Except Freaky-Deaky has been throwing her weight around as usual.'

Freaky-Deaky. Nelson knew that was one of the universal nicknames for Zena Partridge even in the sanctum. She was a control-freak, hence her nick-name, and also known as the Parrot. He flapped his hands and smiled back.

'She does come down a bit heavy at times. She does have a ton of responsibility. Especially to us. Keep your chin up . . .'

Returning to his HQ, he closed the door carefully, sat down and stared round the table. Neither of his brothers said a word. They couldn't possibly have heard any of his conversation with Partridge. The slightly open door still bothered him.

'We've heard a lot of confidential data while that door wasn't completely closed. Refresh my memory.'

'Very confidential,' Noel agreed, his voice high-pitched. 'The water-cannon delivery at Harber's Yard near Tolhaven. The tough training by the team at Harber's Yard. We went into it in some detail. All the details, in fact. You came through that door last. You'll have to be a damn sight more careful in future, brother.'

'Don't call me brother,' Nelson warned with menacing quietness.

'Time to change the subject,' Benton said gently.

'I have decided positively on my next move,' Nelson said firmly. 'In fact, within the hour.'

'Which is?' asked Noel, his V-shaped features compressing into a frown.

'To go over on to the attack,' Nelson said off-handedly, knowing his brother was desperate to keep his fingers on every development. 'You're not the only one who can plan, dear boy.'

'Don't ever call me that again.' In his fury Noel leapt to his feet. 'Did you hear me?' he shouted as Nelson left the room by the outer door as though he hadn't heard.

'No point in getting in a rage,' Benton said quietly.

He spent half his time keeping the peace and he was getting tired of his role as peacemaker.

'I'm checking next door,' Noel snapped.

He opened the door which led into the civil servants' area. No sign of the Parrot. In her corner, diminutive Coral Flenton was bent over her computer. She could see who was coming in the mirror artfully placed on her desk. She made a point of pretending not to notice as Noel hurried over to her.

'Flenton, how long have you been seated at your desk?'

'Ever since I came in. Sir,' she added after a pause.

'Are you sure about that statement?' he asked with a sneer. 'Not been to the loo or any of the other things women take it into their tiny heads to do?'

'I have just answered your question. Sir.'

'All right, then. Get up for a change and bring us some coffee and cakes. Two of us. Get cracking, girl.'

He swung round and headed back for the sanctum. Since he hadn't eyes in the back of his head he missed the look of pure hatred on Coral's face as she left her desk.

I'll go home and change first, Nelson said to himself. And I'll go to see Tweed afterwards in the Merc. Important to display a show of power to Tweed in his hideaway in Park Crescent.

'Home first,' he ordered his chauffeur, Jeff, seated with the guard in the alcove close to the front door. When they arrived at his apartment in Mayfair he leapt out of the car almost before it had pulled up, a habit which always worried Jeff. Couldn't say a word to Nelson Macomber, who went his own way and ignored servants.

Entering the apartment on the first floor after skipping up the stairs like a ten-year-old, Nelson was annoyed to find his wife, Loelia, daughter of an earl, dressed in her velvet suit on the verge of leaving.

Loelia, forty years old and a glamorous brunette, was not pleased to see him. He could tell from the downward slant of her full lips. She spoke rapidly.

'Don't close the door. You're home in the middle of your working day. You might have phoned me first.'

'Why?' He was heading for the bedroom. 'On your way to see your close friend Frederick?'

'Everyone else calls him Freddie . . .'

'To me the conceited playboy is Frederick.'

'He's not conceited,' she snapped, the downward slant of her mouth becoming more pronounced. 'He's got far better manners than you. Who is the cheap floozie you're visiting today? Jeanette would be my guess.'

'As usual you've guessed wrong. This is business. Where is my Armani suit?'

'You're staring at it. Don't forget to fold it neatly before you hop into bed.'

'Get the hell out of here,' he shouted.

'F— you,' she screamed, slamming the bedroom door behind her.

Nelson dressed quickly. He did everything quickly unless he was playing a political game. Then he spoke slowly and not often. He must remember to adopt that pose when he confronted Tweed.

4

In the early hours of the morning, Newman made fast progress down the motorway towards the south-west. Normally smiling, his face was set in a grim expression. Who had attempted to frame Tweed? And why? He had examined the contents of the briefcase during a brief stop, wearing latex gloves. I don't like the look of this one little bit, he thought, echoing Paula's earlier reaction.

Blazing lights came towards him in the murky dawn, the lights of heavy trucks. Newman had already decided which safe house he would use to hide the briefcase. During his stop he had also taken from his pocket the piece of folded paper handed to him by his informant before arriving at Tweed's house where the crisis had started.

Harber's Yard, on the coast south of Tolhaven.

He turned off the motorway to Tolhaven. Once, on a previous case with Tweed, he had visited Buckler's

Hard near Beaulieu. Was this new location the same sort of secretive place? He would find out. His informant seldom made any mistakes.

Reaching the hidden entrance to the safe house, close to the motorway, he parked the Range Rover in a field behind some trees. He was not confident that he had lost the sinister men in black uniforms.

The sky was still heavily overcast as he made his way up the footpath, overgrown with weeds, to the safe house, an isolated single-storey thatched cottage. He approached cautiously, circling the cottage, pausing for long minutes to listen. No sign of anyone.

He was now up above the motorway, and looking down he saw the chain of trucks' lights following each other to London. It was cold as he took out the key to open the shabby front door. It creaked resentfully as he pushed it open, went straight in, Smith & Wesson in his right hand. He had heard a faint sound of movement. There was no security in the cottage – it would have made the place look suspicious – and the sound he'd heard worried him.

He waited just inside the door, half hidden behind it, took out a powerful torch, listened again. There was the furtive sound again. Revolver in one hand, torch in the other, he switched it on. Startled eyes stared back at him. The fox took off, leapt through a broken window, was gone. He let out the breath he'd been holding.

He moved quickly. With the briefcase gripped under his strong arm, he hauled out the only solid chair from an old wooden table. Placing it in the middle of the room, he used the torch for illumination as he stood on the chair. Reaching up between the ancient cross-beams supporting the roof, he pushed at a panel in the wooden ceiling. He kept his eyes closed as dust floated down. Pushing the panel to one side, his hands were covered in spiders' webs. Feeling to his right, he lifted an ancient trunk containing old clothes, slid the briefcase under it, lowered the trunk, closed the panel, stepped down on to the floor. Before he opened his eyes he took out a handkerchief, wiped away a mess of dust and cobwebs.

He carefully replaced the chair in exactly the same place. Opening the creaking door to the outside, he stood listening. It had started to drizzle. He swore to himself, shrugged, went out and locked the door with the rusty key.

Fortunately he was wearing his rainproof jacket with a hood, which he pulled over his head. Tolhaven next – and the mystery of Harber's Yard.

Inside Tweed's flat Paula had completed a second search for incriminating objects. Nothing. Meanwhile, Tweed had taken a long shower, dried and shaved, then dressed. He was beginning to feel more normal. He walked into the bedroom to find the light on and

Paula peering down into the street.

'Another visitor,' she informed him. 'In a limo. It's Professor Saafeld, of all people. I'll go down, let him in . . .'

Tweed was walking up and down to check the stability of his movements when two pairs of feet clattered up the stairs. He was puzzled. Professor Saafeld, his friend, was the most eminent pathologist in Britain, called in by the police on major cases.

With bushy white hair the gnome-like professor, his eyes so alert even at this early hour, smiled as he came in carrying a bag, followed by Paula.

'On the bed,' he ordered Tweed. 'Stretch out.'

'What the hell for?' demanded Tweed.

'Do as you're told. Paula has given me a brief account of your adventures last night. You were drugged, I gather – in a margarita. Clever. That drink conceals most drugs. I'm giving you a blood test. Then I can analyse what was fed into you.'

He was extracting a large hypodermic needle as he spoke. Paula grabbed a towel from the bathroom, spread it on the bed so Tweed needn't take off his shoes. His sleeve rolled up, with a sigh Tweed allowed himself to be subjected to what he regarded as an unnecessary bother. Saafeld extracted his blood sample in no time, applied a sticking plaster, placed the needle in a white metal sleeve.

'Should be able to report to you what it was before

the end of the day,' he explained in his rapid way of speaking. 'I'm on my way to a particularly hideous murder, called in by your friend Commander Roy Buchanan.'

'Who was murdered?' asked Tweed.

'A Miss Viola Vander-Browne, at her flat in Covent Garden. Sounds like a psycho. All her limbs have been chopped off, and her head. The truly hideous aspect is the killer finished up by arranging the severed limbs, and the head, in roughly the way she was when alive. On her bed. Must fly – before some clod of a policeman messes up a vital clue. You have a day in bed,' he called out from the door as he left.

Paula followed him out to make sure the front door was secured behind him, then darted back upstairs, her expression serious.

Tweed was standing perfectly erect in front of a mirror while he adjusted his tie. He swung round and smiled at her. Then he paced back and forth rapidly, smiled again, concealing his sense of shock.

'You're feeling better?' Paula enquired anxiously.

'Thought I'd just demonstrated that. So Saafeld is haring off to the murder scene. Roy called him,' – referring to his old friend Commander Roy Buchanan.

'Was Viola Vander-Browne the woman you had dinner with at Mungano's last night?' she said nervously.

'Don't look so worried. I didn't murder her . . . But I shall always curse myself for not seeing her safely to her apartment.'

He opened the wardrobe, fished out from the top pocket of the coat he'd worn the previous evening the card Viola had tucked in. 'She lives – or lived – in Fox Street.'

'I know it. I used it one evening this winter to visit a girl friend of mine in Covent Garden. It's a short cut to Covent Garden across King Street – this side of King Street. I didn't like it at night. Rather narrow, cobbled, and very lonely. A weird atmosphere. I hurried to get through it. I've something rather ugly to tell you . . .'

She explained how she'd noticed the front door had been tampered with. How she had searched his room while he was unconscious – and what she'd found in a drawer before handing it over to Newman. She described the arrival of two black cars and men with long black coats, how Newman had dealt with them.

'Long black coats,' Tweed responded. 'Any caps? Yes, I see. And with armlets on their sleeves. I don't like the sound of the way things are going. We'll leave for the office.'

In his first-floor office with large windows looking towards Regent's Park, Tweed was settled behind his antique desk (a present from his staff) when the visitor arrived. Paula was seated at her desk in a corner. Monica, a middle-aged woman with her hair tucked up in a bun and his faithful secretary for years, sat behind her desk by the door working at her computer. Two other key members of his team were also present. Harry Butler, a Cockney, wearing an old windcheater and shabby slacks, sat crosslegged on the floor. His partner, Pete Nield, sat in a chair close to Paula's desk.

Partners, but their contrast in personality and dress were striking. Nield, in his late thirties, wore a smart suit with a well-pressed shirt and a smart tie. They had listened in silence while Tweed told them of recent events.

'You was set up,' Harry growled. 'Timing was all worked out by a planner. Chose the wrong man. We'll locate 'im – and when we do if I'm there he'll end up in 'ospital . . .'

He stopped talking as the phone rang, Monica answered, then looked at Tweed.

'You won't believe this but Commander Roy Buchanan is downstairs, requesting to see you urgently.'

'Wheel him up, then.'

They heard feet clumping quickly up the stairs. Paula stared in disbelief as Buchanan entered the room. Instead of his usual business suit, he was clad in full-dress uniform as Commander of the Anti-Terrorist Squad, a temporary appointment since he was normally Superintendent of the CID.

'Good morning, Roy,' Tweed greeted him amiably. 'Why the fancy dress?'

'I'm here in an official capacity,' Buchanan said grimly, his expression stern as he seated himself in front of Tweed's desk.

'Hello, Roy,' Paula called out cheerfully.

'Good morning, Miss Grey,' he replied, glancing at her briefly.

'Oh, it's Miss Grey now,' she said, her tone icy. 'Sorry if I forgot to stand up and salute.'

'Roy, what is all this?' Tweed asked placidly.

'I need to know where you were between the hours of eleven last night and three this morning.'

'No, we don't play it that way. Not after we've known each other for umpteen years,' Tweed replied, still placid. 'What is all this about? Relax for Heaven's sake.'

Tweed's persuasive attitude had an effect on even the strong-minded Buchanan. He grabbed his cap out of his lap, dropped it on the floor as though he disliked the damned thing. He took a deep breath.

'All right. There's been a horrific murder. A Miss Viola Vander-Browne. Saafeld estimates the time of death as roughly between eleven p.m. and one a.m. – probably closer to eleven. The poor woman has been cut to pieces. I had an anonymous tip-off on the phone early this morning that I should check where you were last night. Chief Inspector Hammer is in charge of the case. Back at the Yard he's nicknamed the Bulldozer. He was coming over but I stopped him, came myself. Sergeant Warden, my assistant, will be coming over tomorrow to take a statement from you. You know – knew – Miss Vander-Browne?'

'I'm not making any statement at this stage,' Tweed responded. 'But I think I'll investigate the case myself.'

'I wish you would. In your position you do have the authority. Hammer won't like it, but I don't like him. I hesitated to ask you – for certain reasons.' He stood up. 'Thanks for those reports from your agents abroad. Things seem quiet at the moment. I'd better get back now.'

'You're forgetting your cap,' Paula called out as he moved to the door.

'Oh, thank you.' He came back, picked up the cap. 'Lose my head if this pressure keeps up.' He walked over to her, his hand extended. 'I'm sorry about my attitude earlier, Paula. I was on edge when I arrived.'

She shook his hand, gave him a big smile. 'Aren't we all at times.'

'Roy,' Tweed asked, 'what sort of voice was it, whoever gave you the tip-off?'

'Unrecognizable. Hoarse. Coarse. Keep in touch.'

It was Harry, still cross-legged on the floor, who exploded the moment Buchanan was gone.

'It's that bloody uniform. What does he think he is these days? Admiral of the Fleet? The fleet we haven't got!'

Fifteen minutes later Tweed was checking through reports when the phone rang again. Monica answered, then gazed at Tweed.

'You won't believe this one either. Another visitor. Nelson Macomber, one of the notorious Cabal.'

5

'I think this gentleman would prefer to talk to me on my own,' Tweed said before asking Monica to invite Macomber up. 'Harry, put the recorder on – then you can all listen afterwards. No, Paula, don't go. I want you to stay. You're very good at getting an impression on a new player in this deadly game.'

Monica left to go upstairs, followed by Nield and Butler. Only then did he lift the phone and tell George, the guard in the hall, to ask their visitor to come up.

Macomber came into the office. He wore an Armani suit, and a tie Paula felt sure was Chanel. He moved easily and was smiling. He bowed his head towards Paula, still smiling. She rather liked the look of him.

'Good morning, Mr Macomber,' Tweed greeted him quietly. 'Do please sit down.'

'My apologies,' Macomber said softly, looking at

Paula, 'but I will be speaking to you, Mr Tweed, in great confidence.'

'If I was away or out of action Miss Paula Grey would take over from me,' Tweed explained.

Macomber's reaction was swift. He stood up, and smiling pleasantly he walked over to Paula, held out his large hand to her.

'Miss Grey, my profound apologies. I am not familiar with the ranking here. You are most welcome to hear all I have to say.'

She clasped his hand which squeezed hers, but did not hold on too long. He returned to his chair. His movements were agile for a man she estimated was in his forties.

'Now, Mr Tweed,' Macomber began in his soft voice, 'I have heard you are a man who does not beat about the bush. So am I. I have come to discuss with you the proposed merger of all the security forces under one command. That is the CID, MI5, the police, the coastguard, Special Branch – and the SIS, your own organization. This single organization will be known as State Security. We are thinking you would make an excellent deputy commander.'

'Under whose control?' Tweed asked off-handedly.

He had listened to this revolutionary scheme with a placid expression. Paula, who was appalled, gasped under her breath. She felt sure Tweed would never agree.

'Under the control of a Cabinet Minister heading a new post in the Cabinet, as yet to be created: the Ministry of State Security.'

'Earlier,' Tweed remarked, 'you used the word "proposed". I am interested in what that means.'

'Well . . .' Still smiling, Macomber paused. 'At the moment a bill to establish this organization has been drafted, but not yet presented to Parliament.'

'All the Cabinet agree?' There was a sharper edge in Tweed's voice.

'Well . . .' Another pause. 'At the moment almost half the Cabinet do agree. It's only a matter of time before the slow-coaches come on board.'

'Mr Macomber . . .' Tweed leaned forward over his desk.

'Please call me Nelson.'

'I have heard there are three junior ministers involved. You are one of them. Who are the others?'

'You may find this curious. The other two are brothers of mine. We are offspring of the famous General Lucius Macomber, known for his brilliance in the Gulf War.'

'Tell me about your brothers – and their roles.'

Tweed had folded his arms, leaning over them. His eyes had never left Nelson Macomber's, penetrating and the colour of lapis lazuli, which was rare.

'There is Noel, the youngest. We call him the Planner. Then there is Benton, a year younger than me. He acts as arbiter in the rare cases when there is disagreement on policy.'

'The three of you,' Tweed said thoughtfully.

'We do work closely together in the same room . . .'

'Communications?' Tweed interjected.

'Ah!' Macomber beamed. 'We have the most advanced system in the country. State Security will need to know what is going on everywhere. Phone-tapping, a CCTV system covering the entire country . . .'

'Already installed?' Tweed interjected again.

'In the process of being installed,' Macomber assured him. 'Should be completed within weeks.'

'On whose authority?'

Macomber laughed, glanced over at Paula. 'This is getting to be an interrogation.'

'Which is my job,' Tweed reminded him. 'On whose authority?' he repeated. 'Since the bill you spoke of has not gone anywhere near Parliament.'

'We must be prepared.' Macomber's tone became defensive. 'So, what is your reaction? I have hidden no secrets from you.'

'I'll have to think it over, won't I? All this comes as a surprise.'

No, it doesn't, you wily thing, Paula thought. You knew all about it before Nelson Macomber ever arrived.

'Tell you what,' Tweed continued. 'In the near

41

future I'd like to visit your HQ, meet your brothers. I'd bring Paula with me.'

'Great!' Macomber jumped up. 'I appreciate the time you've given me. Do come and see us soon. Time is breathing down our necks. Needless to say all this is highly confidential.'

'Uniforms,' Tweed said suddenly. Macomber paused on his way to say goodbye to Paula. He looked taken aback. Tweed explained.

'I just wondered whether you proposed that after the merger of all these diverse organizations everyone would wear the same uniform?'

'Well . . .' He was close enough to Paula for her to notice he was clenching and unclenching the fingers of his right hand. 'Bit early to think of that,' he went on cheerfully. 'We had thought of a long black coat, black cap, an armlet identifying the wearer as State Security. But a bit early to decide,' he repeated.

'I see.'

'May I call you Paula?' Macomber asked, holding out a hand. 'I am Nelson.'

'If you wish,' she said quietly, clasping his hand which, again, he withdrew quickly.

'What do you think?' Tweed asked after Macomber had left.

Paula was peering out of the window. 'He does well for himself. He turned up in a whacking great Merc

with chauffeur.' She sat down again. 'I'm flabber-
gasted,' she began. 'I'd expected you to roar at him,
tell him you thought the whole idea was wrong, mad
– that you'd have nothing to do with it!'

'He's a skilled politician,' Tweed told her. 'I can
handle any of them. When he reports back to his two
brothers they won't be at all sure what I'm going to do.'

'So what are you going to do?'

'Everything in my power, however unscrupulous,
to smash them – to destroy the whole plan.' His voice
was a muted growl, his eyes were fierce. 'Strange that
he came to see me a few hours after someone tried to
frame me for committing a horrific murder. And
they're already in uniform. So he lied.'

'So he probably lied about a lot of other things.'

'Undoubtedly. Bring down Monica, Pete and
Harry. When I tell you, play back the recording of the
whole conversation. I don't think it occurred to him
it was all going down on tape.' He looked up at the
cornice in the ceiling above Paula's desk. Harry had
done a marvellous job of concealing the listening
device. 'And you took photos of him?'

'Several. He didn't see me doing it.' She produced
a tiny camera with a long lens which retracted out of
sight when she pressed a button.

She had just finished speaking when the door
opened and Monica walked in, followed by Nield and
Butler. Monica spoke to Tweed quickly.

'While we were upstairs I had a call for you from Professor Saafeld. He has data he wants to show you urgently. At his place in Holland Park . . .'

'Call him back when I've left. Tell him I'm on my way now. While I'm away get the recorder moving.' He looked at all three of the new arrivals. 'You'll hear my conversation with Macomber – Nelson Macomber. Keep what you hear under your hats.'

'Never wear a hat,' Harry told him with a straight face.

Tweed glared, went on speaking.

'Nield, when you've heard it I want you to get moving. Check with your informants. I need to know if the other two brothers, Noel and Benton, are married. If so, who to? We know Nelson is married to Loelia, daughter of the Earl of something. Do any of them have girlfriends? If so, who are they and where do they live?'

'Is that all?' Nield asked with a grin.

'I'm off to Professor Saafeld's place. Could be there for a couple of hours. Have the info for me when I get back.'

'Should give me plenty of time.' Nield grinned again. 'Don't be surprised if I'm still out when you get back.'

Tweed, still speaking rapidly, turned to Monica. 'If a Chief Inspector Hammer arrives or phones tell him I've gone abroad. You don't know where or when I'll be back. Now I must get moving.'

'I'm coming with you,' Paula said firmly.

She had already slipped on a windcheater over her slacks and jumper. Tweed stood uncertainly.

'Thought you were in a hurry,' Paula said, grabbing his arm.

Harry followed them downstairs, talking as they hurried. 'I got here early. Spotted our friends had fixed up cameras to the lampposts on the other side of the road. The cameras are difficult to see. They were aimed to cover the entrance here.'

'Were?' queried Paula.

'I covered them with black goo – same colour as their spy cameras. They'll need new lenses.'

'Don't waste much time, do they?' commented Tweed.

'Neither does Harry,' Paula replied.

The drizzle had stopped. Above was a clear blue sky and it was bitterly cold. Tweed had slipped on his overcoat as he skipped nimbly down the stairs.

They were driving through heavy traffic, approaching Holland Park, when Paula looked back again through the rear window. She swore softly.

'We're still being followed. Big black car picked us up as we left Park Crescent. Look to be two men in the front. Black coats, I think, and black peaked caps.'

'The uniform Nelson said they hadn't got round to. I'll lose them.'

Tweed slowed down as they approached traffic lights on green. He waited for amber, pressed his foot down, passed the lights as they turned red. A police car was parked by the kerb. Tweed recognized the driver, used one hand to hold up his SIS folder. The police driver saluted him.

'That was Ned,' Tweed remarked. 'He knows me well.'

'Well, you've lost our friends,' said Paula after glancing back. 'They were caught by the lights . . .'

Shortly afterwards Tweed swung into the side street where Saafeld's mansion was located. He drove to the end, parked the car round a corner. They walked back quickly to where a pair of high wrought-iron gates were closed at the end of a curving drive. Tweed pressed the button on the speakphone.

'Yes. Who is it?' Saafeld's clear voice enquired.

'Me,' said Tweed. 'The "me" you're expecting.'

The electronically operated gates swung open and they walked quickly up the drive. Little time was given to allow a car to drive in, to stop the vehicle being followed. Rounding a corner of the drive bordered by evergreen shrubs the elegant mansion came into view. The massive front door was open as they mounted the steps. Saafeld, wearing a white gown closed at the neck, ushered them inside, stared at Paula as he shut and relocked the door. They were standing in a large hall with a marble floor.

'Paula,' Saafeld said gently, 'I'm not sure you want to see this.'

Knowing the drill, Tweed and Paula removed overcoat and windcheater. Saafeld slipped them over hangers, put them in one cupboard, opened another, took out white coats, white caps and two pairs of latex gloves. As they put them on quickly their host stared again dubiously at Paula. Her reaction was instant and sharp.

'I've been in there before. Stop treating me like a schoolgirl.'

Saafeld shrugged, walked to a heavy steel door, took out a key card, inserted it in the slot. The door slid open and Paula breathed in powerful disinfectant. They went down several steps to another heavy steel door which Saafeld opened.

Underground now, they followed him into a large room with tables of metal and gutters along each side to catch any blood which spread too far. The first two tables had corpses lying on them while white-coated assistants went about their grisly work. There were large cameras overhead and X-ray machines poised above each table, held by telescopic arms. Now there was another odour which Paula recognized, the odour of bodies that would never move again.

'Here she is, poor woman,' Saafeld said quietly.

It was unusual for him to express any emotion about what was brought into his mortuary. Paula stood very still, her palms clammy. The body of Viola Vander-Browne was lying on the table. The severed head, ashen, was placed an inch or so from the neck, coated with dried blood, now darkish brown in colour. Paula's teeth were clamped tightly behind her closed lips as she continued her survey. The severed left lower arm was also placed an inch or so below the elbow. The same applied to the right arm, to the lower limbs severed below the jagged ends of the knees. Paula found the strange sequence hideous. Saafeld seemed to read her mind. He began talking in his detached professional voice.

'This is exactly how I found the corpse on the bed at Fox Street. The killer had first slammed her naked body on to the wooden floor, by the side of the bed. I think he—'

'Why "he"?' Paula interrupted. 'Couldn't it have been a woman?'

'You could be right, possibly,' Saafeld agreed. 'Except that after gagging her the murderer raped her. He used a condom – no traces of semen. That doesn't rule out a woman completely, if a condom pulled over one of those sex toys was used. After the rape the murderer used a sharp-bladed instrument to cut her up – a meat cleaver, I suspect. The head was severed last – severing the carotid arteries. Hence the jet of blood which covered the window.'

'Excuse me,' Tweed suggested, 'but was there a light on in the room when you arrived?'

'Yes, left on after the killer left, so when the police arrived before me the blood-covered window was very prominent. Now, I said earlier the body was found laid out on the bed. There were blade notches deep into the floor, which is how I know for certain that's where she was killed. He – or she – afterwards lifted the several pieces of the body on to the bed, created an arrangement as I have done on the table.'

'That's horrible,' Paula said after clearing her throat.

'One of the worst cases in my experience – and I've just about seen everything, or so I thought. I think now we ought to adjourn to the drawing room. My wife will provide refreshment. We can discuss the case in more pleasant surroundings.'

He turned to a youngish man who was washing his hands at a deep sink.

'John, I know you've taken X-rays and photos of the lady on my table. I'd like you to take more photos, concentrating on every angle. Thank you . . .'

In the small room they had passed through earlier he relieved them of their white clothes. As he closed the cupboard doors he turned to Tweed.

'I'm very fussy. Those clothes will be burned, in case you picked up something undesirable while in the mortuary. Now for that tea.'

They mounted the steps into the hall. Saafeld closed the heavy door and did not bother to use his key card. Paula guessed it locked again automatically.

They were seated in armchairs in the luxurious comfortable drawing room when a tall grey-haired lady, in her late fifties Paula guessed, came in carrying a large silver tray laden with plates of cakes, Wedgwood china, a teapot and another pot containing coffee.

Saafeld started to get up. 'I'll take that . . .'

'No, you won't, Willy,' she said firmly. 'I can still cope with this.' She laid the tray on a table between the chairs. 'Hello, Paula. So nice to see you again. And you, Mr Tweed.'

'You shouldn't have gone to all this trouble,' Paula said, returning her warm smile.

'You'll have to excuse me,' Mrs Saafeld went on. 'We have people coming to dinner so my place is in the kitchen.'

'We have . . .?' Saafeld began, then stopped as she gave him a certain look, then left the room. She knows what we've seen, Paula thought, so she's tactfully leaving us alone.

Paula accepted tea with a little milk but no sugar when their host also offered her both plates of cakes. She forced herself to smile when she refused. She had arrived hungry but her appetite had deserted her.

Tweed accepted coffee but he also declined anything to eat.

'We had lunch before we came to you,' fibbed Paula.

'Can you tell us anything about the killer?' Tweed asked.

Saafeld settled back in his chair, and stared at the ceiling as though choosing his words carefully.

'The killer is exceptionally strong,' he began. 'That's proved by the fact that each time he wielded the cleaver – if that's what it was, but I think so – it not only sliced through bone, muscle and flesh in one blow but ended up leaving a deep gash in the oak floor. It must have taken more strength to ease the weapon free for the next strike.'

'Surely he must have had blood all over his clothes?' Tweed suggested.

'Not if he was clad as you two were in the mortuary, plus the kind of face mask used by surgeons. Afterwards he'd have taken all his whites off and stuffed them inside some container he took away with him.'

'Any sign of forced entry at Fox Street?'

'None at all. Which suggested Vander-Browne knew whoever killed her. Very premeditated murder,' Saafeld went on. 'The way he – or she –' he glanced over at Paula – 'arrived with all his equipment – weapon, the whites. I suspect he arrived in normal dress. I say this because in the bathroom was cotton

51

wool, traces of powder. Vander-Browne's visitor may have arrived early. He puts on his whites while she is in the bathroom. I think that's about all I can tell you.'

'Is it?' Tweed pressed.

'Well, I'm not a psychiatrist. We may be dealing with a psycho, but that's a vague word. What happens to some people who are strong-blooded and evil is that the pressure starts to build up inside them. The process probably accelerates over a period of days, maybe even a few weeks. They reach the stage when they are ready to murder – and revel in what they are doing.'

'Difficult to detect,' Tweed muttered half to himself.

'I call it blood storm,' Saafeld concluded.

6

As Tweed drove them back towards Park Crescent, Paula glanced several times at him, pretending she was looking at traffic. His expression was unusual – grave, despondent. And he had not said a word since they entered the car.

'Please pull in,' she asked.

He signalled, turned the vehicle to the side of the road, looked at her. She told him to turn off the engine. He did so, then slumped in his seat. She took hold of his arm.

'What is it?' she enquired gently.

'Nothing. I'm OK.'

'You're not – by a long chalk. Tell me. Talking it out always helps.'

He drank half the water from the slim flask she had taken from the pocket in her door. He sipped first as she'd suggested, then drank large quantities. He handed back the flask.

'Thanks. I'm all right now.'

'You're not,' she repeated firmly. 'Tell me. This is Paula.'

'When we were in the mortuary I was thinking of how Viola had looked when we had dinner at Mungano's. Ravishing and young. I liked her. I think she liked me. If only I'd escorted her home – instead of slinking back into that alley and falling asleep. She'd be alive now. I'll never forgive myself . . .'

He paused as Paula's mobile buzzed. She answered, listened, asked very few questions, then slipped the mobile back into her pocket.

'That was Professor Saafeld,' she said quietly. 'He sends you his apology but he forgot to tell you the results of the blood test. He said your margarita was laced with Percodin.' She spelt it. 'Not Percodan, an American drug, but quite different. Percodin dulls the nervous system, neutralizes it. Puts you completely out of action. You told him you'd only drunk about a fifth of the margarita. It creeps up on you, then suddenly you get the full effect. He also said if you'd drunk the lot your mind would have been destabilized for twenty-four hours. So how the hell could you have escorted Viola home? You couldn't have done. Feel a bit better about things now?'

'What I want to do is to find out who fed me that bloody drink.' Tweed had straightened up; his expression was grim, determined, even ferocious. 'I can remember the waitress who served the thing to me. Mungano should be able to identify her. We'd better get moving . . .'

Tweed was still silent when they reached Park Crescent. Thank God Saafeld phoned me, Paula said to herself.

Entering the office they found that Nield had returned, looking rather pleased. Monica relieved Tweed of his coat.

'Your friend Chief Inspector Hammer called,' she said, 'wanted to come and see you, said it was urgent.'

'Urgent to him,' Tweed commented sarcastically as he settled behind his desk.

'I told him you'd left the office and I had an idea you had gone abroad. No, I had no idea where or when you'd be back.'

'One in the eye for him,' Paula commented from behind her desk. 'Where is Harry?'

'He went out, dressed even more like a tramp, if that's possible. Said he had some pals in the East End he wanted to question.'

'Good for Harry. How have you got on, Pete? You're back quickly.'

'You know me,' Nield said, perching on the front edge of Tweed's desk, arms folded. 'I don't waste time. So far I've found out Benton Macomber is married to a woman called Georgina. Has a successful fashion-design business. Is reputed to be very clever and popular. Benton has a house in Hampstead. I've got the address and phone number. Noel, the youngster, is a different proposition. Likes women, plenty of them. He has girlfriends, drops them when he spots something he fancies more. Just dumps them when he wants variety. A real lady-killer. Has charm which he can turn on and off like an electric light. Very brainy. All three brothers were at Oxford together, Noel had junior status because of his age, still came down with three double firsts, which is rare. He has a pad in a street off Pall Mall. It's all in here, addresses and phone numbers – except for Noel, who is ex-directory and keeps his number quiet.'

'You've done amazingly well,' Tweed said, looking at the notebook Nield had dropped on his desk.

'There's a bit more,' Nield went on in his well-educated voice. 'Nelson, Benton and Noel are looked after by a senior civil servant called Zena Partridge, known behind her back as the Parrot or Freaky-Deaky. A control-freak, my informant told me. The father, General Lucius Macomber, has a cottage on a large plot of land down at a tiny hamlet on the Surrey–Sussex border, Peckham Mallet. That's in the notebook. End of the story.'

'This informant is a gold mine,' Tweed remarked. 'Who is she?'

'I don't recall saying it was a woman. And don't ask for a name. You know the rule. None of us reveal anything about an informant. That's it. I'll be going out again in five secs.'

'Good hunting and many thanks,' Tweed said as Nield went out of the office.

'I don't think either you or Paula have eaten,' Monica said firmly, standing up. 'Just before you came in I prepared hot food for you both in the upstairs kitchen. Be back in no time . . .'

'I'm hungry,' Tweed mused.

'So am I now,' Paula exclaimed. 'I'm dropping through my pockets, as they say up north.'

They both cleaned their plates of shepherd's pie, carrots and spinach, followed by hot apple pie and tea and coffee. Paula stood up to collect the plates. Monica took them off her, placed them in a dumb waiter in her corner, pressed the bell informing the kitchen upstairs there was work on the way.

Still on her feet, Paula stared down out of the window into the Crescent leading off the main road. She frowned, turned round as she spoke.

'I think we have yet another visitor. An odd-looking person.'

Monica joined her to peer out from behind the heavy net curtains. A tall slim figure wearing dark trousers, a dark blue coat, a trilby hat pulled well down over the face was striding stiffly but briskly to the entrance. Paula had just caught sight of large horn-rimmed spectacles when the figure climbed their steps.

'He's coming here, whoever he is,' Monica said and sat down to wait for the phone to ring from the guard downstairs. It rang. Monica looked up.

'A Zena Partridge wants to see you. Now!'

'I thought you said it was a man,' Tweed remarked.

'Looked like one.'

'Nield reported on his findings just in time. Send this odd-looking person, as you described her, up. Why on earth would she be calling on me?'

'We'll find out, won't we?' Paula chaffed him.

Heavy heels clacked on the stairs, the door was opened without anyone knocking, and the visitor entered.

Paula stared at the apparition without appearing to do so. Whipping off the man's hat the visitor revealed a thick mop of brown hair which now fell to her shoulders.

She wore the thickest horn-rims Paula had ever seen, with lenses of thick glass. Behind them greenish-yellow eyes surveyed the room quickly. Her mouth was plastered with bright red lipstick and she peered rather than looked when she had checked the room. She took off her coat, ignored Monica's offer to take it, hung it over the back of the chair in front of Tweed's desk. She was wearing a loose white blouse covered with roses.

Tweed had stood up and opened his mouth to suggest she sat down but the visitor plonked her slim backside in the chair without being asked. Tweed sat down, having said nothing.

'You're Tweed,' she began. 'Over there that must be Paula Grey,' she said with a brief glance at Paula. 'I am Zena Partridge,' she continued, 'senior civil servant. My main role is to attend to the three junior ministers, Nelson, Noel and Benton Macomber. I have other responsibilities so it is a back-breaking routine but that doesn't worry me because I have a strong back. I am here to get your advice about hiring protection.'

Lord, another frightened woman, Tweed thought. Partridge ploughed on, speaking in a commanding voice as though addressing the troops.

'The reason for my request is I am being stalked and I want a stop put to it.' She glared at Tweed through the thick lenses. 'But the protection must be invisible. On absolutely no account must the people I work for know what is happening. I can give you no reason why this should be happening but it has to be stopped. I have no enemies or people who would want to harm me. My life is work, work, work . . .'

'Could you describe—' Tweed began.

'He is a short fat creature about fifty years old and he always wears a dark-blue business suit, a red tie and a white shirt. His feet are clad in blue trainers and he smokes a cheap cigar constantly. I have a specimen.' She dived inside the large leather handbag she had slung over her shoulder, produced a transparent envelope containing a half-smoked cigar, dropped it on Tweed's desk.

Tweed glanced at it briefly but made no attempt to examine it. Partridge was talking again.

'Maybe it's a clue – DNA from the saliva and all that – I wouldn't know. I'll pay a reasonable fee for your time and here is my mobile phone number.' As she spoke she dropped on his desk a card which she'd extracted at the same time as the cigar. 'That's all it has on the card. I have no intention of letting anyone know where I live. What alerted me to the need to take action was the description in the newspaper about that brutal murder of the Vander-Browne woman. There's a lunatic on the loose. I have no intention of risking being his next victim.

She was still talking at top speed. She opened her mouth again but Tweed hammered his clenched fist on the desk and she stared with indignation at him.

'Where did you get the cigar from,' he asked her, 'and how long has this persecution been going on?'

'I picked up the cigar in Whitehall,' Partridge rattled on. 'Turning round, I began to walk back to challenge him just as a police car came slowly cruising up the street. The fat man threw his cigar into a side street and disappeared after it. He only reappeared when the police car had passed. He hailed a cab when he saw me coming towards him. After he'd gone I used my gloved hand to pick up the cigar and dropped it inside that evidence envelope. I carry them so I can stuff used handkerchiefs inside one. Germs are everywhere. I have been stalked for two days and every time I leave the building. While I think of it, Paula Grey over there is in great danger. Don't ask me how I know that because I won't tell you. Highly confidential.'

'Medfords Security Agency,' Tweed said suddenly. 'I can give you the address and the name of the man to see. We do not handle work or problems like yours. I am sorry.'

'So am I!' she snapped, jumping up, slipping on her coat. 'And I do know where Medfords are. I've wasted my time coming here. I'm going now. No, keep the cigar.'

When Partridge had gone Monica stood up and let out a long sigh.

'Phew! She never stopped talking for over five minutes. No wonder back at the civil service they call her the Parrot. To say nothing of Freaky-Deaky. Pete knew what he was talking about. As to enemies, she must have a horde of them with all those subordinate to her.'

'Did you believe what she said?' Tweed asked Paula.

'Not one single word.'

'The only thing she said which worries me is her warning that you are in danger. Could be the reason she came here. I'm thinking the Cabal are launching a campaign against us to persuade me to withdraw opposition to their crazy plan for a merger.'

'Don't think so,' Paula said as her mobile phone began to buzz. She answered it. 'Hello.'

'Recognize my voice?' a man asked. Newman's.

'Yes, I do.'

'I need your help urgently. I'm at the Monk's Head Hotel in Tolhaven, west Dorset. Can you get down here?'

'I'm practically on my way.'

'Bring a camera. Something very weird. Come armed . . .'

The line went dead. Paula had scribbled the address on a pad. She opened a locked drawer, took out her Browning, checked the mechanism, inserted a magazine, tucked it inside her shoulder holster. Next she took out a small 6.35mm Beretta, checked it, and slid the automatic inside another neat holster strapped to her leg. She took the pad with the address over to Tweed, told him what Newman had said.

'Things are warming up,' she remarked. 'About time.'

'I'd come with you,' Tweed said. 'But the situation here . . .'

'Bob didn't ask for you,' she said with a cheeky smile. 'I will keep you informed as far as I can. Borrow a mobile off Pete Nield. See you.'

'Don't take your Saab to drive down there,' Tweed warned. 'You are known to have that car and the enemy has done his homework. Take my old battered Ford with the souped-up engine. That might confuse them.'

'Will do.'

She was almost at the door when she stooped to pick something up off the carpet. It was a contact lens with a greenish-yellow tint. She took it back and laid it on Tweed's desk.

'The Parrot must have dropped this as she left in a fury.'

'I wonder,' said Tweed very thoughtfully, looking at the lens.

'And here,' Paula said, handing him a camera, 'inside is the film. I took two shots of our visitor.'

Tweed called over to Monica. He gave her the camera.

'Take this down to the basement. Tell them to print what's inside. Then they should give the prints to that clever artist, Joel, and ask him to come up. I have experienced his talented hand at creating people's images.'

7

Paula was racing down the motorway, the same one Newman had driven along earlier. Before leaving Park Crescent she had used a map to check the location of Tolhaven, a place she'd never heard of. A souped-up engine, Tweed had said. She was having to concentrate to stop the car carrying her away, and as a result she passed the exit leading to the safe house Newman had used without giving it a thought. Shortly afterwards she turned off the motorway down a road leading more to the south.

The end of March. It was a gloriously sunny afternoon and cold. She had her window open a few inches to keep herself alert. She frequently checked her rear-view mirror but there was no sign of black cars. She had eluded State Security – no, Special Branch as they still were, despite their black uniforms, the long overcoats, the peaked caps.

She was driving through open country with rolling

hills on either side. Here and there a field had crusted brown sods of soil. Ploughing was well under way. She sighed with pleasure. Such a relief to be in the country and away from the crammed streets and buildings of London.

The road was straight for long stretches and she risked increasing her speed. Eventually she crossed the Dorset Downs and a panoramic view opened up. The road descended, hedge-lined on both sides, but ahead in the distance the sun glowed off a vast stretch of blue sea. The English Channel. She crawled through the first village she had encountered for ages, saw a signpost bearing the legend Tolhaven.

No traffic. She was thinking of the contact lens she had given Tweed, along with the camera she'd used to photograph the Parrot. She had a twin camera in her pocket. 'I wonder,' Tweed had said and asked Monica to give it to the basement boffins, develop the film, then send it to Joel, the artist. Why? What had occurred to him in his agile brain?

Tolhaven was a dull place, small and with stone buildings, most of which had small shops at ground level. She saw the Monk's Head, turned into a parking area under an arch. Newman's Range Rover was parked in a corner.

In reception a woman in late middle-age, wearing a crumpled grey dress, told her Mr Newman had said he was expecting a lady guest. His room was 25, hers was 24, both on the first floor.

'You made good time,' Newman greeted her when Paula had tapped on his door, and entered his large bedroom, its windows overlooking the main street. 'Are you armed?'

'Yes. Sounds as though you expect trouble.'

'I do. Thanks for coming. I need someone sensitive to weird atmospheres. We ought to get moving. On foot. It will be dark soon.'

'Mind if I dump my emergency bag in my room and change into walking boots? You can come with me . . .'

She had noticed Newman was exuding energy, but that his expression was grim after his welcoming smile. He was clad in a camouflage jacket and trousers tucked into boots. She worked quickly in her room while Newman peered out of a window looking down on the car park.

'Don't miss a trick, do you?' he said sharply. 'Parked your car like mine facing out for a quick getaway.'

'That's on the cards?'

'I've paid in advance for both rooms for two nights. If we have to we can take off in an emergency.'

'You expect one?'

'State Security have been here for hours in full battledress. I've done a recce, so I can show you.' He looked towards the bathroom. 'We may not be back for a while.'

'I'm OK. What are we waiting for?'

'Have you eaten?' Newman paused on the pavement outside the hotel. 'I should have asked earlier.'

'Yes. Shouldn't we keep moving?'

He led them down a side street near the hotel and over to the far side of the High Street. They emerged into the open and the small town was gone. The road climbed to an ancient bridge. Paula peered over a crumbling stone wall. Below a fast-flowing river headed seaward. On one bank an old wooden dock was gradually collapsing into the water.

'Ages ago, before the Channel decided to recede,' Newman explained briskly, 'Tolhaven was on the edge of the sea. The town has a history of smugglers and savage fights with the equivalent of the coast-guard.'

'It's eerily quiet, apart from the water lapping,' she remarked as they walked quickly beyond the bridge.

'It's a riot here compared with where we're going.'

'Can't wait . . .'

The road became a lane with forests of fir trees hemming it in on both sides. To their right, in a break in the trees, a path curved away marked with a sign: Ferry.

'Where does that go to, then?' she asked.

'To Black Island,' Newman replied, 'not far off the coast. I've been there for a quick shufti . . .'

'What was that? Think I've heard it before.'

'Arabic for look-see. Philip Cardon used the word when we had fun down in Marseilles.'

'Fun? We nearly got killed.'

'That was a honeymoon compared with what this could be. I want you to keep quiet, crouch down after me.'

Newman's whole attitude, his remarks, made Paula check the Browning in the shoulder holster. They had turned off into another gap in the forest. The grass and dead bracken were squashed down with what looked to Paula like wheel-tracks. He held up a hand to halt her as they arrived at an opening. Three large cars were parked facing the track. Newman checked each one with small powerful field glasses. He had laid the golfer's bag which he'd carried casually slung over his shoulder down on the grass. He completed his survey, tucked away the glasses.

'Empty,' he announced in a whisper.

'What's in the golf bag? Not irons, I suspect.'

'A powerful automatic weapon with plenty of ammo,' he told her casually. 'I think we'll risk crossing over to Black Island by ferry. The thugs had overhead lights fixed up where they were working, so maybe they carry on at night.'

'What work?'

'That's what I want you to see. If I tell you to do something like "drop flat" you do it damned fast.'

They had returned along the track to the road, went back to where the signpost pointed to the ferry.

'I thought I always did when you said something. I was with you down at the training mansion in Surrey. I seem to recall I scored more bulls than you on the firing range.'

'You did,' Newman agreed. 'I said that because my impression is the thugs in State Security gear are also well trained. And they're armed . . .'

Walking along the other path Newman stopped frequently to listen, then resumed his long strides. She had to hurry to keep up with his pace. The forest ended, they were in the open, the smell of the sea even stronger. The ferry was like a large barge with a small ladder at its stern, a short distance from a large engine. One weather-beaten rustic wearing oilskins stood on the shore, smoking a curved pipe.

'Going across?' he called out in a West Country accent. 'It's calm today so don't bother with oilskins. I'm Abe,' he introduced himself as Newman handed him the fare for two people.

'Had any other passengers?' Newman enquired with a smile.

'Only six of those bastards . . . excuse me, miss . . .

in their black fancy-dress uniform. Came over early this morning, asked if the old tub, as they called my ferry, crossed at night. I told them the last crossing is at 8.30 p.m. I bring her back through the channel marked with lights. You mention us to anyone and you're in hospital one of 'em said. So I won't be sayin' another word to people like that . . .'

They climbed the small ladder and Paula saw there were long continuous seats on either side of the barge. Newman led her to the front and as they settled themselves Abe started the engine. The barge slid out along a channel between long reeds, then they were in open sea.

'Black Island is shaped like a triangle,' Newman explained, 'with the apex pointing south into the Channel. We land at a small village called Lydford. Has a pub and not much else.'

'No holidaymakers?'

'A lot at the eastern end, which has small hotels and good beaches. There's another ferry – one that takes cars. At this end there are locals in places like Lydford. That's it. Nothing on the western side, where the fancy-dress lot are building like mad. It's sinister. Which is why I want photos.'

He stopped talking as Abe fixed the tiller, walked down to them. There was hardly any motion as Lydford's church spire hove into clear view.

'Don't know what they can be buildin' over on the

west side,' Abe began, talking with his pipe in his mouth. 'I've seen cargo ships comin' in, unloadin' steel bars and Gawd knows 'ow many breezeblocks.'

'Probably another holiday centre,' Newman suggested.

'Don't look like it. We'll be landin' soon. I comes over to collect any passengers on the hour. You'll be comin' back?'

'I hope so,' Paula said under her breath.

There was a bump as the barge gently hit the wooden dock. Slinging his golf bag over his shoulder, Newman helped Paula up on to the dock. He grinned as he tapped the bag with one hand while they walked off the dock into the tiny village.

'Good job there are golf courses on the eastern cost. So this won't look odd.'

'No one about to notice,' Paula observed.

The village was very small. On either side of the road were old one-storey thatched cottages. The postage-stamp-size garden in front of each was neatly tended. The church was also small and constructed years before of black stone.

'Not very welcoming,' Paula commented as they walked down the street. 'Black stone. Why?'

'Because this island has the only granite quarries I know of in the south. Black granite, hence its name.'

'There are some nice expensive-looking houses over there,' Paula commented. 'You can just see them in gaps between the fir trees. Some oaks too.'

'We turn down this lane,' Newman said, not interested in her observations as he kept turning his head to scan for any sign of life. 'This is where it could get hairy . . .'

They walked some distance west along the curving lane. Fir trees arched above their heads, as if they were walking inside a tunnel. Rounding a corner they saw a track leading away to their left, its broken surface carrying the wheel marks of wide heavy trucks. A sentry was posted there, wearing a long black coat, peaked cap, an armlet with the legend State Security, an automatic weapon slung over his left shoulder.

'Get back the way you came,' he ordered. Beneath the peaked cap his face was coarse and ugly. He barked as Newman came up to him, Paula by his side, 'Back to the friggin' mainland. Restricted area here. You can always lay her in the grass and do it other side of the channel.'

'Manners . . .' Newman began.

The sentry was starting to slip his weapon off his shoulder, watching Newman. Paula had her gun in her hand, holding it by the muzzle. She slammed it down on the sentry's nose, aiming for the bridge. The sentry opened both eyes wide, then closed them as he slumped backwards on to the verge.

Newman crouched over him, checked his pulse. He grinned at Paula as he looked up at her.

'Nice work.'

'He was watching you, not bothering about a woman.'

'He'll be out for quite a while. Now we have to hide him and I know just the place. Found it when I came over here this morning.' With ease he lifted the body of the six-foot thug, called over his shoulder as he began walking quickly along the track, 'You bring his weapon.'

At a turning Newman walked a few paces off the track. Paula caught him up, to find him staring down into an abandoned quarry. The slope was fairly gradual. Newman bent down, lowered the unconscious man to the edge, pushed. He slithered down a long way, lay still at the bottom. Without being asked Paula tossed the weapon down so it lay a few feet away from the inert body.

'Now it gets dangerous,' Newman commented as they returned to the track. Paula caught him up.

'What do you call what's just happened?'

'Just an opening shot.'

The enclosing trees ended and they were in open rolling country. A distance to the south she could see a green down with the blue horizon of the sea on either side. No sign of anyone.

'What's that hill?' she asked.

'Hog's Nose Down. Well named, considering the sort of people who have taken over the western end.'

Newman was carrying his automatic weapon which he'd hauled out from the golf bag. Noting this, Paula kept hold of her Browning, close to her bag so that she could slip it inside if it seemed wiser. They arrived at a long low ridge. Newman stopped, dropped down behind it, poked his weapon over its crest. Paula dropped down beside him.

'Why are we doing this?'

'I'm a student of the Duke of Wellington's campaigns in Iberia. At Vimeiro he placed his troops behind a ridge to save them from the enemy's initial heavy artillery bombardment. When their infantry followed they couldn't see them and were shot down in their hundreds. Time to keep moving . . .'

They crossed the ridge, went down the other side and walked over a grassy plain until they reached another ridge. The sky was a clear blue; a bitter wind blew, almost freezing, so Paula buttoned her windcheater at the neck.

Newman climbed it, went over the crest, dropped flat on the far side, poking his automatic rifle over the top. Paula did not follow his example. Her tone had an edge to it when she spoke.

'Can we stop playing soldiers and get moving? It's perishingly cold.'

'Nearly there,' Newman said with a smile as he jumped up. 'You brought your camera? Good. Lots to photograph if it's quiet. The beginning of the prison state . . .'

Only half-built, it was located in a vast hollow. Newman used his field glasses. Swivelling them everywhere, he grunted with satisfaction.

'No one about. All gone to get lunch at the pub. We go in now. Prepare for a shock. This is a new idea for a prison. Take plenty of pics.'

There were frameworks for more buildings everywhere, a series of tall steel posts with breeze block walls behind them. Newman led Paula into a large completed building. The entry door was solid steel but no lock had been attached yet.

Paula shuddered inwardly as they went inside. The floor was solid concrete. She thanked Heaven she was wearing her boots. The straight corridor which ran into the distance was surprisingly narrow. She was expecting cells with bars separating them from the corridor. No bars. Newman opened the steel door of a cell. She peered inside.

Hardly room for a big dog. A hole in the floor which Newman explained would be the only toilet facility. Along one side of the cell was a steel slab fixed to the wall. Newman pointed to it as she worked her camera.

'That's the bed. Imagine trying to sleep on it. No sign of mattresses. Not quite like the British police accommodation.'

'What are those shower-like objects in the roof?' Paula asked as she continued photographing.

'If they don't like the prisoner they turn on the water and you're soaked. I checked the system. First cold water, then very hot, scalding probably.'

'It's inhuman.'

'Wait till you see the punishment chamber.'

She counted fifty cells on one side as Newman led her towards the end. So fifty on the other side. This cramped hell accommodated one hundred prisoners. Near the end Newman opened a larger steel door. She peered into a much bigger cell. Newman beckoned to her to come inside.

A steel floor sloped on all four sides towards a central drain. She gazed at hooks let into the walls about seven feet above the floor. Hanging from one wall were six cat-o'-nine tail whips, a sharp needle at the tip of each tail. She spoke as she used the camera.

'What are those for?'

'To whip aggressive prisoners into submission. Their bodies will be slashed and dripping blood. Hence the drain to take it away. Nice people, the hoped-for State Security mob.' Newman walked to the far end, bent down, took hold of a handle attached to a round lid about five feet in diameter.

When he heaved it open Paula looked down into a deep circular area. High up in the walls were radio speakers and showerheads.

'What are the speakers for?' Paula wondered.

'I'd say when they have a prisoner down there they turn on the showers and the speakers play ghastly music at top pitch – enough to burst their eardrums.'

Newman shone a powerful torch down inside the tubelike cell. Paula used the illumination to take a number of photos. When she had finished Newman replaced the lid in the position he had found it.

'Time to get out,' he said, 'after I've checked that giant American-style fridge outside.'

'I wonder why those hooks are there, high up in the walls?' Paula enquired, pointing up.

Newman opened the metal drawer of a steel cabinet built into a side wall. They peered inside. It was full of metal handcuffs. Newman closed the drawer quietly, his expression grim.

'They plan to handcuff prisoners, then lift them up so they can hang the chain between the cuffs from the hooks. Being so high up, no matter how tall the prisoner is he'll find himself with his legs dangling in space, the whole weight of his body hanging from his wrists. Now, that fridge.'

As they re-entered the corridor, Newman closed the punishment-cell door quietly behind them. He opened the huge fridge that stood at the end of the corridor. The electric power was working, and it was crammed with ice.

'Got it,' Newman explained. 'Before they drop a prisoner into that tube cell they empty a load of ice down inside. My guess is they half-freeze the poor devil first, then turn on the showers emitting scalding water. Let's get out of here while we can . . .'

They traversed the entire length of the corridor. Newman cautiously opened the door a few inches, nodded, stepped out as Paula hurried after him. A damp cloying mist had drifted in off the sea while they were inside. They were walking swiftly alongside the prison wall when Newman grabbed Paula, pushed her against the wall and flattened himself.

'Keep very still,' he whispered. 'Movement attracts attention.'

Some distance away, blurred in the mist, four men in uniform were walking towards a distant half-erected building like the one they had explored. Two carried steel bars while the couple behind them pushed a trolley laden with breeze blocks.

When they had arrived Paula and Newman had seen the whole area was surrounded with high coils of barbed wire. They had entered through a gap with a huge roll of barbed wire pushed to one side.

'Let's hope they haven't closed our exit,' Paula whispered.

'If they have I can shift it,' Newman assured her,

taking out of his pocket a pair of thick gardening gloves.

They reached the exit point to find it still open. Once they had climbed out of the vast hollow, they crossed the flat grassy plain. They had reached the first ridge when Paula grabbed Newman's arm.

'We've been seen. Three men with automatic weapons are running up behind us.' Newman glanced back, saw three figures blurred in the mist coming after them. He took Paula's arm, hustled her over the first ridge, then moved at the double towards the second ridge. They had just reached the far side when Paula pointed ahead. Three more uniformed men with weapons were walking towards them.

'Caught in a cross-fire,' she hissed.

'Drop flat behind the ridge.'

He did so, facing the way they had come, and she flattened herself behind him. He gave the order fiercely.

'Whatever happens, you stay still. You do not fire.'

He glanced over his shoulder, saw the three men as blurred figures, like ghosts, weapons at the ready. He looked in front over the crest, aimed his rifle. He timed it carefully. As the three in front stood on top of the other ridge Newman aimed, fired, deliberately hit one man in the kneecap. A shriek as he fired two more shots over their heads, dipped his own head.

The mist made his tactic work. The three in front

thought the three blurred figures coming from the other direction had opened fire on them. A fusillade opened up on the men behind Newman and Paula, immediately returned by a rattle of automatic weapons. The three men on the ridge nearest the prison dropped, slumped like dead men. Newman looked over his shoulder. The three behind him were collapsing on their ridge. No further movement anywhere.

'Let's get out of this,' Newman ordered urgently.

They ran to the ridge behind them. Newman paused to check the bodies on the ridge. All dead. Bless the Duke of Wellington, he said to himself.

They ran all the way after Paula had checked her watch and said they were going to miss the return ferry. As they arrived on the dock, Abe, his motor running, waved at them. Newman glanced down into a powerful motorboat tied to the other side of the jetty. The earlier wind had blown overboard a canvas covering, now floating in the water. He saw the contents.

'We've made it,' Paula panted as she hauled herself aboard the ferry.

'Don't be too sure of that,' Newman warned.

8

Abe had the barge leaving the dock as soon as they were aboard. A strong breeze had blown up, curling the smooth water into waves. It had dispersed any fragments of mist. Above the sky was a clear cerulean blue.

'Thank heavens,' Paula said to Newman as they sat near the stern. 'What we saw was quite terrible.'

'Main thing is we have the evidence – your photos. Soon as we get back to Park Crescent, take the camera down into the basement. I want the film developed immediately and five sets of prints.'

'Five?'

'That's what I said,' he told her abruptly, then grinned.

They were in mid-channel, halfway to the mainland landing point, when Paula turned in her seat, stared back towards Black Island. Newman was also looking in that direction. The speedboat had left

Lydford dock and was roaring towards them. Paula took out her field glasses, steadied herself, then slipped them back inside her pocket.

'We may never reach the mainland,' she said quietly.

Newman was using his own field glasses. He sucked in his breath, then lowered them. He looked at Paula, who had taken out her Browning, holding it out of sight of Abe. She looked at Newman.

'You've seen what's coming after us like a bat out of hell?'

'The powerboat moored to the dock back there. I peered down inside it and neatly stacked next to each other inside the craft were grenades.'

'Do you think, if we survive, they could sink this barge?'

'I've no doubt they could.'

When their lives were in mortal danger Newman never concealed the situation from Paula. She was tough enough and experienced enough to face the truth. She looked back at Abe attending the engine behind them, just far enough away not to overhear them.

'There are three of those swine in black uniforms aboard it,' she mused. 'One is concentrating on steering and the other two are holding automatic weapons. I guess they could spray us with bullets.'

'They'll use the grenades.'

The breeze had dropped. The sea was now a calm sheet of blue. The roar of the oncoming powerboat was louder. Newman calculated it was a question of minutes before the killers arrived. He turned round to Abe.

'Abe, whatever you do don't increase speed.'

'I'm doing that. Don't like the look of that speed job coming straight for us.'

'Do not increase speed if you want to live,' Newman ordered.

Something in his tone, his expression, got through to Abe. Reluctantly he ceased powering up the motor, then looked back, his ancient face distorted with fear. Newman called out again.

'It's going to be all right. Maintain present speed.'

'Hope you knows what you's doin',' Abe shouted back.

Paula had lifted her gun, perched the muzzle on the side of the barge. Newman's tone was quiet but intense.

'Put that damned thing away. Stay very still.'

'If you say so,' she replied, obeying him.

Newman turned his head again, estimating the course the powerboat would take. Earlier it had been roaring towards the stern of the barge, now it veered to their port side; close enough when it was parallel to the barge to hurl grenades into the target, far enough away to elude the results of the expected detonation.

The powerboat was catching them up at a rate of knots. One minute hence and they'd have their craft alongside the barge, but far enough away for their own safety. Newman delved inside a pocket in the golf bag, brought out his clenched hand grasping something. He showed it to Paula. She stared at a large grenade.

'That's a biggie,' she commented.

'One of Harry's specials. Gets them made up by a pal working in an ironworks. Then Harry fills it himself with high explosive, inserts the four-second fuse.'

He held it up so Abe could see only a portion of it. Abe, whose gaze had been fixed on the nearby powerboat, stared, called out.

'What's that?'

'Firework,' Newman lied. 'Left over from Guy Fawkes' day.'

'Lot of friggin' use that will—'

He stopped speaking as Newman, seeing the powerboat had now drawn level with them, jumped swiftly to his feet after removing the grenade's pin. He was on his feet only seconds as he lobbed the grenade. Paula watched it curve in an arc, fall straight inside the powerboat. Newman dropped flat as the first bullets were fired, grabbing Paula, hauling her down with him.

The grenade detonated with an ear-splitting crack. This was nothing compared to the tremendous explosion as it detonated the explosives inside the enemy craft. The menacing prow soared into the air, followed by large fragments of the stern. Abe was knocked flat with the shockwave.

Paula sat up, gazed at where the boat had been only moments before. The surface of the sea was boiling and bubbling. Small pieces of the enemy boat drifted on the surface, then sank. As the sea settled a large red lake spread. Blood. No sign of the recent occupants.

Abe clambered to his feet, a stunned expression on his face. He opened his mouth, burbled something. Then he regained control of his voice.

'What the 'ell was that?'

Newman stood up, walked back to him, laid one hand on his shoulder, showed him his folder with the other. Abe frowned, blinked, looked at Newman.

'Secret Service,' he gulped. 'Gawd!'

'So you don't mention that we were here – not to a soul. And if anyone heard that bang in Tolhaven, you simply say they're using explosives in Black Island's quarry. Got it?'

'Sure I 'ave, and I keeps me mouth closed tight. Now I'll get you both back to the mainland . . .'

'We're leaving for Park Crescent right away,' Newman decided as they approached the Monk's Head. 'Grab your stuff and I'll get mine, then we link up in the car park.'

They left Tolhaven behind, Newman in his Range Rover with Paula behind him in the Ford. Again she had to fight to stop the car running away from her. They paused for a quick tea at an old farmhouse, sitting in the garden despite the cold so no one could hear them.

'Where's Harber's Yard?' Paula wondered. 'We never found it.'

'Remember the old bridge we crossed where you peered over at the river? It flows on and widens into a lake. Then it continues on through woodland to the sea. I explored down there before you arrived, then took the ferry and found the prison. It was important to show you.'

'You're satisfied with our expedition?' she asked.

'I am.' He put his arm round her. 'You've been such a great help taking all those photos. We now have powerful evidence of the lengths to which the so-called State Security lot are going in plotting to turn Britain into a police state. On top of that, at the battle of the ridges six of the bastards killed each other. Add to them the crew in the speedboat and that makes nine less of them to worry about. The first phase of the war went well.'

'You're right,' Paula agreed, 'it is a war. I wonder what's been going on in London while we were away in Dorset.'

9

The Cabal was holding yet another of its brainstorming sessions. All three men were seated round the strange triangular rosewood table. Outside dusk was falling and they had the lights on. Nelson was playing with his fountain pen, still wearing his Armani suit. As usual, Noel was holding forth.

'The Parrot has reported to me about the informant she sent to spy outside Tweed's office. He was still there, so the plan to involve him in that horrible murder in Fox Street didn't work.'

'What horrible murder?' enquired Nelson.

'Obviously you don't read the *Daily Nation*,' Noel sneered. 'It might help if you kept up with the news. There's a lurid article on the murder by that swine of a lead reporter, Drew Franklin. We ought to do something about him, put him out of action . . .'

'You've just made two mistakes in a few sentences,' Nelson said severely. 'First, you must call Miss

Partridge by her proper name. If she ever heard you use the nickname Parrot we could lose her loyalty, which is important to us. And, in addition, don't try any of your funny tricks on Drew Franklin. He may be a nuisance but he has great influence. Just watch it, Horlick.'

Noel, his face livid, jumped up, ran round the table, his long hands reaching for Nelson's neck. 'Don't ever call me by that name again,' he screamed.

Benton stood up just in time to stop him reaching Nelson. He grasped Noel's outstretched arms, forced them down by his side. Breathing rapidly, Noel glared at Benton, who was smiling.

'Go back to your chair, Noel.' He looked over his shoulder. 'Nelson, I think you'd be wise to remember his name is now Macomber. An apology would help – otherwise I'm adjourning the meeting.'

'My sincere apologies, Noel,' Nelson said quickly. 'I made a blunder, which you can rest assured will never be repeated.'

'I should damned well hope not,' Noel snapped.

He returned to his seat, mopping his sweating forehead with a handkerchief. To calm himself down he poured water from a carafe into a glass, drank the lot. He waited and there was silence while he got a grip on himself. He resumed talking.

'As I was saying, Miss Partridge's informant visited Tweed, found him seated in his office, his normal self. She, the informant, did notice one relationship we might exploit to throw Tweed off balance. I refer to his senior assistant, Paula.'

'What about her?' asked Benton.

'She is Tweed's weak point. He appears to be fond of her. If she was kidnapped—'

'What!' demanded Benton. 'Who gave you that idea?' he went on, his tone ominously quiet.

'Thought it up myself,' Noel replied with a smug grin.

'In that case,' Benton leaned across the table, his eyes fixed on Noel's, 'you can remove the thought from your evil mind.'

'In any case,' Nelson interjected, 'first, who is the informant Miss Partridge used who is capable of penetrating Tweed's fortress?'

'That's restricted info,' Noel replied. 'Not to be told to anyone under any circumstances.'

'I see.' Benton pressed on. 'Had you anyone in mind to carry out this dangerous folly?'

'As a matter of fact,' Noel continued in the same smug way, 'I have the perfect operator for the job.'

'Who *is*? This time you tell me,' Benton demanded.

'Amos Fitch.'

He was not able to proceed any further. Benton's full face became red, red as a man with high blood pressure.

'Oh, my God!' He lifted a hand, ran it through his

thick greying hair. 'Amos Fitch. You've lost your mind. We can't be involved with a brute like that. About eight years ago he was charged with knifing a man to death. The not guilty verdict was due to his brilliant lawyer discrediting the circumstantial evidence.'

'Just a thought,' Noel said, smiling. 'Forget it. And no one has noticed that all the time we've been talking the door to the next room has been left open a few inches. Who left us last?'

'Actually,' Nelson observed airily, 'it was Miss Partridge.'

'I'm checking,' Noel whispered.

He crept over to the door, moved it slightly. Well-oiled hinges. He closed it quietly, testing the latch. He pulled at it quietly. It was firmly closed. He looked at the other two.

'I'm going to see if anyone is there.'

Again he opened the door, slipped into the next room, closing the door carefully. On their own now, Benton looked at Nelson.

'That was a bad slip, using the name Horlick. You saw the effect it had on him.'

'My mistake, but I have apologized.'

Noel surveyed the spacious room next door. No sign of Partridge at her large desk. The only occupant was her assistant, Coral Flenton, seated with her back to him at a corner desk as she worked at a computer. Noel crept up behind her, laid a hand on her shoulder.

'Oh, please! Don't do that.' She had moved her mirror and she had nearly jumped out of her chair, which amused Noel. She swung round in her swivel chair, her large hazel eyes glaring at him. She put up a hand to push back a lock of red hair. 'What is it?' she snapped.

'No "sir"? I am a junior minister,' Noel said genially and gave her a wide smile. He perched himself on a nearby desk, looming over her small neat figure.

He had a winning smile and she responded with a faint smile of her own, but ignored the reference to 'sir'. He folded his arms. He still looked youthful and she had mixed feelings about him.

'The door to our sanctum was open, not properly closed,' he began. 'Not that I'm suggesting it has anything to do with you. Has Miss Partridge been lingering near that door?'

'I doubt it. In any case,' she went on, emboldened, 'with my back to it how would I know who comes and goes?'

'Of course you wouldn't. When you leave the office tonight maybe you would join me for coffee or a drink?'

'That's very nice of you,' she replied in a neutral tone, 'but I'm attending a girl friend's birthday party.'

'Pity.' He stood up, still smiling. 'Maybe some other time.'

He walked slowly back across the wide room to the door and voiced his thoughts to himself, barely muttering.

'Paula is the key. And Amos Fitch is the man for the job.'

Amos Fitch was at the greyhound races. He kept at the back of the crowd, always remaining as inconspicuous as possible. Five feet eight inches tall, he wore a brown overcoat and as usual he also wore a large trilby hat, the brim pulled well down, exposing only the lower half of his face. Which, unintentionally, was kinder to the rest of the world.

His restless brown eyes hardly ever stopped moving while they checked his surroundings. The thick upper lids were frequently half-closed so only part of the searching eyes were seen. His bent nose above a thin twisted mouth added to the cunning look, almost his trademark. His mouth was little more than a slit with a heavy jaw below. He was known in certain not-so-law-abiding circles as Sly. He was pondering the brief message on his mobile inviting him to meet Canal at 9.30 p.m. in an East End pub called the Pig's Nest.

Tony Canal was a dubious go-between who never revealed the identity of his employer. This habit had caused Sly to follow Canal on an earlier occasion. Canal was an old Etonian who had gone to the bad, as they said at the Yard. So Sly knew that the real employer was a toff. A real toff, called Noel Macomber.

10

Tweed was driving slowly in the country near the border of Surrey and Sussex. He was searching for Peckham Mallet, where General Lucius Macomber, father of the three Cabal brothers, had a cottage. He'd decided it was time he met the General, had a chat with him.

It was early afternoon, the sky was a clear blue, sunlight illuminated the forested area. He had been driving for over an hour, searching for this tiny village. He hadn't found it on the map back at Park Crescent. It was only when Monica suggested checking the index that he'd located it. Should have thought of that first. Was that drug still fogging his system? Percodin, Saafeld had called it.

There were no houses in the forested area, no pubs, no one he could ask for directions. He drove slowly on and almost missed an ancient signpost at the entrance to a turning. He reversed to read it, barely able to make out the words on the worn signpost. Peckham Mallet.

He proceeded slowly down the narrow lane. After about half a mile he saw an old codger, dressed in working-man's clothes, scything the grass verge. He stopped, got out, smiled as he approached the man. His shoulders were permanently bent, probably due to the nature of his work. About seventy, Tweed assessed. His face was lined, his chin was shrunken and he'd not had a shave for days.

'Can you help me, please?' Tweed began. 'I've been asked to give General Macomber some information. I need to speak to him urgently.'

'Who might you be?'

Tweed produced his folder, held it under the old boy's nose. The workman studied it. He attempted to straighten up but the shoulders stayed bent. He gazed at the folder, then gazed at Tweed.

'SIS? That wouldn't be Secret Service, would it?'

'It would be and is. I'm asking for your help, please.'

'Won't find the General round 'ere. Comes up to the cottage on his way to Lunnon. Spends a few days up there and then goes back 'ome. On his way up he calls 'ere to pay me wages, checks the cottage back there.'

He waved with the scythe he was still holding. Tweed stepped back quickly to stay clear of the deadly blade. He looked up a pathway to a cottage set in the fields as he spoke.

'Would you mind putting down that scythe while we chat for a moment?'

'Means I'll 'ave to bend over to lift it again. If I'm able to manage that . . .'

'I'll pick it up for you,' Tweed said quickly.

Without bending, the workman threw the scythe a foot or so away from them. What a dreadful way to spend the later years of your life, Tweed thought as he looked up the pathway at the cottage. Built of brick with a renewed tiled roof and a brilliantly polished brass knob on the freshly painted wooden front door that gleamed in the sun. The General was obviously a stickler for appearances.

'Stays there overnight sometimes. Just sleeps there, then buzzes off to Lunnon.'

'When was he last here – and in London?' Tweed asked in an off-hand tone.

'A week ago. Stayed up in the Smoke a few days, then came back here this morning on his way 'ome.'

That places General Lucius Macomber in town at the time of the murder of Viola Vander-Browne. Interesting, Tweed thought. He bent down, picked up the scythe carefully, handed it to its owner.

'Where is his real home, then?' Tweed asked. 'The MoD had lost his permanent address,' he concluded, making it up as he went along.

'That be a distance from 'ere. He's a large house on Black Island, near Tolhaven. You takes the ferry, gets off at Lydford, walks past the village, takes the first road to the left and he's a short way along on your left. I goes down there to look after his garden, more like a park. Other people 'elps 'im but he likes me to trim edges. I'm Pat,' he added.

'You've been very helpful, Pat.' Tweed paused. He was absorbing the shock that the General lived in the location where Newman and Paula were exploring. 'Oh, where does this lane lead to?'

'Mountain 'igh. See all over Sussex and Surrey from the top. I'd take the car, if I was you. It's a long pull walkin' up there.'

Tweed drove up the lane, which swiftly became very steep as the trees disappeared, with green grass spreading up the slope. Tweed was aware he was climbing a considerable height. He'd never heard of Mountain High. Too difficult to find the lane up, he decided.

He had another surprise when he reached the summit. It was flat as a billiard table and extensive. An airsock to show wind direction suggested private planes landed there. He parked on the edge of the landing field, climbed out and took in a deep breath of the marvellous fresh air. He was on top of the world.

Pat had not exaggerated. The panoramic view in every direction was stunning in the sunlight. Tweed could see for miles, and in the far distance he could make out a small plane high in the sky. He went back to his car to fetch his powerful field glasses.

He had already located the General's cottage, which from where he stood looked no bigger than a doll's house. What had attracted his attention was a large enclosed truck moving away from the back of the cottage. Through his lenses he read the legend painted on its side: Windrush & Carne Removals. Take Anything But A Tank.

He watched it heading towards a large barn whose rear doors were wide open. The truck entered the barn. The driver appeared at the back and Tweed had a clear view of the contents. Heavy old furniture – and a black metal box. The driver climbed inside the truck, inserted a key, lifted the lid of the black box. Tweed had a brief glimpse inside – a maze of wires. His lips tightened. High explosive.

He had a clearer view of the driver. Grabbing a small sketch pad from his pocket, he used a pencil to draw his impression of the driver's face. A brown trilby pulled down at a slanting angle over his forehead. Thick upper lids were closed down over half his eyes, a bent nose, a slit of a mouth, heavy jaw, the whole expression had a cunning look. The driver turned his head away. Tweed slipped the pad back into his pocket, continued watching through the glasses.

The driver jumped agilely out of the furniture van, fixed a large padlock after closing the heavy doors. He then repeated the process after leaving the barn. He ran across to a Saab parked nearby, jumped in behind the wheel. Tweed noted the plate number and the car was moving fast down the field on to the road leading back to London.

Tweed turned round as the light aircraft he'd seen flew closer, dipped and was landing on the airstrip. The moment it was stationary the pilot leapt out, removed his goggles and helmet. He grinned at Tweed.

'First person I've ever found up here.' He was youngish, his voice was cultured, his personality friendly. He marched towards Tweed.

'Care for a spin? Half an hour and you'll look down on the beauties of this part of the world. I love it.'

'Thank you,' Tweed replied, 'but I have to go now to an urgent appointment in London. I appreciate the offer.'

'Maybe another time.'

Tweed walked briskly back to his car. This landing point might just be useful one day, he thought. Newman is an expert pilot. He could get us down here in no time.

*

The Cabal's meeting had resumed after lunch. Nelson insisted that they must keep checking on progress. So many aspects to keep moving. Benton spoke gently, gazing up at the ceiling. His words were aimed at Noel.

'Still wasting our time chasing the girls, are we?'

'Of course. What better way of spending a free evening? I've dumped Eve. She was too prissy when it came to the point. Women are useful for only one thing. Not to mind. I'm on with a girl called Tina. Very hoity-toity, but I'm sure she knows what men need.'

He's younger, Benton thought. He'll grow out of it. Or will he? Another anxiety surfaced. He stared at Noel.

'The idea you had about kidnapping Paula Grey isn't going anywhere, I trust?'

'Gone clean out of my mind,' Noel lied. 'Too many other problems to sort out. There's the prison – the one on Black Island . . .'

'We haven't seen any plans,' Benton snapped. 'Before we even consider starting building I want to see the plans. So, I'm sure, does Nelson.'

'Yes indeed,' Nelson agreed.

'No work's done yet,' Noel lied again. 'As to the plans, the project is so secret the only plan is with the surveyor on Black Island. I thought it too risky to have photocopies floating about.'

'Well,' Benton persisted, 'not a brick is to be laid until we have seen them. I'm worried about the idea.'

'Benton,' Nelson interjected, 'we do need somewhere to park social saboteurs.'

'And what does that sinister phrase mean?'

'Anyone who tries to disagree with the new society we are creating.'

'Too vague,' snapped Benton. 'If we give the State Security staff too much rope some will use it to pay off old scores. I won't sanction that.'

'Well,' Noel interjected, 'let's leave that problem until later. There's no hurry on that front. Benton could be right.'

Noel was playing a game he'd thought up in the past: act as reasonable peacemaker, then they'd leave him alone. He had been feeling under pressure.

'When do we play the terrorist card?' boomed Nelson.

There was dead silence. Nelson had decided the atmosphere must be tougher. There were rumours in Parliament that he might be nearer to full promotion – to become a member of the Cabinet as Minister of Internal Security. He waited for the outburst of disagreement. Benton was more subtle.

'Noel,' he said casually, staring up at the ceiling, 'have you yet explored the dangers of playing the terrorist card, as Nelson suggested?'

'No, not really,' Noel said, lying once again. 'I had

the idea of getting someone to drive a truck with a modest amount of explosives into a side entrance to Richmond Park, an area which, at this time of the year, has no one about. I'm not at all sure it's a good idea.'

'It isn't!' Benton thundered. 'Kill one civilian and we all end up in Belmarsh prison.'

'I did say I felt it was a bad idea,' Noel assured him smoothly. He checked his watch. 'Isn't it time we ended this session? You all agree? Good.'

He had an appointment to take Tina out that evening.

Tweed parked his car, locked it, walked through the dark at Park Crescent, found his whole team assembled in his office. He greedily drank the coffee Monica supplied, then produced his sketch book. What he had drawn of the driver was a caricature.

'I've been down to Mountain High,' he announced.

'Switzerland?' Paula teased him from behind her desk. 'You were quick.'

Tweed grinned, then turned round the sketch pad and asked if anyone recognized who it was. Newman loped over from beside Paula's desk, picked up the pad, stared at it for only a few moments.

'God!' he exclaimed. 'That's Amos Fitch. He wasn't close to you, I hope?'

Tweed leaned back in his chair, tersely gave them

the details of his excursion. Harry, seated cross-legged on the floor, looked up sharply at the mention of high explosives. This was his speciality. He kept quiet as Tweed spoke.

'Then I drove back here,' Tweed concluded. 'Now I want to hear what you, Bob, have been up to with Paula.'

He listened without interrupting as Newman related the events of their day. When Newman described the details of the prison on Black Island, Tweed's expression changed, became grim.

'I see,' he said as Newman sat down. 'Then that does it. We will use any unorthodox method to remove the Cabal from any contact with politics. Any method, however ruthless. The gloves are off. I'm glad you killed those State Security thugs. We may have to eliminate many more. From this moment on no one leaves this building without carrying weapons. And I want a guard to accompany Paula wherever she goes.' He held up a hand as she started to protest. 'I have a premonition you may be one of their main targets – from the way Partridge looked at you when she pretended to visit us on her own.'

'You think the Cabal knew?' she asked.

'I doubt if they knew everything she told us, but she's too smart to come here without their knowledge.'

'May I report something?' Pete Nield requested.

'While you were away I had another long talk with my informant. She told me the Parrot is crazy over Nelson. At least she was. For some reason now she hates him.'

'Paula,' Tweed asked, 'what emotion is most likely to cause a woman to turn into a murderous rage?'

'Jealousy.'

'It opens up a new possibility.'

'Well,' Paula said, 'at Professor Saafeld's didn't I correct him when he kept saying "he" for the murderer? I suggested it could be a woman who was responsible for Vander-Browne's awful fate.'

'We'll keep all our options open.'

'You know,' remarked Newman to Tweed, 'you do have so much on your plate now. First this merger of the security services you're fighting. Second, the investigation into the Fox Street murder. Two separate problems. A bit much?'

'Not necessarily. I'm beginning to wonder if there isn't a link between the two.' Tweed produced a sketch from a locked drawer, invited his team to come and look at it.

It was a retouched photo produced by Joel, the artist in the basement. They crowded behind Tweed and stared at the result. It showed an attractive woman's head and shoulders. Her dark hair was close to the side of her head, like a helmet.

'Joel worked on one of those photos of the Parrot

you took, Paula,' Tweed explained. 'I gave him a description of someone. You are now looking at the picture of the waitress, so-called, who laced my margarita with Percodin and brought it to the table. "With the compliments of Mr Mungano." On the way back from Peckham Mallet I called in at Mungano's, saw the proprietor. I knew he'd been adding to his staff of waiters by hiring a few suitable girls. I showed him this.'

'Go on,' Paula urged, 'what did he say?'

'That he'd never hired anyone who looked a bit like her.'

'So that links her directly with the plot to frame you for the Fox Street murder,' Paula said, concealing her excitement. 'Now we can concentrate on the Parrot.'

'She was never out of my calculations – among a range of suspects,' Tweed replied. 'What triggered me off was that contact lens you found on the floor. The fake waitress who drugged me had blue eyes. I'm going to see the Cabal soon. It will be interesting if Partridge appears so I can see the real colour of her eyes.'

'May I come with you when the time comes?' Paula asked.

'I was going to take you with me in any case.' Tweed looked at Newman. 'Bob, I also want to go down with you and Paula to Black Island, urgently. I found out General Lucius Macomber lives there. Not far from the village of Lydford. I think it's important I have a long talk with him. He is the father of the three men composing the Cabal.'

'What about those explosives in that furniture van? I'd like to go down and check out that black box, maybe muck it up,' said Harry.

'Do that. But Peckham Mallet is the devil of a place to locate. Mainly because it doesn't really exist. I'll draw you a plan marking the lane to the General's cottage, the cottage itself and location of the barn. Both the van and the doors to the barn it's inside have very heavy padlocks.'

'Piece of cake for me.' Harry bent down, lifted up the bag with his tools he carried almost everywhere. 'I've already located Peckham Mallet on the map.'

'Then we don't waste time,' Tweed decided firmly. 'Tomorrow, Harry, you go check out that furniture van.'

'Excuse me,' Monica broke in, 'I checked the name on the side of the van, as you asked me to. No firm with that name exists. I also checked the number plate. Stolen from a car in a police compound.'

'Fitch has a nerve,' Newman commented grimly.

As they were talking, Marler walked in.

Marler was a key member of Tweed's team. He dressed at least as smartly as Pete Nield. This afternoon he was sporting a blue Aquascutum suit, a cream shirt and a blue tie decorated with herons in flight. His feet were clad in black handmade shoes with concealed razor-sharp blades in the tips.

In his early forties, but looking like a man in his thirties, he was slim, and five feet nine tall. Women found him good-looking. His hair was fair, he was clean shaven with features which suggested he felt superior, although he had perfect manners and an upper-crust voice. He was also reputed to be the most deadly marksman in Europe. He walked across to his usual corner by Paula's desk, leaned against the wall, took out a cigarette and inserted it into a black holder before lighting it.

'Thought I heard the name Fitch, my old sparring partner Amos. Weird that such a murderous villain has a biblical name. Last time I met him he tried to knife me. He ended up on the floor, cold to the world. I've often thought I should have killed him,' he remarked casually. 'World would have been a better place without him.'

'It certainly would,' Paula said coldly.

Tweed heard this uncharacteristic tone in her voice. Paula had become even tougher. He guessed it was since seeing Viola's shattered body. He stood up.

'It's been a long day. Tomorrow will be another one. So I suggest you all go home and relax in whatever way you prefer.'

'I'm taking my girlfriend, Roma, out to dinner,'

Newman announced. 'She's very bright and enter-taining. Two degrees from Cambridge. I have to be alert to keep up with her.'

'Then make the most of it,' Paula teased him. 'It won't last long.'

'You might be more polite. I'm escorting you home.' He saw her expression. 'No option, Tweed's orders. I'll call back later to make sure everything is secure.'

'That will be about 4 a.m.,' she said wickedly. 'When you've torn yourself away from Roma. That's a curious name.'

'She was born in Rome, daughter of the British Ambassador. She was born in the Embassy, so she's as British as you are. Ready to leave?'

'Not for half an hour at least, maybe longer. I have a report to type. If that's going to mess up your date with Roma . . .'

'It isn't. I'm not seeing her until eight o'clock.'

'I'm off to prowl the East End,' Harry called out as he left.

'I'm off too,' Marler said. 'To have a drink with some Members of Parliament. To see whether they've heard of State Security. If so, get their reaction. Toodle-oo . . .'

Nield said he had a job to do. He left the building, climbed into his car. He was waiting for Tweed to leave so he could follow him home. No good telling him. He'd blow up.

'I'm off too,' Tweed decided. 'Let's hope we have a quiet night.'

It was a statement he later regretted.

11

That afternoon Fitch had used his mobile to contact his accomplice, Tony Canal. They had arranged to meet at 9.30 p.m. at the Pig's Nest in the East End but Fitch had used this tactic before. It was important to show who was boss, to throw his henchmen off balance. He called Canal again in an hour.

'Meet me at the warehouse now!' he snarled.

He switched off before Canal could reply. Fitch was inside the abandoned warehouse. The old wooden floor was still solid but the skylights were missing several panes of glass. The large room, once used by a shipping company for storage, had been rented by Fitch for a song. In a fictitious name.

While he waited his booted feet clunked up and down the floorboards, pacing impatiently. He was smoking a cigar, a Havana. Only the best was good enough for Amos Fitch, and he had a nice balance in a small bank, the fruits of his criminal exploits.

When Canal entered after climbing the rickety staircase Fitch blew smoke in his weird face. Tony Canal was an ex-prize-fighter in matches held in private houses where no holds were barred. A broken nose and a lopsided jaw were the earnings from his underworld life.

'Show you something,' Fitch growled at him.

Bending down, he lifted a handle set into the floor, raised a thick wooden lid about two feet in diameter. Canal heard the gurgle of rushing water a long way down. Roughly, Fitch grabbed his arm, used the other hand to point a torch.

'Take a look, thickhead.'

Canal peered down. The torch beam lit up a steel shaft with a large hook about a foot down. The beam was just strong enough to illuminate rushing black water at the very bottom. Canal didn't like it. He stepped back as Fitch replaced the lid, spoke.

'That's where we'll put 'er when we've grabbed 'er.'

'Put who, may I ask?' Canal enquired.

'You may ask, dear boy,' Fitch told him, mimicking Canal's public-school accent. 'You just damned well did,' he rasped in normal coarse voice. 'Miss Paula Grey goes down the chute.'

He picked up a coil of rope from the floor. One end was twisted into a loop, but without a slip knot. Fitch pointed this out to Canal, who was looking worried.

'With that round her neck,' he explained with a sadistic smile.

'When we get 'er 'ere, we wrap a scarf round 'er neck, then we slip this rope loop over the scarf. With that round 'er neck we lower 'er into the chute, then fasten one end of the rope over the 'ook sticking out from the side of the tube.'

'I don't understand, I'm afraid,' Canal protested.

'No, you wouldn't. You've noticed the loop goin' round 'er neck is frayed, have you? Good. Miracles 'appen. She's suspended down in the tube. She'll try to remove the rope. When she keeps tryin' to do that the frayed part gives way. Down goes Tweed's pet into the water and gets carried into the river. End of the lady.'

'Sounds horrible – and strangely complex.'

'Heaven give us strength. Don't you see? The body will be carried down the river towards the barrage. At some point the body will be seen and dragged out – or she'll get washed up on the river edge. The police autopsy will check her. No sign of strangulation. The scarf has protected her neck against the grazin' of the rope. Rope and scarf will have got washed away. She'll have lungs full of water. Verdict? She drowned. No risk of it lookin' like murder. See?'

'I think so. Do we have to do this?'

'Monkey, we're being paid good money to kidnap Miss Paula Grey. To hit Tweed hard. Imagine how much harder it'll hit him when she's dragged out dead. Get it?'

'I guess so. I'm not happy about her dying.'

'Who asked you to be 'appy? This is business. Now we've got to go out and grab 'er. You've nicked a car, fitted it with stolen plates?'

'Of course I have. It's parked out of sight at the back of the warehouse here.'

'Good. We'll grab 'er tonight. Bring 'er back 'ere.'

'You're not going to put her down that awful shaft?'

'Listen, mate,' Fitch snarled, 'your job is to do what I tell you to do. And yes, she'll be food for the fishes in the river before the night is out. I've done my 'omework. She often arrives back at 'er Fulham Road pad at about 9 p.m. So we get there early, park further down the Fulham Road, chew the fat until she arrives.'

12

Newman insisted on escorting Paula home despite her protests. She was not best pleased when Tweed ordered her to drive home while Newman followed her in his own car.

'You've got your dinner with Roma,' she protested as they went down the stairs.

'I've phoned her, made a later appointment.'

'Great, she must have loved that.'

'She knows I'm very busy and said she'd phone the restaurant to warn them to keep the table. She's very amenable.'

'I still don't like it.'

As she pulled up outside the entrance to the large yard where she'd park her car outside her apartment she didn't notice the battered Ford parked further behind her. Inside it Fitch grunted with satisfaction, lifted a tin off the floor, took out the airtight bag containing a cloth soaked in chloroform.

'Got 'er,' he gloated.

Then he stared as another car pulled up behind her Saab. A man jumped out, walked alongside the Saab as she drove it inside the yard. Fitch rammed the bag back inside the tin.

'Friggin' 'ell,' he said to Canal beside him. 'That's Newman going in with 'er. He's a tough bastard.' He started his engine. 'We'll 'ave to come back about 4 a.m. What 'e's goin' to do with her could take a while,' he commented coarsely. 'We'd better make ourselves scarce.'

He drove at moderate speed past Newman's car and continued along the Fulham Road.

Newman searched her flat on the first floor thoroughly. Paula, feeling guilty, offered him a drink. He was in the main corridor, staring up at a flat panel let into the ceiling. He called out to Paula, who was hanging up her windcheater. He pointed.

'What's up there?'

'Just a loft. I never use it. Some people put all their junk up there. I don't. Now, have a nice evening with Roma. I'm sure you will.'

He'd refused the drink. She kissed him on the cheek, then hugged him, smiling as she let him go. She'd seen no point in mentioning there was a large skylight in the loft.

'I do appreciate your looking after me. Go wild tonight.'

'It's early days with her.'

★

He met Roma at Santorini's, a luxurious restaurant with a section projecting over the Thames. No one was using that area tonight – it was too cold.

Roma was an attractive woman in her mid-thirties with perfectly coiffeured black hair. She had large blue eyes, a well-shaped profile and a wicked sense of humour with a habit of laughing a lot, a low husky laugh.

Her father was rich, owning a large chain of retail stores he'd inherited from his father. She'd been to private school at Benenden but had no airs and graces. He had no trouble talking to her.

'You're in insurance, I gather,' she remarked later in the evening over coffee and the rest of the wine. 'A special sort, I've heard.'

'The General & Cumbria Insurance,' Newman said, quoting the name on the plate outside SIS headquarters in Park Crescent. It was a cover for the real activities they engaged in. 'It is a bit special. We only insure wealthy men and their families against being kidnapped. The ransom demand.'

'You just pay up, Bob? I can't quite imagine that's how you always operate.'

'Shrewd lady.' He smiled again. 'We have been known to track down the kidnappers. It can get a bit hairy sometimes.'

'You lead a dangerous life . . .'

'I suppose I do, now and then.'

Her remark made him check his watch under the tablecloth. It was 4 a.m. Roma had just suppressed a yawn.

After escorting Roma to her apartment nearby Newman sat for a moment in the car. He remembered the battered old Ford parked further along the Fulham Road when he'd arrived with Paula. Automatically he'd swung round, caught a glimpse of the driver. He'd seemed familiar. Alarm bells began ringing now inside his head.

Fitch. He'd seen police photos of the brutal villain. He drove as fast as he dared back to the Fulham Road. A few yards beyond the entrance to Paula's place the same battered Ford was parked. One man inside, in the front passenger seat.

Newman pulled up, switched off the engine, dived out on to the pavement. He then walked casually up to the Ford. The driver's window was lowered. Newman tested the door handle. It opened. He leaned inside.

The passenger had slipped something into the side pocket of his jacket. He looked at Newman nervously. Didn't say anything. Which was odd.

'Why are you parked here in the middle of the night?' Newman demanded in an unfriendly tone.

'I've . . . had too much . . . to drink. Waiting till it's safe . . . to drive.'

'Really?' Newman had leaned in closer. No smell of any liquor on his breath. 'Where's the driver?' he snapped.

'He had to . . .'

'You kidded me up you were the driver. What's going on?'

'Nothing. I told you . . .'

Newman jumped inside, sat in the driver's seat, grasped his captive round the neck. He pressed a thumb against the windpipe. Canal's eyes bulged, he began to choke.

'Who is the driver?' Newman demanded in an unpleasant voice. 'And where is he now?'

With the hands removed from his throat Canal started talking. Newman listened. Canal admitted that they were going to kidnap Paula. The moment he heard this Newman hit him on the jaw, hard enough to knock him out. He left Canal, who had given his name, slumped half on the floor.

Newman ran back towards Paula's flat. No sign of Fitch. He walked quietly on his rubber-soled shoes over the cobbles, glanced at Paula's window. No light. He walked round the side. A strong-looking drainpipe was attached to the wall. Fitch was nearly at the top. Newman recalled that on his crime sheet among many other more villainous crimes Fitch had been a cat burglar.

'Come on down, pal,' he called up loudly. He had

his Smith & Wesson in his right hand. 'Unless you'd prefer a bullet up the rear end.'

Fitch, startled, nearly lost his grip. He regained it as he glared viciously down at Newman, his eyes like those of a snake, then descended quickly when he saw the revolver. Newman had holstered his gun when Fitch landed expertly on the cobbles, bending his knees. He was swinging round when Newman grabbed both his shoulders, hauled him across the yard, slammed him forcefully into a wall. Fitch's head met the wall with a loud crunch. He was tough. He pretended to be winded, crouched down, grasped a knife from a sheath strapped to his leg.

Newman raised his right foot, kicked Fitch hard between the legs. Fitch groaned, dropped his knife, used both hands to clutch the injury. Newman grasped his hair, hauled him out of the yard and along the deserted pavement to the car. Before opening the rear door he slammed Fitch's head hard against the car's roof. Fitch was unconscious as he heaved him on to the floor in the rear of the Ford.

As Newman had hoped, Canal was sitting up, staring as though he couldn't believe what he'd witnessed. Newman climbed into the back of the car, placed his feet on Fitch's face.

'Canal,' he said grimly, 'you can drive now, can't you?'

'I guess so.'

'Don't guess, just do it. Slide behind the wheel. Then you drive to that warehouse you told me about . . .'

It was still dark. Canal made a better job of driving than Newman had expected. The East End was still quiet as they pulled up in front of the warehouse entrance. On Newman's ferocious order Canal got out, opened the padlock, went inside. Newman followed, Fitch's unconscious body looped over his shoulder. They entered the large bare room. Newman saw the handle to the round lid let into the dirty wooden floor. He dumped Fitch, then turned on Canal.

'Listen, pie-face, where do you come from? You're not East End.'

'Blackpool.'

'Any contacts up there?'

'My sister has a place I stay at.'

'Then you catch the first train north and never come back. If you do I'll report you to Commander Buchanan at the Yard. Tell him you were involved in a kidnap attempt. Should get you five years inside. Maybe more. So better keep your stupid trap shut. Get moving.'

'You'll tell Fitch where I've gone?'

'I'll tell him you're hiding away locally. Can you imagine what he'll do to you if he ever catches up with you?'

'I'm on my way.'

Alone with Fitch, who was stirring feebly on the floor, Newman put on latex gloves. No fingerprints. He lifted the lid off, used a torch to stare down into the metal shell, saw the rushing water at the bottom heading for the river. He was in a fierce mood when he recalled Canal's babbling account of what had been planned for Paula.

Picking up the large coil of rope from the floor, he checked it, saw the loop for Paula's neck, the frayed section which wouldn't have lasted long. Taking out a knife, he cut away that section, then re-formed the loop without a slip knot so it would hold.

Using the woollen scarf he'd taken from the back seat of the car (Fitch was a well-organized piece of filth), he wrapped the scarf round Fitch's neck not too tightly, so he could breathe easily. Next he slipped the safe loop he had prepared round the scarf. Fitch suddenly came wide awake.

'What the 'ell you doin' now? I'll get you for this, Newman.'

'You think so?'

Grabbing both Fitch's legs he hauled him to the chute, dropped them over. Fitch was now mixing the worst swear words with pleas for mercy. Newman looped the long length of rope over the hook a short distance down the chute, then lowered Fitch slowly down inside the metal tube. His head was now a short distance below the hook. His voice echoed weirdly inside the metal tube.

'For Gawd's sake, Newman, don't do this to me. I've a pile of money. It's all yours . . .'

The rest of his maundering plea was shut off as Newman replaced the lid. It was now up to fate. Newman couldn't bring himself to use the frayed loop. That would be cold-blooded murder. Not his style.

13

It was still dark. Newman walked some distance before he hailed a cab driver, told him to drop him outside a block of flats in the Fulham Road. He didn't want any witnesses who could report where he had boarded the cab, where he had left it.

A promising dawn was casting first light as he walked quickly to Paula's place. He'd intended to get into his car and drive quietly away. Paula, fully dressed, appeared at her bedroom window, called down to him.

'Come on up. Here's the key to the front door . . .'

He caught it, went inside and up to her flat. The ground-floor flat was occupied by a woman who spent little time there. Paula was waiting for him at the head of the stairs, took him by the arm, led him inside. She was clad in what she called her 'battle-dress' – smart blue slacks tucked into the tops of knee-length boots, a warm blue windcheater. Her hair was well brushed, as though she'd just been to the hairdresser's.

'I was worried when I saw your car still parked out there . . .'

'I've been up the last twenty-four hours.'

'So you had a great night with Roma.' Paula smiled as she said it. 'I'm not asking for details.'

'You can have them. I left Santorini's with Roma at 4 a.m., drove her home, then came straight on up here. Which may be why you're still alive.'

He'd decided to tell her part of his encounter with Fitch. She needed to grasp the danger of this mission. He cut off the story with shoving an unconscious Fitch in the rear of the Ford, ordering Canal to drive off and never to come back.

'He was climbing up the drainpipe,' Paula said nervously.

'What's in the loft? Another way in?'

'There's a large skylight.'

'Fitch must have done a recce earlier. That's where he planned to get in, to grab you. He had a bag containing cloth soaked with chloroform. You'd have ended up in the river.'

'Are you trying to frighten me? If so, you're doing a good job. And you look fagged out. You need sleep – in my back bedroom. Now!'

'Tweed wants us to go down to Black Island, to interview the General. Then there's his trip to confront the Cabal.'

'Shut up! Sleep.'

Newman stumbled, she grasped his arm, led him to the back bedroom. He found the sight of the made-up bed alluring; his head was throbbing. He was taking off his shoes when Paula reappeared with a glass and a large carafe of water. He swallowed the whole of the glass she poured for him, drank half the refill. Taking off his windcheater he stripped off his tie, loosened his collar.

'I'll phone Tweed, explain the position,' Paula assured him.

He flopped full-length on the bed. He was asleep when she tucked the pillow more comfortably under his head. Then she went into the kitchen, prepared two thermoses, one with coffee, the other with tea, a jug of milk, two cups and saucers, a plate of currant buns, carried everything on a tray, left it on the table by his bedside. Newman was motionless, breathing steadily, out of this world.

Paula drove to Park Crescent, was the first person in the office except for Monica. She had phoned Tweed at home from her flat. Everyone else arrived later, including Marler, who took up his favourite position, leaning against the wall, inserting a cigarette into his holder.

When he'd settled behind his desk, Tweed's first question was addressed to Paula.

'How is Bob?'

'Sleeping like a babe. I think he'd had a tougher night than I relayed to you on the phone.'

'I suspected that. Marler, you were going to contact some of your pals in Parliament, to check what they'd heard.'

'Not my pals,' Marler drawled, 'my contacts. Fed them plenty of booze in the visitors' room or whatever they call it – and they talked their heads off. One of the brighter characters had heard the rumours about the formation of State Security. Didn't like it a bit. Said this land of freedom was going to be converted into a police state. A number of others agreed. A number of Cabinet Ministers are in favour, but not quite enough yet to agree to a bill being presented. It's on a knife-edge.'

'So we can expect further incentives to scare everyone stiff. Hooligans smashing up inner cities. God knows what other villainy . . .'

Tweed paused as Newman roared into the office. Paula checked the time. Newman couldn't have had more than four hours' sleep but his mood was tigerish.

'I've been thinking,' he began. 'We're not moving quickly enough. Tweed has a horrific murder to solve, then we have the State Security lot to smash. Anyone with scruples about using unorthodox methods had better wake up. Now I'm ready to drive down with Tweed and Paula to Black Island as a starter.'

Paula was marvelling at Newman's speedy recovery, his vitality. His appearance was intimidating. He was wearing a camouflage jacket and trousers tucked inside his boots. He had crammed a black beret over his tousled hair. Like a Commando, she thought. But at one time he had trained with the SAS to write an article on them. His experience had included joining potential recruits in a gruelling march over the Welsh mountains. To everyone's astonishment, including the SAS commander's, Newman had reached the far-away stop line as Number Two.

'Pete,' Tweed interjected, wanting to give him a difficult task so he'd not feel put down by Newman, 'I need you to do a tricky thing while we're down south. I want you to take photos of the three members of the Cabal when they leave their HQ. They must not see what you are doing.'

What a devil of a job, Paula thought.

'One other point,' Newman roared on. 'Remembering our last experience down there with Paula, we need a strike force. So I'd like Harry and Marler to come with us. All heavily armed.'

'You are starting a war,' Paula commented.

'Only if the other side shoots first. Agreed, Tweed?'

'Yes. And Paula comes too.'

'So,' Newman decided, 'we'll travel in the ancient Bentley with the souped-up engine, courtesy of Harry.'

'What are we waiting for, then?' Tweed demanded as he checked his Walther and slid it back into his shoulder holster.

They parked the car in the area near the ferry where a striped pole was lifted. Tweed gave a local a generous tip to keep an eye on the Bentley.

The drive down to Dorset had been a pleasure, with the sun shining out of a clear blue sky. It was warmer as they neared the sea. This time Abe was no longer operating the barge. His replacement, a local man called Judd, explained Abe had gone on holiday. Newman smiled as they settled down, the only passengers aboard the barge.

'Poor Abe has been scared off by that powerboat which blew up,' he remarked.

The crossing to Black Island was like travelling over a lake. Paula revelled in the experience, sitting so she could see the approach to Lydford. They disembarked at the dock. The streets were deserted as they passed through the village and turned along the road to the left. It was very quiet. As Paula walked in front Harry was wary.

'It's too quiet,' he remarked, bringing up the rear. Inside a long leather pouch he carried an automatic weapon. In the capacious pockets of his camouflage jacket was a collection of hand grenades. Tweed walked alongside Paula as they went down a wooded lane. Entrances to drives leading to large houses had names but there was no sign of Lockwood, the General's house. The previous evening a friend at the MoD had given Tweed the name. He stopped in front of wrought-iron gates which were closed. The name board merely gave the owner's name: 'Macomber'.

There was no sign of life along the curving drive behind the gates, and no speakphone. Tweed shrugged.

'He likes his privacy,' he observed. 'We'll walk a bit further. There must be someone about . . .'

Paula clutched his sleeve. On either side of the tall gates was a massive stone pillar. She pointed to the top of the right-hand pillar, her voice expressing distaste.

'Look at the top of that pillar. It's really rather awful.'

Perched on top of the pillar was a stone sculpture of a cat. It was crouched down but its head was twisted round the wrong way, twisted through an angle of a hundred and eighty degrees. There was something horrible about the distortion.

Turning a corner in the lane, Paula stopped. A freshly repainted sign board carried the legend 'Crooked Village'. What lay beyond was extraordinary. With little space between each very un-English one-storey cottage was a scene which reminded Tweed of Provence.

The walls, and the steeply angled roofs above them, were painted with white paint, piled on thickly. Some had spike-like rafters protruding beyond the roof-line. Each cottage had only a few small windows and the doors were painted, again thickly, in blue.

Tweed stared. The sunlight gave the brilliant colours a powerful blinding effect. A mass of cacti were placed close to the front walls. They turned a corner and now the steeply slanted roofs were painted red. It was not like England at all. They felt they had been transferred to another world.

'Someone round here likes Van Gogh,' Tweed observed. 'This village is like one of his paintings.'

'There's someone working inside this one,' Paula pointed out.

'So we can ask about the General,' Tweed said and walked inside, followed by Paula.

Another surprise. The large room was a potter's working area. The potter, working a wheel, was a small heavily built man with a crooked face, one side of his jaw lower than the other. He stopped working and gave Paula the pleasantest of smiles. His gnarled hands were enormous. He wore a white smock, woollen leggings and suede slippers smeared with white paint.

'Welcome to France,' he greeted them. 'I am

François. I hope you like our village. The General paid all the costs. General Lucius Macomber. He loves France.'

He sat on a three-legged stool, indicated for them to sit in wicker chairs. Tweed lowered himself gingerly but the chair was solidly constructed. He introduced himself and jumped in with a reference to the General.

'I was intrigued by the sculpture of a cat on one of his pillars. The cat with its head the wrong way round. Rather unusual.'

'The story behind that is unusual, even macabre. The General has three offspring, Nelson, Benton and Noel. This goes back to when they were boys, approaching their teens. There was a cat the General worshipped, called Tommy. An old name for army privates. The General used to feed Tommy – no one else could give it milk or food. I had better demonstrate . . .'

François picked up a large chunk of malleable clay from a table. Paula watched, fascinated, as he used his large hands skilfully, moulding the clay until, quickly, it became a cat. He held it up so they could see how lifelike it looked. He then did something which horrified her. He took hold of it by the neck, slowly twisted it until the head was the wrong way round.

'That,' he said quietly, 'is what one of the offspring did to the cat.'

'How beastly,' Paula exclaimed.

'The General went almost out of his mind with grief and fury. He did everything possible to find out which of the boys had committed this atrocity. He never did. So, to punish the culprit, he asked me to create that sculpture in stone, to fix it to the top of the pillar. His idea was that every time the culprit walked out of the grounds they would see this aberration.'

'I think that too is quite horrible,' Paula muttered. 'So he never knew who was responsible?'

'Never.'

'What about his relationship with his three sons now?' Tweed asked.

'Not all is as it seems.'

'I don't understand.'

'The General is a virile man, even now when he is eighty. His wife died three years ago. Years before that he had an affair with a woman called Horlick. She became pregnant. He told his wife, a remarkable woman. She agreed to tell the neighbours she was pregnant and went on to the mainland. When Mrs Horlick gave birth to Noel the General's wife came back with the baby and everyone thought that it was hers.'

'So Nelson and Benton never knew the truth?'

'Not then. When they were grown up they did find out. I'm not sure how.'

'So how did they react to having a half-brother instead of a real one? Not pleasantly, I imagine.'

'You're wrong there,' François told him. 'First, Noel turned out to have a brilliant brain, especially on the planning front. He also took wrestling lessons at a specialist gym on the other side of the island. Nelson is pretty tough but he wouldn't mix it with Noel. If he did he'd end up with a broken arm. When none of them would own up to screwing the cat's neck the General took his revenge.'

'The stone sculpture, you mean?' Tweed suggested.

'More than that. The General is rich. His father was a billionaire, left it all to him. The General used a top lawyer in London to create three trusts. One for each of his offspring. Every year the boys get a handsome amount which enables them to live well – but nothing like a fortune. They were furious. Greed. The General never sees any of them when he goes on one of his three-day trips to London.'

'You did say,' Tweed began, phrasing it delicately, 'that the General is virile. Has he still an interest in women? These trips to London.'

François stopped what he was doing. He stood up suddenly and Tweed was surprised to see him standing straight as a ramrod.

'That is personal. The General's private life is his own business.'

He stared hard to Tweed, cocked his head to one side as though he couldn't quite make Tweed out. He sat on the stool again, still gazing at Tweed.

'What is it about you, sir? I'm telling you things I've never told another soul. I presume you will never repeat any of this to anyone. And my real name is Frank. The General calls me François to fit in with the atmosphere of the Crooked Village.'

'I give you my word I will never repeat anything you have told me,' Tweed said firmly, his eyes fixed on Frank's.

'You didn't introduce me to the charming lady,' Frank said, gazing at Paula.

'I'm sorry,' Tweed said quickly. 'My manners must be slipping. This is Miss Paula Grey, my confidential assistant.'

'May I call you Paula?' Frank suggested, taking off his working gloves and extending his hand.

'Of course you may,' she said with a smile, shaking his hand.

'I can tell,' Frank went on, 'that she is a trust-worthy and most able assistant. Tight-lipped, I am sure.'

He didn't seem bothered about Newman, who had been standing a distance away by the open heavy door at the entrance. Newman kept glancing outside. He had posted Harry with his weapon at the entrance to the village to warn of any intruders. He also had very acute hearing and had heard every word.

'You're going now?' Frank said as Tweed held out his hand. 'I was going to offer you some refreshment.'

'Thank you, but I want to have a word with the General. Is it all right if I tell him we have been here, that we chatted with you about your pottery and the village?'

'Of course it is. He is very proud of his village. When it was built he brought over architects and workmen from France. They advised me about the paint to use. The colours are deliberately exaggerated – the light in Provence is so much stronger than here. Go well . . .'

14

In a daze, Paula turned to look at the village they had left. The startling effect of being in France seemed stronger than ever. She took out her camera, pressed the button three times.

'That was a unique experience,' she said to Tweed with a lilt in her voice. 'And I liked Frank.'

'He liked you. Otherwise he wouldn't have told us so much. A shrewd old boy. And one of the happiest men I've ever met.'

They walked quickly, Harry in the vanguard, his eyes everywhere. Behind him Newman strode briskly along, also very alert. He was worried about Paula. He hoped they wouldn't have another grim experience. To Tweed's surprise the wrought-iron gates guarding the General's estate were swinging open. He stopped, listening.

Thud . . .

Thud . . .

Thud . . .

The sounds were coming from round a curve in the wide drive. For no reason he could fathom Tweed thought of the trip to the mortuary, and what Professor Saafeld had said about the murder of Viola Vander-Browne.

Tweed walked round the bend. He was in the lead and Paula was close behind him. He stopped abruptly. Newman came up behind him.

'Trouble? You're disturbed.'

Tweed was staring at the stretch of drive leading up to a large gracious mansion. Red-brick, Georgian in style, a long terrace perched above a flight of stone steps.

The sounds were being made by a tall agile man swinging a huge axe up and down, chopping large logs into smaller pieces with the flat base of a tree trunk as the chopping block.

The General, wearing a peaked army cap to protect his face against flying chips, laid down the axe, took off his gloves and turned to face Tweed. When he took off the cap he revealed a sun-tanned face with a large hooked nose, piercing blue eyes, a firm mouth, a strong jaw – all of which reminded Tweed of paintings he'd seen of the Duke of Wellington.

'Mr Tweed, I presume, with Miss Paula Grey and the formidable Robert Newman,' he called out in his commanding voice.

No suggestion of the pompous brass-hat in the voice. Rather the voice acquired over the years when addressing officers. Despite his age his skin was leathery rather than lined and he moved briskly as he walked to greet them. Upright as a telegraph pole.

'I was expecting you,' he continued, hand extended. 'Your friend Allenby at the MoD phoned to say you might be visiting me.'

You can't trust anyone these days not to babble, Tweed thought. His hand was ready for the General's crushing grip, but the hand that grasped his was strong but not aggressive. After shaking hands with Tweed he turned immediately to Paula, clasping her hand gently, bowing slightly.

'Tweed is an able fellow otherwise I would not have opened the gate,' he told her. 'But without you I suspect he'd find life very difficult indeed. Ability and charm – not something I often encounter.'

'You overestimate me, sir,' she replied. 'But you are correct in your assessment of my chief.'

'And here is the tough guy, Robert Newman. Not a man I'd trifle with.'

Newman was ready for a bone-crushing grip and that was what he experienced. He squeezed as hard as he could while smiling. The General's expression changed briefly. He'd felt the pressure.

'Of course, Newman, you are younger, so you have the advantage over ancient material. You should start

writing more of those articles on the state of the world.
I have read them all. You are the best journalist I've
read. Of course there is Drew Franklin. Good, but lacks
sharpness, which is just one of your strong points.' He
spotted Harry, who was a few paces behind the others.
He strode over, hand extended. 'You must be Harry
Butler, another key member of Tweed's amazing team.
Explosives are your speciality.' He was shaking hands
as he continued talking. 'Tricky job, yours. Suppose
you cut the wrong wire on a time bomb . . .'

'If I was not sure which wire to cut I'd leave the
damned thing alone,' Harry said emphatically.

'Which is why you're still here.' He put an arm
round Harry's shoulders. 'Come on now. We'll have
drinks inside to celebrate your courtesy in calling on
me. A sundowner, as they called it in the Far East. I
know that because my favourite author is Somerset
Maugham. He knew a thing or two . . .'

They followed the General up the steps and Tweed
asked the question on the terrace before they entered
the mansion.

'One thing intrigues me. How did you know we
were coming? The gates opened automatically for us.'

'See that object fixed to that tree at the corner of
the drive where it turns?'

Tweed stared at where the General was pointing.
Attached to a lower branch was a large mirror. The
General chuckled.

'That mirror shows me who is outside the gates. If it's someone interesting – like you and your team – I operate a lever behind the trunk where I was chopping the logs. At night glare-lights illuminate the entrance and the road outside. Have to get organized in these decadent days. Now, let's get those drinks.'

Double doors of oak opened into a spacious hall. The floor was covered with a huge Persian rug. On one wall Tweed was not surprised to see a portrait of the Duke of Wellington. On another a self-portrait of Van Gogh, the colours so reminiscent of the Crooked Village.

A white-painted door off the hall led into a comfortable living room with windows on three sides. A girl appeared, obviously the maid. The General checked what everyone preferred, then spoke in French.

'Celeste, our guests would appreciate drinks . . .'

He rattled off what was required. In an astonishingly short time she reappeared with the drinks on a silver tray, served them, left the room. Paula, who was intrigued by the French maid and understood the language, asked a question.

'General, are all your staff French?'

'Yes, indeed. These days most British people think a servant's job is below their dignity. I have four girls who look after this rather large house. And a dragon of a French housekeeper. They all live in the cottages in Crooked Village. They seem to feel at home there.' He stared at Tweed. 'The murder of the Vander-Browne lady sounds quite ghastly. We are descending into barbarism.'

'How did you hear about that?' Tweed enquired.

'I have the *Daily Nation* delivered every day. Like to keep up with what's going on. Drew Franklin has written a long article on the subject. Sounds gruesome.'

'I understand it was certainly that,' Tweed replied.

'And now,' the General continued, 'we have the Blackshirts, the Fascists, the so-called State Security lot taking over the western tip of this island, building strange buildings. You know, I wouldn't be surprised' – he paused, ran a finger over his lower lip – 'if one dark evening those buildings and anyone still working on them were blown sky high. What I've just said is off the record and you never heard me say it.'

'Say what?' asked Tweed with an innocent expression.

'My mind was elsewhere,' Paula remarked.

'And I've gone deaf,' Newman said.

'That's the ticket.' The General smiled as he stood up. 'Now you've finished your drinks perhaps I could show you my little Versailles.'

He led the way into the hall and down a long corridor towards the back of the house. Opening a door he stood aside to let Paula walk out on to a spacious terrace running the width of the back of the house. She stopped, gasped as the others followed her. The white stone terrace was elevated with a flight of wide steps leading down into a small paradise – although not so small: the estate spread out on both sides, with stretches of green lawn like a vast putting green. There were pergolas and stone arches, arrangements of evergreen shrubs such as she had never seen before, all trimmed neatly. In the distance, beyond a lake shaped like a swan, was a large maze of evergreen hedges. The General stood beside her.

'Walk into that maze without the map and you'd never find your way out. There's more.'

He walked across to a chrome wheel in the balustrade wall, turned it. All over the endless vista great fountains of water rose up high, each creating a different shape. He explained the jets were sunk in the lawn.

'I've never seen anything like it,' she enthused, rhapsodized.

'Better than Versailles,' Tweed commented. 'Which is too large for my taste. This is a jewel.'

'Don't need a gardener do you, sir?' joked Harry.

'I have twelve from a village to the east but I can always do with someone else,' the General chuckled, joining in the joke.

'Breathtaking,' Newman commented, placing his hands on the balustrade. 'You had people from

France to create this?'

'Yes, I did. Experts from outside Paris.'

They lingered for a while, unable to tear themselves away from the spectacle. Then Tweed checked his watch.

'We thank you for your hospitality, General, but if we leave now I think we'll just catch the return ferry to the mainland.' He looked at his host. 'You look very fit. How do you do it?'

'I get up early, have a glass of orange juice, then jog over Hog's Nose Down. They say you can just see the Isle of Wight to the east but I never have. Not even on a clear day.'

He accompanied them to the end of the drive, then turned back as the gates automatically closed behind him.

Returning aboard the ferry, Paula had expected to recall the powerboat roaring close to them, the explosion when Harry's jumbo-size grenade landed inside it. Instead she found her imagination filled with visions of the Crooked Village, then the amazing garden at the back of the General's house.

They had quick refreshment in the bar of the Monk's Head and settled themselves in the Bentley. The sun was still blazing as Newman pressed his foot down. He called out to Marler, who had stayed in Tolhaven.

'You missed some extraordinary experiences.'

'I was chatting to the barman. They're often funds of info. He's counted fifty of those infernal Special Branch – beg their pardon, State Security – men coming in and heading for the ferry. So they have a small army to build those appalling prisons I saw in the photos Paula took.'

'As many as that?' Paula exclaimed. 'They're breeding like ants.'

'That's valuable information,' Tweed commented. 'Now we know what we're up against. They have to be stopped and quickly.'

'But how?' Paula asked.

'I'll think of something,' Newman assured her with a wide smile.

They were approaching Park Crescent, crawling through a jungle of traffic, when Paula voiced her thought to Tweed.

'Did you notice the General never mentioned that you are in charge of the murder investigation? I thought it odd.'

'I did notice,' he replied. 'I thought it very odd too. I am sure he knows.'

She opened the day's copy of the *Daily Nation* Newman had just bought. She stared at the article by Drew Franklin, splashed on the front page.

HORRIFIC MURDER IN LONDON

Only two days ago Viola Vander-Browne, society beauty, was raped, then her body chopped up into pieces like a butcher using his cleaver to chop meat. No photos are available from the police, on the grounds they are too horrible for circulation. It is understood this case, exceptionally, has been put in the hands of a top SIS officer, a man who previously was an ace detective at Scotland Yard, solving three murder cases which baffled everyone else at the Yard. Londoners, do not go out after dark. Check your windows and doors. This psycho may well strike again. He has a liking for women victims.

She sighed, handed the paper to Tweed as she reacted to what she had read.

'Drew has really gone to town this time. The General seemed to know so much about many things, including us, I'd have thought he'd have caught on as to who the chief investigator was. You.'

'I'd have thought so too,' Tweed replied as he rapidly read the lurid article. 'He does everything except print my name.'

'I'm going to see Drew as soon as I can. He'll talk, if I have to put my hands round his throat,' said Newman.

Paula, seated beside him, glanced at his expression. It confirmed her earlier opinion that Newman was in the most ferocious and determined mood she had ever seen.

Arriving back in the office they found only two occupants: Monica, as ever, behind her machine, and Pete Nield pacing up and down with a worried expression.

'Something wrong?' Tweed asked him.

'Just turning things over in my mind.'

As soon as Tweed had settled behind the desk, Monica jumped up, a large white envelope in her hand. She wore gloves as she placed the envelope on his desk.

'That was pushed through our letterbox at lunchtime.'

'By whom?'

'We don't know. I was out collecting my lunch from the deli. I was only away about twenty minutes. I think someone chose their time carefully.'

'What about George?' Tweed asked, referring to the ex-army CSM who was their guard behind a desk near the front door. It would take someone very strong and agile to mix it with George.

'He was in the loo for about five minutes. Came back and this was on the floor below the letterbox. George opened the door and couldn't see anyone in particular among the lunchtime pedestrians on the main road. He handled it with gloves.'

'So will I.'

Tweed put on latex gloves, weighed the envelope in his hand. Not much inside. A good-class envelope which could be purchased at any decent stationer's. The flap was tucked inside the envelope, in spite of the fact that it had glue which most people would lick. So no saliva, no DNA. He carefully pulled out the flap, then what was inside.

A large colour photograph, taken at night, showing a man from the rear, wearing a coat with the collar turned up, which concealed whether the neck was thick or slim. No more than a silhouette of a heavily built figure in a narrow cobbled street, a first-floor window on the left covered with bright red. An ancient street lamp attached on an arm protruding from a wall gave some illumination.

Tweed looked at Paula.

'What is it?' she called out as she hurried across to him, holding a magnifying glass she had been using to check a map of Black Island. He looked up at her as she stooped over his shoulder.

'You tell me.'

'I'm sure that's Fox Street,' she said. 'Oh, my God, that looks like blood spread all over the first-floor frosted-glass window.'

She used her magnifying glass to examine the

window. She looked at Tweed with a grim expression. 'It's recent blood, hasn't had time to turn brown. Didn't Saafeld say when the killer of Viola chopped off her head he severed the main arteries, which would have sent a powerful jet of blood across the room? It hit the window and covered it with solid streaks. This must be where Viola lived. In Fox Street.'

'Turn it over,' he said.

She did so. In crude block lettering were the words Portrait of a Murderer. Tweed showed her the envelope, addressed to Mista Tweed, again in crude block letters.

'Can't spell,' she said without thinking.

'You think not? I'd say whoever wrote the wording and delivered it here is well educated. The spelling and the crude lettering is to cover up that fact.'

'It was a big man, difficult to tell his height.'

'Not necessarily big, not necessarily a man, as you keep reminding me. Someone wearing three raincoats and then an overcoat could bulk out their figure. It could be a man or a woman. The key question is who took the photo – and how did they come to be there at just the right moment?'

'The killer was followed earlier.'

'And the motive?'

'I take your point,' she admitted. 'Jealousy?'

'So all we have to do is to identify the photographer,' he said ironically.

'The Parrot would be my best guess,' she told him.

'During an investigation we don't rely on guesses. And I was under the impression the Parrot was at the head of your list of murder suspects.'

'It's confusing . . .'

'So take this photo down to the basement when you can. I want three copies and the original.'

During this conversation Newman had marched up to Pete Nield. He jerked his head towards the door.

'A quiet word in your shell-like ear. Visitors' room downstairs would be best.'

Paula had the unusual ability to carry on a conversation and at the same time overhear someone else's. She dashed down to the basement ahead of Newman and Nield.

Inside the visitors' room, a spartanly furnished room opposite George's post, Newman sat Nield down, then sat down himself, facing him across the table. His tone was grim.

'I need to speak to your informant urgently, which means as quickly as possible. Not tonight – now!'

'I don't like it,' Nield protested strongly. 'It's an iron rule that none of us ever reveal to any of the team—'

'In the diabolical situation Tweed finds himself in – and so do the rest of us – the rules go out of the window.' His tone became sarcastic, which was out of character. 'Unless you look forward to wearing a long black coat and cap, with an armlet carrying the legend State Security. Secret police would be a better description. Knocking on people's doors in the middle of the night, then dragging them away for brutal interrogation. What's the informant's name?'

'Coral Flenton,' Nield said quietly.

'That's better. Don't make me drag every detail out of you. Who is she? Where does she work – if she does work?'

'She's a civil servant. Assistant to the Parrot, who treats her abominably. Very dominating, the Parrot, always hoping she can catch Coral out in a mistake. And, Newman . . .' Nield had raised his voice, 'she's sensitive so I won't have you upsetting her. You've become a bit of a bastard on occasions recently.'

'I have,' Newman agreed, lighting one of his rare cigarettes. 'But when you're dealing with characters like Fitch, who was on the verge of kidnapping Paula from her home, the Marquess of Queensberry rules are pretty useless.'

'You could meet her in about half an hour's time,' Nield said after checking his watch. 'I've agreed to meet her at a cafe in Covent Garden – Popsies. I'll introduce you then make myself scarce.'

'I would appreciate that,' Newman replied, standing up.

What Newman didn't know was that Paula had

guessed what he was up to. And it bothered her. After leaving the photo with a boffin she darted out of the front door. She chose Harry's Fiat, locating the spare ignition key under the cheap floor covering. Typical of Harry that he hadn't had the covering replaced.

She pushed the seat back, kept an eye on the door to Park Crescent, bobbed her head out of sight when Newman emerged with Pete.

15

Paula carefully followed Newman's car. He was good at spotting tails, but Paula was expert at not being seen. Newman was clever in the route he took to Covent Garden, using the back streets from Leicester Square favoured by experienced cabbies. Once there, he drove very slowly, glancing out of his window at a cafe. Paula had trouble reading the elaborate script but then made out the name. Popsies.

Most people were going home so Newman soon found an empty parking spot. Paula drove straight past him, found another empty spot. She put coins in the meter as Newman and Nield entered the cafe.

If Nield's informant was a man she wouldn't worry. If it was a woman she'd fume. Newman was in no mood to be subtle. Paula understood why and he had saved her life on Black Island. She jumped inside a shop entrance when Nield reappeared and went off towards the market.

Paula took her sunshade out of the car where she'd thrown it after collecting it from the office. Tweed, thank Heaven, had been absorbed on the phone. He'd have had a fit if he'd known she was out on her own.

She strolled along slowly under her sunshade even though it was by now dusk. As she passed the entrance to Popsies she saw Newman's back seated stiffly and a good view of a small attractive girl. She took out her camera, took two quick shots, walked on.

'So you're some sort of friend of Pete's,' Coral Flenton said with an edge to her tone.

'That's right. We work closely together . . .'

'On special insurance. You take premiums from rich men frightened of being kidnapped.'

She had made it sound like a racket. Her large hazel eyes never left Newman's. He knew she was suspicious, hostile. Pity, because he liked her.

'That's right,' he answered. 'But we've been landed with a grim murder investigation. May I ask what you do in the way of work?'

'I'm a civil servant. I think you knew that.'

Newman sipped the coffee he'd ordered. It was very good. He could bring Roma here one evening before taking her on to dinner.

'I believe you work for the Parrot,' he struggled on.

'You mean Miss Partridge.'

Her expression was blank and those penetrating eyes never left his. He was beginning to lose the plot. He really liked her but was getting nowhere.

'Do you have anything to do with Nelson, Benton and Noel Macomber?' he asked with another forced smile.

'No, they're in another room.'

'So who does look after them?'

'Miss Partridge.'

'Ever heard of State Security?' he asked, moving in deeper.

'What?'

'State Security.'

'That's a new one on me.'

Newman forced himself to relax in the comfortable chair. He kept smiling and she kept the blank expression. Newman did not give up easily.

'Another life may be at stake after one horrific murder and that's why I'm asking these questions.'

'I'm sorry to hear that.'

'I'm referring to the murder of Viola Vander-Browne. It's in the papers today.'

'Now you're putting me off my dinner this evening. I read about it.'

'May I ask you out to dinner? I promise not to ask you any more questions.'

'Certainly not. I already have a date, Mr Newman.'

'I think I'd better go now.' Newman stood up and called the waitress for the bill.

'Don't pay for me,' she said through clenched teeth.

Newman walked out into the street. He spread out his hands wide in frustration as he saw Nield approaching. Seated now in the Fiat with her head hunched down, Paula saw, understood the gesture. She was not surprised. She waited until Newman with Nield by his side had driven away, then got out, put more coins in the meter and walked along and entered Popsies.

The cafe was empty except for Coral Flenton, who had ordered more coffee, as if to get over her annoyance. Paula stood, staring round vaguely, caught Coral's eye, walked slowly to her table.

'Excuse me, but if you're not waiting for someone I dislike having even coffee alone.'

'Sit down,' Coral invited with a flashing smile. 'The coffee here is rather good.' She waved to the waitress and ordered another cup.

'I'm a bit of a fake,' Paula confessed. 'I'm a friend of Pete Nield, work closely with him.'

'Really.' Coral became guarded. 'And also a friend of Mr Bob Newman?'

'I'm senior to him.' She paused. 'Friend is the wrong word,' she said, implying she didn't much like him. 'He is a very able man but he has to be careful with me otherwise I'd rip him to bits – verbally.'

'So you work for the same insurance outfit,' Coral pressed her.

'Yes, I do . . .' Paula paused. 'I rarely say this to anyone because it sounds so egotistical but I'm second in command. I heard Pete saying he was going to Covent Garden so I thought I'd see if I could find him – to tell him to take the evening off.'

God, I'm awful, Paula thought, making all this up – but this woman could be important. She saw Coral's features relax and when she spoke her manner was animated and friendly.

'You then saw it was Newman so you waited until he had pushed off. If I can help in any way to solve that dreadful murder I will. You see I knew Viola, that is Miss Vander-Browne.'

'Do you know any of her men friends by chance?'

'No, I don't. I do know the Parrot – that's my boss, Miss Partridge – was in a fury and I wondered if she was having a thing with the murderer.'

'Why would she do that? Be in a fury, I mean.'

'Because Viola was very much a woman of the world. I don't wish to speak ill of the dead but Viola, a really nice person, spent the night with rich men for a lot of money. She spent so much on clothes the generous legacy she inherited didn't always cover her wants. I don't think Viola would have minded my telling you if it helps to track down the hideous killer.'

'Did she do this often?'

'Only about three times a year, she told me. We were old friends because we went to the same boarding school. I'm small and you know how vicious some girls can be. Viola used to protect me.'

'So you know Fox Street?'

'Quite well. I used to go and see her and we'd have a meal in her flat. She was a marvellous cook. I'm not going to the police because if they came to my work place the Parrot might use it to have me chucked out of the Civil Service. I need the job, you see.'

'Don't go to the police, then. A very able man, no longer in the police, is investigating the murder. May I tell him what you've told me? It's up to you.'

'I could do with some support.' Coral finished her coffee. 'I trust you, so if you trust this investigator – and you must – then it's OK by me to pass it all on to him. If you're ready to go I'd like you to come and see me sometime. My pad is just down the road. I could show you.'

'I'd like that,' Paula said with a smile.

Coral insisted on paying the small bill. As they were leaving the cafe, which was beginning to fill up, she took a plain visiting card from her handbag. She slipped it to Paula, who palmed it.

'It's got my address, phone number, mobile number,' Coral went on as they turned right towards the main part of Covent Garden. 'The mortgage was terrifying but I liked the place. Tucked away. Here it is.'

They paused before the entrance to a slim three-storey building, recently built after the demolition of several small shops, Paula guessed. She looked up as Coral pointed, gazed up. Paula had a shock.

'That window on the first floor is my living room,' Coral explained. 'The window is frosted glass for privacy. Not much to look out at anyway.'

Paula stared at the tall frosted-glass window. It had a horrible similarity to the blood-drenched window in Fox Street, where Viola had been slaughtered. She forced herself to smile as Coral continued speaking.

'Not much space except in the living room. You see now why I put up with the Parrot – I need the salary.'

'Here is my card,' Paula said, giving her the version with General & Cumbria Assurance, the cover name on the plate outside the SIS headquarters. 'If I'm out speak to Monica, give her your first name only. If you're worried I'll come as soon as I can.'

'I have enjoyed your company,' Coral said as they shook hands. 'Let's see each other soon.'

'I have a photograph of the murderer of Vander-Browne,' Tweed was saying on the phone when Paula returned. Newman and Nield were sitting down, facing each other like antagonists.

Tweed clapped his hand over the phone to inform Paula.

'I'm on the phone to Chief Inspector Hammerhead.' He removed his hand, continued. 'Yes, a photo of the murderer . . .'

'What!' Everyone in the room heard the policeman's explosive outburst.

'You heard me correctly,' Tweed replied calmly. 'I'm sending it over to the Yard for your attention by courier. No, I've no idea who pushed the envelope containing it through my letterbox. The lettering on both envelope and back of the photo is in deliberately crude block lettering. Yes, I've had both items checked for fingerprints. None at all, as you'd expect. I must go now. Sorry. Goodbye.'

'Is it the original?' Paula asked. 'And why send it to him anyway?'

'Because as well as me he's investigating the case. I don't like the man but I play fair, when necessary. You never know, he might just stumble over something.'

'The only thing he'll stumble over will be his own feet,' she replied.

'And how did you get on?' Tweed asked, looking at Newman.

'I made a complete and utter balls-up,' Newman began bluntly. 'Pete introduced me to the informant and I couldn't get a word out of them. I think I went about talking to the person concerned in one hundred per cent the wrong way. I've apologized to Pete.'

Paula admired Newman's frankness about his failure. She also noticed he'd made no reference which could even vaguely identify Coral. Tweed must have read her mind, which he often did, as she frequently read his.

'Man or woman?' Tweed demanded.

'I don't remember,' Newman replied, staring hard at his chief.

'A washout, then,' Tweed suggested.

'Absolutely. I think it's done me good. Brought my big feet back on the ground. I'm taking Pete out for a drink in a minute.'

'I've had a thought,' Paula began. All eyes turned to her. She stood up, walked to the far side of Tweed's desk, folded her arms.

'I can't get out of my mind that cat with its neck screwed round the wrong way. It was an act of sadistic cruelty – done by the sort of person who in later years could chop Viola into pieces for the fun of it.'

'Interesting.' Tweed frowned. 'I think you have detected a significant pointer to the killer. Trouble is, we don't know which of the three teenagers mal-treated the cat in such a beastly fashion.'

'Unless it was the General himself,' she remarked.

'Oh, my Lord.' Tweed clasped both hands behind

his neck. 'That would be a very strange twist in the plot.'

'And,' Paula went on, 'we know from Frank that the General makes three-day trips up to London. Frank called him "virile". Just a thought which crept into my head.'

'I could phone every decent hotel in London and persuade them to tell me if he stayed there – and if so when,' volunteered Monica.

'Do it,' said Tweed.

Except, Paula thought as she returned to her desk and not voicing the idea aloud, he's clever. He'd probably stay at some rundown boarding house, giving a false name, and never the same place twice.

When Tweed had started talking to Chief Inspector Hammer, Marler had glided into the room. The Invisible Man, as he was nicknamed in the office, had followed Paula, parked his car in Covent Garden, had seen everyone who had entered and left Popsies.

Now he announced, 'I'm going out on the prowl. Never know what I might see.'

'You've just been out somewhere,' Paula said with a smile.

He squeezed her shoulder. 'And I'm just going out again. Toodle-pip.'

He saw no point in revealing that his destination was Covent Garden.

16

On the Thames, Mugger Morgan was steering his barge in close to the dock. He was the only crew aboard his huge vessel but that was because of what he was carrying in his pocket – a large packet of cocaine which would bring him a load of money when he handed it over to the waiting dealer.

He swore when his mobile phone started buzzing. The last diversion he wanted at this moment was someone asking him to do a job. Knowing he'd wonder all the time who had called, he kept one hand on the wheel, used the other to take out the mobile and answer the call.

'Yes,' he growled.

'It's Fitch, Mugger. Need your help bloody fast or I'm a goner . . .'

'What is this crap?'

'Mugger, I've been shoved down the chute at the warehouse. I'm 'angin' with a rope round me bleedin' neck. I've got me feet propped against the side of the chute but they won't hold much longer. For Christ's sake . . .'

'How much?'

'What!'

'How much for me to come and haul you out? I'm a businessman. You should know that by now.'

'Five 'undred nicker. In cash. For Gawd's sake, Mugger!'

'I'm on me way. You 'ang on.'

Mugger chuckled as he put away the mobile. He rather liked the humour of his remark.

The barge's prow bumped the wharf. He manoeuvred it alongside, switched off the engine, jumped ashore. Swiftly he roped the barge safely to the bollards, looked round for the dealer. Not here. He was always late and then he'd try to lower the price. Frig him. He would go for the five hundred nicker first.

He hurried along the crowded street. If he didn't get there in time Fitch would go down the chute. That didn't worry Mugger so much as the fact that he'd take the five hundred pounds with him.

Mugger was a big man, six foot one tall, fifteen stone, with a brutal face. He was in his forties: he had earned the nickname Mugger in his teens, christened by the police who had never brought him to justice. His technique in those days had been to prowl

Mayfair and Regent Street, looking for well-dressed women, snatch their handbags and scarper. He'd made a lot of money that way, but gave it up when police patrols began to walk those areas.

Buying himself a large barge, he'd entered the drugs trade. He collected the cocaine packets from downriver, sailed back to the East End and charged his dealer three times what he'd paid.

Arriving at the padlocked entrance to the warehouse he took out a bunch of keys, which included a pick-lock. He was inside the place in minutes. Opening the door into the room where the chute was located, he bent down, grabbed the handle, hauled off the lid. Sure enough there was Fitch, a rope round his neck over a scarf. He'd agilely managed to use his exceptional strength to manoeuvre himself at right angles to the vertical shaft. Both his feet were rammed into the side of the shaft, both hands holding on to the rope. He knew he couldn't last out much longer. He looked up.

'Reach down, grab the rope and haul me up,' he ordered.

'I'll need my five 'undred nicker before I do any work,' Mugger informed him with a hideous grin.

Bastard! Fitch muttered under his breath. He let go of the rope with one hand. It was tricky, but he managed to feel inside his pocket for a sheaf of twenty-pound notes held together with an elastic band. He threw it up and sighed with relief as it shot up through the hole, landing on the warehouse floor.

Mugger picked up the bundle, counted it quickly. Then he shouted down.

'Only two 'undred and forty here. We said five 'undred.'

'You get the rest in my pocket when I'm up there with you. If you don't get me out fast I'm going down – with the money.'

Mugger reacted quickly. He knelt down, stretched one long arm, grasped the rope. Despite the awkward position and Fitch's weight, he hauled him up. Fitch flopped on the floor, worked his stiff legs, clambered to his feet.

He was wondering whether to catch Mugger off guard, tip him down the chute. He changed his mind as he used a dirty handkerchief to wipe sweat off his forehead and face. He had thought that Mugger could be useful to him.

'Money. Now.'

Mugger was holding out a huge hand, working his fingers in the money gesture. Fitch took a battered pack of cigarettes from his pocket, lit one with a jewelled lighter. He stared at his saviour.

'Like to make a lot more? Say two thou?'

'Talk about that after the two 'undred and sixty you owe.'

Fitch reached in his other pocket, took out another

roll of twenties. He gave it to Mugger, who counted it carefully. While he was doing this Fitch replaced the lid over the chute. He wouldn't send Mugger down to the pearly depths. He could use him, he'd finally decided.

'What job?' Mugger demanded aggressively.

'To put away – permanently – a woman and a man. Use any method you like but they must both disappear.'

'For two thou? You must be jokin', mucker. For five thou I'd consider it.'

'Four . . .'

'I said five!' Mugger roared.

'OK,' Fitch agreed, after a long pause. 'Five.'

'So who are the bodies?' Mugger asked.

'A man and a woman.'

'I could have fun with the woman before we finish them . . .'

'No!' Fitch shouted.

He leapt forward, grabbed Mugger round the throat with both his strong hands, pushed him over backwards, fell on top of him, his hands still round the neck. Mugger was stunned. He'd not realized before how strong Fitch was. 'NO!' Fitch yelled again. 'This has to be a quick job. You can get up now.'

Fitch jumped to his feet. Mugger climbed upright more slowly. His hands were soothing his neck. He was scared now. Fitch realized this and set about making him forget what he'd done.

'Five thousand nicker,' Fitch repeated. 'How long would it take for you to earn that drug dealing?'

'A little while,' Mugger admitted. 'I only deal in small packets. Then if I'm stopped by the river patrol they'd never find it even if they turned the barge upside down.' He regained his toughness. 'Name of these parties?'

'Tweed and Paula Grey. I'll be with you when we grab them. Take them in the back of my car – no, the boot.'

'Then dump them in the river? We'll need heavy chains.'

'No we won't.' Fitch grinned sadistically. 'Chloroform first to knock them out, then a trip to the burner.'

'The burner?'

'I have a pal further east who operates a metal foundry – with a huge furnace. He clears out of the place for a consideration. He'll think I'm getting rid of dud banknotes.'

'I'm still not sure I know . . .'

'Stupid! We take the bodies and shove them into the furnace. You can watch them burn. Only takes a minute. OK?'

'I guess so.'

17

Marler was 'prowling'. He had returned to Covent Garden, and was standing on the opposite side of the street to the building where he had seen the small woman with Paula say goodbye and then enter her flat.

Earlier he had witnessed Newman's fiasco in his attempt to get on with Coral, had seen him emerge and wave both hands in frustration. Then Paula had entered Popsies. Strolling past he had seen the back of Paula's head as she had talked to the woman.

Marler was shrewd. He'd realized this must be Pete Nield's secret informant. He was always suspicious of informants, mistrusting half his own sources. He now stood, watching the door to the flat, on the street under a striped blind projecting from a bar entrance. In his hand he held a mug of coffee. He sipped it occasionally. It gave him a reason for hanging about.

It was dark when a tall woman, good figure, brown

hair neatly coiffeured, well dressed in a silk frock and expensive shoes, pressed the bell to the flat. Marler perched the coffee on a nearby ledge, took out a miniature camera which was non-flash, pressed a button for bad light since by now it was dark.

Paula's friend from Popsies appeared, smiled, shook hands with her visitor. As the visitor turned her head Marler took three quick shots of both of them. He followed them until they went into a good restaurant. He immediately returned to the building, checked the bell he'd seen the visitor push. A small card alongside had the owner's name. C. Flenton.

Marler then continued his prowl. He hailed a cab, asked to be dropped in the East End. He got out near a pub called the Pig's Nest, not the most salubrious establishment in London. Mixing with the crowd, he was strolling towards the pub's entrance when he nearly stopped short. His instinct and his training saved him. He continued to stroll.

Marler was startled. For him the immediate reaction was rare. Its cause was hurrying towards him, then turned into the Pig's Nest. Before he did so Marler used his camera to take two shots. His target was Amos Fitch, the man Newman had 'dealt with'.

At Park Crescent, Newman was still out with Pete Nield. Monica thought they must really be knocking it back. Harry had left, telling Monica he was on his way to paradise.

'Some people call it the East End,' he added as he left.

Paula went over to Tweed, leant over his desk, whispered a suggestion.

'I have info to pass on, just between us. Would your house be the best place?'

'I'm leaving now, so it would be.'

She followed him in her car, stopping several times to pick up some shopping. She arrived after dark to find two new locks on the front door. A Banham and a Chubb. Tweed appeared quickly when she'd pressed the bell three times, then twice.

Taking two of her three carrier bags he ran up the stairs. Paula followed, noting the locks closed automatically when she shut the door. Tweed was sitting at his desk, studying files when she walked in, picked up the two bags.

'You haven't eaten today,' she told him. 'I'm cooking a meal for both of us. Liver, bacon, fried egg – followed by crème brûlée.'

'Appreciate that,' he said not looking up.

She went into the kitchen, closed the door. She knew where everything was. She donned an apron, set to work. He had laid the table when she returned with the meal. She frowned.

'That's my job. Come and get it while it's hot. I can

tell you about my afternoon while we eat . . .'

Tweed ate voraciously, congratulated her on another first-class meal. He fixed his eyes on hers as he posed the question.

'You have information?'

She told him about following Newman and Nield. Their meeting in Popsies with Coral Flenton. Newman, frustrated, driving off with Nield. Her own meeting with Coral, their conversation.

'So Coral and Viola Vander-Browne were friends, went back a long way – to their schooldays,' Tweed observed. 'A strange twist. I find it odd.'

'I found something about Coral odd, but I can't put my finger on what it was. And she emphasized how far away her desk in the next room is from the Cabal's hideaway . . .'

Paula stopped as the front-door bell rang three times, then twice, the signal that it was someone from Park Crescent. Ever cautious, Tweed in his shirt sleeves extracted his Walther, ran down. A large cardboard-backed envelope had been pushed through the letterbox. On the front in neat lettering was Mr Tweed, from M—r. Marler.

Taking the envelope back upstairs he sank into his favourite armchair. Paula perched on an arm. She watched his expression as he took out a batch of colour photos and hid them from her. The reaction to the first one told her nothing. He looked at two more, then at Paula as he handed her the three photos.

'Who are these women? Any idea? The smaller one is Coral Flenton – Marler has written her name on the back.'

'Glory! This is crazy,' Paula exclaimed. 'The woman who is calling on Coral is the Parrot, I'm sure. She was disguised when she came to see you but I'm sure it's her.'

'And Coral told you in Popsies she hated the Parrot. No sign of hatred there. They look the best of friends.'

'What the devil is going on?'

'Loose strands are beginning to link up. First, Coral knew poor Viola. Now she has the Parrot as a friend.'

'I'm confused,' Paula admitted.

'Well, you know I never trust anyone. Nield's informant has been playing a double game, but how?'

'I'm shaken – after what Coral told me. And I've just grasped what I thought was odd about her. While talking she kept looking down at her coffee as though she didn't want to meet my eyes.'

'There are four more colour pics Marler took. In the East End, this time. Fitch is on the loose again.'

He handed her the pic showing Fitch walking towards Newman, then three more. One showed the sign board of the Pig's Nest. Another of Fitch inside the pub talking to another man. There were two of the same view. Marler must have stood at the open door. He had a lot of nerve, Tweed thought as he handed her the last photos.

'I recognize Fitch at the bar,' she said. 'But not the thug he's drinking with.'

'Thug is too mild a word. That's Mugger Morgan, a very nasty piece of work. Buchanan once showed me a picture of him leaving court. Once again his lawyer had got him off a serious charge of brutal manslaughter. On a technicality. Newman caught Fitch trying to invade your home. He may try again. Wherever you go now you need someone with you from the team.'

'I think you're right.'

'And I'd better follow you home in my car.'

'Couldn't I stay in the spare bedroom tonight? I've done so before. I did bring some night things with me.'

'Good idea. Sleep well.'

She bent down and gave him a kiss on the cheek, then headed for the spare bedroom. Tweed continued checking his files on agents operating abroad, recent reports. Nothing from Philip Cardon, who could be anywhere.

Paula reappeared in her pyjamas and dressing-gown.

'Any idea of what time it is?'

'I thought you'd be asleep.'

'My mind was churning over those photos and other developments. It's 2 a.m.' From behind him she placed both hands firmly on his shoulders. 'Up you get and off to bed.'

'I suppose you're right.' He suppressed a yawn. 'I need to be fresh for tomorrow, that is today in the morning.'

'Why?'

'We have a meeting with the Cabal at their HQ in Whitehall. The two of us. I want to study those three brothers.'

'Two brothers, one half-brother.' She increased the pressure on his shoulders. 'I want to see you actually go to bed.'

For discretion's sake, Paula left early, collected her car from behind Tweed's in the nearby mews where he'd rented space. When Tweed arrived three-quarters of an hour later the whole team was assembled in his office. Monica spoke up immediately.

'I've got someone hanging on the line you will want to talk to,' she said.

'Hello,' Tweed answered.

'Wonder if you still recognize my voice,' the caller began.

'Philip! Where the hell are you now? Or maybe you'd sooner . . .'

'Just listen. You need to fly to Aix-en-Provence today. By this flight. Here are the details . . . You land at Marignane Airport, in the middle of nowhere. I'll have a car waiting to drive you to your Aix hotel, the one in the north of the city. It would be safer if you brought two members of the team.'

'Paula and Newman?'

'Perfect. Something very weird is going on. A certain Noel Macomber is arriving late tonight to meet a most dubious character tomorrow evening. Twenty-four hours should do the trick. OK?'

'Yes.'

The line went dead. Tweed looked round the room. Paula could tell he was delighted. He gave them the news.

'So,' Newman commented, 'our wandering boy Philip Cardon has surfaced again. Bet he knows what is going on over here. Strange that Noel Macomber is flying out to Aix. To meet whom?'

'We'll find out, won't we,' Tweed told him. 'Heathrow is the worst part. All those queues on security grounds. I hate that.'

'That's all right,' Monica called out. 'I'll phone your old friend, Jim Corcoran, chief of security. He'll slip you through the queues.'

'Good idea,' Tweed agreed. 'Now Paula and I have an appointment with the magic circle. All the Macombers. I'm anxious to detect which one is the boss.'

*

Tweed found a parking space as a car pulled out. They walked the rest of the way down Whitehall and into the side street – into the dragons' lair, as he called it.

'Bet I spot the chief dragon,' Paula teased him.

The side street was narrow and deserted. Tweed stopped in front of a building which bore a wall plate: Special Branch. He pointed.

'Let's hope that's never altered to State Security. And they've converted the place into a fortress.'

The ground floor windows had been blocked up with steel sheets. On the first floor all the windows had bars and wire netting over them. To reach the speakphone Tweed had to perch on a big stone slab with a rubber pressure pad attached to its top.

'How do we get into Fort Knox?' he demanded after pressing the bell.

'Identify yourself,' a metallic voice demanded.

'Oh, for Heaven's sake, you know we're coming. Tweed – and don't forget Paula Grey. Now open up, if you can.'

Tweed was about to add something even more caustic when Paula pulled at his sleeve, a finger to her lips. She eased him off the stone slab.

'Probably nothing will open while you're on the pressure pad,' she whispered, then grinned.

They waited. Tweed put his executive case, which

contained nothing but blank sheets of paper, over the lens of a camera let into the large metal door. Paula frowned, pulled his arm away.

There was an electronic buzzing sound and the door slid up, disappeared. In the opening stood Noel Macomber, smiling as he checked out Paula. She stared back until his gaze dropped.

'Welcome to you both,' Noel began in a cultured voice. 'In you both trot.'

Trot? Tweed wondered. 'Electronics? Is the fire exit also opened by gizmos? Because if it is and there is a fire you'll all burn to a frazzle.'

If he keeps on like this, Paula thought, we'll get nowhere.

They stepped on to an escalator which purred up to the first floor. Noel had pressed something, there was more buzzing and the entrance door slid back to the closed position.

'We have to take all precautions,' Noel explained as they stepped off the escalator.

'So if anyone wanted to wipe you out,' Tweed replied, 'a truck with a very large bomb could just get down the narrow street by riding its wheels on the pavement.'

Paula wanted to punch Tweed but resisted as Noel opened a mahogany door into a large room, the walls painted cream, the only furniture a triangular table of rosewood with a chair on each of the sides. A large square table stood further back, at which two men were seated. They stood up and came forward to greet their visitors with outstretched hands.

'I'm Nelson,' the largest brother said. 'My father was an admirer of the famous admiral.' After shaking hands with Tweed he turned to Paula, a wide smile on his face as he grasped her hand, then released it. 'Bit of a joke – if I'm in a rowing boat on a lake I feel seasick.'

'Didn't your father realize this later on?' she asked, smiling back.

He laughed. 'A bit late to do anything about it. Not that he'd have bothered. This is Benton, my brother.'

'I am glad to make your acquaintance.' He was smaller than his brother but also heavily built. He also smiled warmly. 'Do come and sit down.' His voice was soft, gentle, unlike Nelson's, who spoke with force.

'Then there is an equally important member of our little group, or perhaps the most important,' Nelson boomed. 'Noel is our planner. He has a head for detail which I fear I lack!'

By now they were close to the large square table. Noel smiled at Paula, a very pleasant wide smile as he studied her. 'I am glad Tweed brought you along. You would have an important part to play in the new organization. We do know something of your remarkable ability.' He held out a chair for her. She looked up, smiled, thanked him.

Tweed, who was rather left out at this stage, was amused. They were all concentrating on Paula. He thought he knew why. When they were all seated Nelson asked whether they would like tea or coffee. Both guests opted for coffee. Black.

Nelson pressed a bell under the table. A side door was opened at once and the Parrot appeared. Tweed looked straight at her, betraying no recognition. Coffee was brought quickly, but was served by a red-haired girl who did not even look at Paula. Coral Flenton.

'I expect,' Benton said, 'that Mr Tweed has heard a few details of what is proposed. May I ask you, sir, what is your reaction? You do have a veto.'

'Veto?' Tweed queried.

'Yes,' Nelson said in his loud voice, 'a veto. You don't like some aspect of the new system, then we eliminate it—'

'I hadn't finished,' Benton interrupted, smiling at Paula now. 'And you will have an important role to play, as Noel told you. We all admire your decisive mind, your courage. You may well be second-in-command to Tweed, as you are now.'

His whole manner was persuasive, the ever present smile warm. Paula showed no reaction, staring at his greenish eyes below his fair hair. He was very convincing. She looked at Tweed, who started speaking.

'Details. How would this so-called State Security operate?'

There was a tap on the door connecting with the next room. Nelson called out, 'Come.' The Parrot entered, stared at Benton. 'A call for you on the phone next door, Mr Macomber.'

'I'd better take it, I suppose, please excuse me. I'll make sure whatever this is it doesn't take long.'

'Details,' Tweed repeated. Visitors come first.

Nelson began to outline how he saw the merger of the security services would work.

18

'First,' Nelson explained, 'I'm sure you'll agree Britain is now full of frightened citizens. In the suburbs people install glare-lights which illuminate anyone approaching their houses. They sleep with all the doors and windows secured with a variety of locks. Women don't dare walk the streets alone after dark. We live today in an atmosphere of terror. Right?'

'Go on.'

'You agree with what I just said.'

'Yes.'

'So why is this?' Nelson threw his hands wide. 'Because we have let in through Dover alien forces from the Continent, from Africa, from the East. The government fiddles the figures to conceal the truth. We are being inundated with a tidal wave of criminals from all over the world. Hence the atmosphere of terror.' He raised his voice. 'We propose to deport this trash – dangerous trash – back to where it came from. No argument. No stupid tribunals to hear their efforts to stay here. We call on these people in the dead of night, knock on their doors, grab them, take them to the nearest deportation station . . .'

Benton returned in time to hear some of this. He walked to his chair, sat down.

'Veto,' snapped Tweed.

'Why, for God's sake?' thundered Nelson.

'Because it sounds too much like the KGB. Knocking on doors at the dead of night, hauling people out, taking them away. President Putin of Russia, an ex-KGB officer, is moving in the same direction. Veto!'

Benton interceded. 'Now, Nelson, I suspect you have, as you do, dramatized what we really propose,' he said in his calm voice.

'We shall convert Britain into a country for the British,' Nelson rolled on, in full blood. 'Social saboteurs will be rounded up . . .'

'What is a social saboteur?' Tweed demanded.

'Anyone who disagrees with the government,' Nelson told him. 'Don't you agree that the whole moral structure of society has broken down? That our young people are confused, have no rules to guide their behaviour?'

'Something in that, yes,' Tweed agreed.

'You see,' Benton broke in, 'Tweed is a realist. A

very worried realist, Nelson, if I have understood him. You have so exaggerated what we must do, he has compared us to the KGB. We are not monsters, Mr Tweed. Nelson does go over the top at times. We are democrats. Perhaps, Mr Tweed, you would look at that peculiar three-sided table over there where we hold our consultations.'

'So who is the boss?' Tweed enquired. 'Who is in charge here?'

Tweed gazed straight at Benton's small greenish eyes. His face was flushed red, as though he had high blood pressure. The strain of coping with his brother, Nelson? Tweed thought.

'There is no boss,' Benton told him. 'I said we are democrats. We sit at that neutral table and work together. The table is symbolic of our relationship.'

'That should convince you,' Noel said, speaking for the first time. He was lightly spoken and was smiling. Paula thought she rather liked him. So controlled, so charming. His V-shaped features suggested character.

'What about uniforms for this merged State Security?' Tweed asked suddenly.

There was a long silence. Nelson glanced at Benton as if he wished him to answer the question. He did.

'Noel,' Benton explained, 'has designed a distinctive uniform. We think that will give the population a feeling of safety. To see them patrolling the streets day and night. A symbol that protection is available, which is not the case now.'

'I've seen some of them already. Before the bill has been passed – even presented to Parliament. That's illegal.'

'Indeed it is,' agreed Benton. 'Their commander must have jumped the gun. Where did you see them, Mr Tweed?'

'Outside my London house – in the middle of the night.'

'Then someone has tripped up,' Noel spoke again. 'We shall have to investigate that, make sure it doesn't happen again. I am surprised.'

'Building up a completely new organization,' Nelson said in a quieter voice, 'you always get glitches.'

'Big glitch,' Tweed told him. 'Veto.'

Benton finished his coffee. Neither Tweed nor Paula had touched theirs. Tweed stood up and Paula, with relief, followed suit. At his most amiable, Tweed explained they had to leave, thanked them for their explanations, said he would have to think over their conversation before he reacted in his report to the PM.

'The PM?'

Nelson had jumped up, his expression a mix of frustration and anger. He walked over to Tweed, grasped him by the arm.

'I do not see any reason to send a report to

Downing Street. This meeting was confidential, off the record completely.'

'You didn't say that at the beginning, did you?' Tweed replied with a smile.

'Of course,' Benton said quietly, 'Mr Tweed must react however he thinks best . . .'

'We would appreciate seeing a copy before you submit it to the PM,' Nelson said brusquely.

'You will have a copy in due course,' Tweed told him.

'We are all forgetting our manners,' Noel said. He turned to Paula. 'Your reaction is equally important. So what do you think of our proposals?'

'Like Tweed, I need time to think it over.' She smiled because he was smiling at her. 'There was so much to take in.'

'Yes, there was.' He walked with them towards the exit. 'Nelson is the oldest brother and rather runs away with himself at times. I'll escort you out. That wretched escalator has to be got moving, then there's the electronically operated door. I think they went mad when they designed security for this place. On behalf of my brothers I'd like to thank you both for sparing so much time to see us. May I keep in touch with you?'

'Of course,' she replied.

'I thought I saw Marler a moment ago,' Paula said as

they walked down the narrow street. 'Strolling along on the opposite side of Whitehall.'

'You must have been mistaken. What would he be doing here?'

They walked in silence until they reached the car. Once inside Tweed started the engine. He backed cautiously from the parking space into heavy traffic. It never seemed to stop. They were well on their way back to Park Crescent before Tweed asked the question.

'What did you think of the play they performed for us?'

'Play?'

'You don't really think we've seen the real Cabal, do you? Before we arrived they'd decided who would play which part. How did you weigh up the three of them?'

'Well, the most polite and, apparently, the most civilized was Noel.'

'You were rather taken by him?' Tweed said with a grin.

'Of course not,' she snapped.

'What about the others? Who is the boss? Because there is one.'

'I've no idea. At first I thought it was Nelson, he was so dominating. Then I wondered about Benton. He really is an enigma, the peacemaker. The way he intercepted Nelson as soon as he thought he was going over the top. He was very pacific.'

'And Noel?' Tweed asked. 'He may be the youngest but I had the impression he's very clever. And he was the one who talked about reining in the State Security men in uniform. Could be any of the three.'

The traffic was either crawling like a snail or stationary. When he couldn't do anything about a problem Tweed was eternally patient.

'Anything else occur to you,' he asked, 'while you sat and watched them?'

'I was trying to imagine which pair of hands had strangled the cat so horribly all those years ago. Came to no conclusion at all. One of them had a viciously cruel streak in those days.'

'Probably still has. Which could link up with the horrific murder of Viola. That's only a theory,' he warned.

Eventually arriving back at Park Crescent they were met in the office by Marler. He handed Tweed an envelope.

'More snaps for your photo album. I waited near the exit of Special Branch HQ. Saw you both leave, then three men came out one by one, with intervals between them. I took their pics.'

'That's Nelson,' Tweed said, showing Paula who had darted over from her desk. 'Then this is Benton. Finally, we have Noel. You followed them, of course?' he said, looking at Marler.

'Of course. They left at intervals, and one by one they met inside a restaurant beyond Trafalgar Square. Cunning lot. They didn't want to be seen going to lunch together.'

'So how on earth,' queried Paula, 'did you get back here ahead of us – and in time to get these printed downstairs?'

'Motorbike. I passed your stopped car, nipping in and out of traffic. Knew you wouldn't spot me. Not with my helmet and visor. Any good? The pics.'

'First rate,' said Paula, picking them up again. 'You have their features so clearly.' She handed them to Pete and Harry. She told them who was who. 'In case you ever encounter one of them.'

'Maybe I could get a word in edgeways,' Monica piped up. She brought over a thick envelope, dropped it on Tweed's desk. 'Return tickets for you, Newman and Paula. To Marignane on your way to Aix. Phoned Jim Corcoran. He'll be on the lookout for you – to slip you past security.'

'Economy,' Tweed replied. 'Thank you.'

'Well, Newman told me Philip had warned us Noel Macomber was on his way to Aix. If he's delayed he might be on the same flight. I'm gambling that, if he is, he'll hide himself in economy.'

'Clever lady. What would I do without you?'

'Get the paperwork in a proper mess,' she joked.

'So where is Newman?' he asked.

'Back at his flat in bed with Roma, would be my guess. She has lasted longer than any of her predecessors.'

The Cabal had waited until they returned from lunch to talk about their visitors, and were seated at the three-sided table. Nelson set the ball rolling.

'I don't think we're going to get Tweed to join us . . .'

'No doubt about that,' agreed Benton. 'So the next item on the agenda is: how do we stop him cold?'

'By elimination,' Noel decided. 'I'll be thinking about the best method to deal with them – Paula has to go too – while I'm flying out to Aix. Best thing would be if they both disappeared for ever. Bodies never found. I've set the wheels in motion in case it comes to this.'

'Won't involve Fitch, I hope,' mused Benton.

'I'm the Planner,' snapped Noel, glaring at Benton. 'So you leave the problem to me. You don't want to know.'

19

Tweed was in a hurry. Monica had warned him they should leave soon or miss the Air France flight. He gave orders to Pete Nield to see Coral Flenton again, to extract more information from her – about the Parrot, about her friendship with Viola from their schooldays on.

'Harry,' he called out. 'You are coming with us to Aix, flying tonight. At the special late request of Philip.'

'Now we're in April,' Paula told him, 'it's warmer. I have checked Provence. It's warmer still down there. So in that bag you'll find lighter-weight clothes.'

Monica walked over, handed Harry an envelope. 'There's a return ticket for you also,' she said. 'So make sure you come back.'

'Thanks for the vote of confidence,' he replied.

Within minutes they were all inside Newman's

Range Rover, on their way to Heathrow. Tweed told Newman to park in Short Stay. Crossing the bridge from the car park to the airport they met Jim Corcoran.

'You go aboard first,' he told them. 'Get a move on. I'll be with you until you're aboard . . .'

At the check-in desk Paula became aware of a passenger behind her who appeared to have survived a car crash. He was a tall man, smartly dressed, but his head was covered with a bandage. He gazed round through dark tinted glasses. As Paula presented her ticket he muttered something like 'wrong check-in . . .'

As he walked away Newman watched him and Paula did the same. The bandaged victim was standing near the exit talking into a sophisticated mobile. Newman grunted, smiled.

'A spy reporting the flight we're on. Maybe a reception committee waiting for us.'

'That was Mugger Morgan,' Harry said. 'Forgot to bandage his jaw. I broke it once.'

They settled in their seats. Very quickly the engines built up power, they were rolling towards the departure slot, straight on to the runway, then taking off.

Newman found two cushions, slipped one behind Paula's back, seated in front of him, the other behind her head. She rested her head, fell fast asleep. It was almost dark but in the seat beside her Tweed remained alert. He hated sleeping when flying.

Paula woke suddenly, looked out of the window. A moon cast a luminous glow over a landscape with rows of sticks on a south-facing slope. Vineyards were beginning to show signs of life. The plane was dropping rapidly. She'd slept during the whole flight.

'That man at the airport,' she whispered to Tweed. 'I wonder what will happen at Aix's airport?'

'Philip will have foreseen that development. Never misses a trick. I don't understand his late request for Harry.'

He kept his voice very low since Harry was seated across the aisle.

'He'll have a reason,' she replied, gazing out of the window.

In the distance she could see several new buildings. Beyond them nothing but a flat endless plain. Marignane was in the middle of nowhere. We have no weapons if there's trouble, Paula thought. Leave it all up to Philip.

They disembarked down the staircase and walked to the airport buildings. Paula was immediately aware it was much warmer. Philip met them the moment they entered. He was accompanied by a small Frenchman in an elaborate uniform.

'Armand,' Philip introduced. 'Chef du Securité. We must keep moving. Good flight?'

'Must have been,' said Paula, trotting to keep up with the two men. Tweed by her side, Newman and

Harry guarding their rear. Armand unlocked a door, led them down a long corridor well away from the arrivals hall. Outside again, Newman shook hands with Armand, hustled them inside a grey people-carrier with small windows. No one had checked their tickets or the small bags they were carrying.

Behind the wheel, Philip Cardon smiled at Paula. He drove at speed along a narrow road, emerged on to an autoroute, pressed his foot down. Now they were really moving. Tweed, who had again given Paula the window seat, grunted.

'When we stop somewhere I'll catch my breath.'

'Soon,' Philip called back, 'we will stop briefly. So I can hand out cutlery, the weapons you're all used to.'

'So it's that sort of a trip,' Harry called out behind Paula. 'I guessed it might be when I was hauled in at the last minute. Fair enough . . .'

Paula gazed out of her window. The vineyards had disappeared. In their place were dense forests of evergreens. Between gaps she caught sight of high rolling hills, everything glowing in the luminous moonlight. Philip slowed down, glanced again in his rear-view mirror, then swung off the main road up a cutting fenced in by trees, arrived at a concrete circle. He turned round it, stopped, switched off headlights, engine.

After telling everyone to stay in their seats, Philip

pressed a button. The door opened and a small fat man with an automatic weapon slung over his shoulder appeared. Philip called down in French, which Paula caught the gist of.

'Pierre, everything clear? Nothing suspicious.'

'You see no bodies. I haven't shot anyone yet tonight.'

'Everyone out,' Philip ordered in English.

He was delving into a large bag when they surrounded him. He carefully brought out what to Paula looked like the first of several metal pancakes.

'Limpet mines, special type,' Philip explained. 'We'll need them later in Paris.'

Paris? Paula thought.

'They are switched off?' Harry asked as he took the first mine.

'Of course,' snapped Philip. 'Turn that lever to the right and they're active.' He showed Harry three more mines, put them back in the leather bag with thick cloth between each one. From the next container he brought out a Browning, shoulder holster, a Beretta, a leg holster, spare mags. Handed them to Paula, grinned.

'Feel dressed now?'

'I do. What about registration?'

'Don't worry. Dollars satisfy many officials. As they did Armand at the airport. Now, Tweed . . .'

When he had finished distributing the 'cutlery', Harry also had a large automatic weapon and spare mags, concealed inside a golf bag; Newman had his beloved Smith & Wesson with holster and ammo. Philip handed Pierre two fat envelopes which Paula guessed were stuffed with banknotes, then clapped his hands.

'All aboard. Must keep moving.'

They had just settled in their seats when Philip was driving them down the side road back on to the main route. Paula was savouring the perfume from some plant on the side road. It had seeped into her clothes. She took deep breaths.

'Be in Aix soon,' Philip called out. 'Tweed, you won't be staying at the Violette, which I know you favour. It's too obvious a place where Noel's friends might check to find you. Instead you're at the swish Negre-Coste on the famous Cours Mirabeau. They won't expect you to choose that. Both you and Paula have rooms overlooking the *cours*. A treat. Food's wonderful.'

'So Noel has arrived?' asked Tweed.

'Came in a few hours ago. Staying at a pokey little joint in the old town. Thinks it makes him inconspicuous. But it doesn't.'

'And who are Noel's friends?' Paula wondered.

'Not to be recommended as dining companions. Bit of a mix,' he went on casually. 'Arabs and Slovaks.

Need watching. Cut your throat for sixpence – or the equivalent in dollars.'

'Can't wait to meet them,' said Paula.

'Just pray you don't. We are now entering the ancient city of Aix, first built by the Romans. Getting back to Slovaks, Noel's lot come from the High Tatra mountains in Slovakia. I have been up there in the snow. Tweed, they have a training ground for those selected for the corps d'élite of State Security planned by Noel.'

'What sort of training ground? I don't like the sound of this,' Tweed commented.

'You shouldn't. It's well organized, has been created months ago. They are taught how to kill silently. Also they're taught English. Noel has fifty of them infiltrated inside Aix. I've heard he hopes to transport them to Britain tomorrow. I know the route. Here we are. The Cours Mirabeau.'

Paula peered out of her window, alternating that with staring through the windscreen. She was impressed. The *cours* was a long wide straight street with plane trees along the pavements on both sides. The warmth was bringing out their leaves. It was a beautiful boulevard with huge old mansions to her right. Philip saw her looking at them.

'Once they housed wealthy families. These days most are converted into company offices. This is the gem of Aix.'

Gem was the right word, she thought. There was not much traffic at this hour, and locals were strolling, gazing at the mansions, the older ones remembering the grander days, she thought. Philip parked by the kerb outside a large imposing building.

'Journey's end,' Philip announced. 'The Negre-Coste. I've booked front rooms overlooking the *cours* for Tweed and Paula. Very expensive. Let's explore.'

The rooms were huge. Refurbished, as Philip explained, it still retained some of the character of the original mansion. Inside her first-floor room Paula revelled in the luxury as she swiftly unpacked her few things, including one evening dress protected with tissue.

She walked to the windows, opened them, gazed down at the *cours*. They were double-glazed, probably to muffle the sound of daytime traffic. After showering, she dressed quickly, sat in front of an elegant mirror and applied the minimum of makeup. A tap on the door sent her to unlock it and Tweed, in a smart suit, walked in.

'You look terrific,' he said and kissed her on both cheeks. 'It's lucky we all keep small cases packed at Park Crescent ready for instant departure. You have money?'

'A stack of dollars. I tipped the chap who brought up my bag with a twenty-dollar bill and he was pleased. He doesn't like euros, said they were only good for lighting fires!'

'Philip gave me this for you,' he said, producing an envelope from his pocket. 'Take a quick look.'

She extracted a photo and pulled a face of distaste. 'Don't like the look of him. Who is he?'

'Radek, boss of the fifty Slovaks Noel hopes to smuggle into Britain. Favours a knife for killing.'

She studied the photo again. A small but well-built man, Slavic features, prominent cheekbones, dead-looking eyes, sharp nose, a pointed jaw. He had thick black hair, a curving moustache, a sneering expression.

'Keep it in case you ever spot him. I've got a copy, so have Newman and Harry. Philip thinks of everything. Now we'd better get down to dinner . . .'

The dining room was spacious and only a few of the large tables were occupied. Out of season. Philip complimented her on her dress and beauty, kissing her hand. It was something she normally disliked but with Philip she liked it. They drank aperitifs while studying the enormous menu.

They had a table in the corner, so when they were eating and the waiters were distant, they could talk frankly. It was Tweed who got down to business.

'Philip, how were you able to obtain this valuable information about the Tatra training camp?'

'Oh, simple. I have a trustworthy contact who

knows the Tatra well. We've skied quite a lot up there. My contact had a Slovak mother and a French father. The info cost me two thousand dollars – part of the funds you sent me months ago. Incidentally, their villainous chief's name isn't really Radek. No idea of what his real name is. Doesn't matter.'

After the meal, Philip, seated next to Paula, suggested she might like a short walk since it would still be warm outside. 'Freak weather,' he remarked.

'We'll go north just a bit,' he said as they strolled in the *cours*. 'That's where the original houses are still standing. Just a bit, not far.'

'I love the big fountains,' Paula said glancing down the *cours*.

'They have them where we're going. Smaller efforts but I find the sound of running water soothing.'

Down a side street they plunged into a different world. Narrow streets twisting and turning. Some illumination from ancient lamps but long dark areas of shadow between them. Paula was beginning to wonder whether this was a good idea. The occasional Arab in a long white gown drifted past them.

They reached a deserted square and again there was the sound of running water. Paula darted away from Philip to see a small fountain spraying in from a stone well in the corner of the square.

She never heard him coming or saw where he had

been hiding. One arm wrapped round her breast from behind and a large knife just touched her throat. She glanced up, saw an Arab with only one eye grinning horribly at her. She was terrified. She had no chance of reaching for the Browning under her armpit, even less chance of hauling the Beretta from the holster strapped to her right leg. Any movement and this beast would slash her throat open. Where the hell was Philip?

Philip appeared in front of them out of nowhere. In his right hand he held a revolver with a silencer attached. Pointing his weapon, Philip said something in Arabic.

Her assailant's response was to move the blade closer in. Paula could feel the razor edge touching her skin. For some idiotic reason she wanted to sneeze. She suppressed it. Philip was speaking in Arabic again. The Arab replied, his tone vicious.

Philip smiled, waved both hands as though accepting he could do nothing. Oh God, she thought. Philip's next movement was so swift she hardly saw it happen. Then he was pressing the tip of his weapon against the Arab's good eye. He snarled something in Arabic. She felt the Arab shudder. Then he removed the knife and stood back behind her.

She was much smaller than her attacker so from where Philip stood his neck and head loomed well above Paula's. Phut! Philip had shot him in the head. The man fell over backwards, lay still on the cobbles.

'You'd better take this gun for a moment,' Philip said, speaking quietly but rapidly. 'I have to dump the body in that huge rubbish bin over there. Just in case some of his chums arrive.'

'I'm armed.'

She had already grasped the Browning so Philip could see it. He nodded, stooped, grasped the corpse round the waist, began to hurry towards the bin. She followed him. Without being asked, she lifted the lid. It was heavy, but she managed to hold it high up.

A foul smell drifted up from the interior, half full of rubbish. Philip heaved the body inside. She lowered the lid slowly to avoid a noise. Philip was already running away from her after a quick searching glance round the square. He had a glove on his hand as Paula ran after him, unwilling to be alone for another moment. Picking up the long blade by the handle, he dropped the knife down a nearby drain, then grabbed her arm.

'Back to the *cours* now!'

'How did you manage that?' she asked as they hurried.

'He had one precious possession, his one good eye. Without that he'd be at the mercy of other Arabs. The thought of a bullet through it made him release you instantly.'

'Quick thinking, thank God,' she replied. 'You saved my life.'

'No, I endangered it with my stupid idea of showing you the old quarter. I'll never forgive myself. There's the *cours*. Pause just for a second.'

He unscrewed the silencer, dropped it down a drain, holstered his weapon. She was puzzled as they entered the *cours* and civilization – as it seemed to Paula.

'Why throw that away?' she wondered.

'Silencers are tricky. One shot, OK. Then a silencer can jam a gun. I have more. Back to the hotel. You must tell Tweed what happened.'

'I wasn't going to say a word . . .'

'I insist. Promise me. He's my chief. He trusts me. So he's entitled to know everything that happens.'

Tweed was sitting in an armchair near the main reception area. Philip sent Paula off to brief him while he had a drink in the bar. She was beginning to feel rattled. She was familiar with this reaction. With the Arab's knife at her throat she had been scared stiff but in control, staying quite still. When a danger was behind her, her nerves played her up.

Tweed nodded as she sat on a chair close to his. He waited until the glass of Chardonnay he had ordered was placed before her. There was no one else in the room. He looked straight at her, his tone grim.

'What went wrong while you were out?'

'Nothing dramatic. Why do you ask?'

'Because I'm observant,' he continued in the same serious tone, unsmiling. 'I know something did because your face has lost colour. Added to which Philip has gone off to the bar so you can talk to me.'

'Philip saved my life,' she said, beginning on what she hoped was a positive note. She then told him of the incident. He gazed straight at her, the same expression on his face. When she had finished he drank the rest of his wine.

'So, he saved your life after putting it in terrible danger. I thought the two of you were just walking down the *cours*. Now I know he ventured with you into the north side, which is to be avoided at all costs. You know I was here some years ago, staying at the Violette hotel in the north. There were a few Arabs creeping about in those days. So when I walked down through that area I had a gun in my hand. Any Arab who saw me disappeared immediately. Because of the gun. Now there are many more Arabs.'

'You're not going to have a row with Philip?'

'Of course not. We are dependent on him while we are here. Also, he is the most valuable agent I have abroad. Here he comes.' Tweed stood up. 'Hello, Philip. Could the three of us take a stroll along the *cours*?'

Paula admired Tweed's masterful self-control. She

sensed he was seething with anger, but nothing showed in the amiable way he greeted Philip. They left the hotel and wandered down the *cours*. Tweed was in the middle with Paula on his right, Philip on his left. Paula was drinking in the atmosphere of the famous street. Tweed kept his comments to himself. So much had been modernized, including the Negre-Coste. Still a magnificent hotel but without some of the character he recalled. Even the bathroom in his room had been 'upgraded'. The French had been influenced by the American fetish for advanced plumbing. Aix he'd visited once before to meet a contact.

'Dreamy,' enthused Paula.

'Unique,' said Tweed.

'I've paid your hotel bills,' Philip said suddenly. 'We leave tomorrow, which may be an exciting day.'

'How exciting?' Tweed asked.

'Noel is moving his fifty Slovaks to Paris tomorrow, on their way to Britain. They're travelling in two separate grey coaches. I was talking to Harry earlier. You remember that old stone hump-backed bridge we crossed – where the road was rough?'

'I do,' said Paula. 'We went up steeply, then dropped down the other side. It was over a river.'

'We'll eliminate half of them at the bridge,' Philip said casually. 'The twenty-five in the other coach we'll finish off in Paris. Up at six tomorrow for early breakfast. It may not be a joy-ride.'

20

It was dark when they left the hotel for the south side of the town. They were on foot, led by Philip. Paula noticed it was more modern. Down an alley Philip opened an automatic door to a garage. Inside was parked their people-carrier.

As they climbed aboard he remarked: 'Should have told you earlier. All windows are bullet-proof, the sides and roof have been reconstructed with armour plate. So rest easy on our way to Paris . . .'

Harry emerged from underneath the vehicle, gave a thumbs-up sign to Philip.

'No explosives attached underneath. I checked the engine.'

'You're a thorough chap,' Philip thanked him.

'I'm a bloody suspicious chap,' Harry shot back as he got into the car. Philip drove out to the end of the alley, pausing to use his controller to close the garage door. Leaving the alley he turned left. Paula sighed with nostalgia when they moved into open country. Tweed sighed with relief. Place is a death-trap these days, he muttered to himself.

'We're well ahead of the first Slovak coach,' Philip called out. 'They're just loading up. The second one will follow some distance behind. Both with twenty-five killers aboard. We'll take the second one in Paris,' he reminded them.

'How does he know all these things?' Paula wondered aloud to Tweed.

'Contacts,' Philip called back. He riffled his right fingers as though shuffling a wad of banknotes. 'Dollars are more than acceptable.'

'And where has Noel been all this time?' Paula asked from her seat by the window.

'Staying under cover in a dump on the north side,' Philip told her. 'Visited by nice Mr Radek.'

'Radek?'

'The chief of the Slovak mob, remember? I gave you a photo of him. A very nice chap, to watch while he drowns. Noel is driving back to Paris in a hired Citroën, some distance behind the second coach. With Radek for company. The villain had a Slovak mother, a French father. And a Czech uncle who taught him languages, so Radek is fluent in quite a few tongues. We'll soon be at the bridge.'

Tweed observed Harry place a large leather container in his lap. From inside he carefully extracted a large landmine and a trowel. Paula, peering out of her window, didn't see this. It was still dark and Philip's headlights were on full beam as the carrier moved round a series of curves. As the road climbed steeply, Philip slowed, then dropped down the other side. He switched off the headlights, joined Harry and they both left the carrier, walked the short distance back to the bridge.

Not wishing to miss anything, Paula left her seat, moved forward and sat in the driving seat. Through the windscreen she had a good view of what was happening, her eyes now accustomed to the dark which was showing traces of dawn.

Philip reappeared, handed a pair of night-glasses up to Tweed. 'If you'd watch out for their first coach. Warn me when you see its lights.'

Harry was digging a large wide hole in the soft earth at the top of the bridge. He worked quickly, then with care slipped in the landmine. Equally quickly, he scooped loose soil over it to conceal it. As he stood up Tweed called out from the exit.

'Lights in the distance. Looks like a coach. About a mile back, roughly. Difficult to be sure in this light.'

Philip with Harry rushed aboard, closing the door behind them. Harry went back to his seat, as did Paula. Philip told Tweed he could keep the night-glasses.

'Then you can see the fun,' he said.

Jumping behind the wheel he started the engine, turned on the headlights to low beam, drove on a short distance. He swung right off the road up the same small cul-de-sac where he had parked on their way in to distribute weapons.

At the top he moved round the small concrete circle so he was facing the exit. He suggested to everyone that they got out with him. Paula was surprised when he pointed out how clearly they could see the bridge now silver bands of dawn were shafting across the eastern sky. Philip borrowed the night-glasses from Tweed, stared east, handed them back.

'Coach is coming too fast. Slovak at the wheel, they're mad drivers . . .'

It was chilly. Paula, now wearing her denims and windcheater, buttoned it up to the neck. The coach was racing along, its headlights on full beam. She half-expected it to drive into the wall and off the bridge. At the last moment the man behind the wheel slowed, crawled up on to the top of the bridge.

The explosion was devastating. A blinding flash coinciding with a deafening roar. The vehicle soared into the sky, broke in half. Body parts were hurled in all directions. She thought she saw a leg as she gazed through the night-glasses Tweed had loaned her. Then a headless trunk caught in the blazing inferno illuminating the wreckage of the bridge. The dawn light was red with fire. One half of the vehicle dropped into the river. Paula heard a brief hiss as water absorbed the red-hot metal. Then a sudden silence.

'That worked rather well,' Philip commented.

'I think a long way off I can see headlights. The second coach?' suggested Paula, her mouth dry.

'Probably,' Philip agreed. 'They have night-glasses so they'll see what's happened. They'll have to make a long diversion to reach the autoroute. That means we arrive in Paris before them. Ready to sort out that lot.'

Sort out? Paula, her mind still full of the massacre on the bridge, wondered how Philip would manage this. He always seemed so calm, so matter-of-fact in the face of the most murderous danger.

Well along the autoroute, Philip pulled in to a remote lay-by. He stood up, turned to address them.

'I want you to hand in all your weapons now. We could be stopped by a patrol car.'

He even collected the three remaining slim landmines from Harry. Everything was secreted inside a special compartment in the side of the carrier. Harry was indignant.

'I thought I'd be using those to polish off the thugs inside the second coach.'

'No, you won't,' Philip said firmly. 'Change of plan. I've been thinking. I can do that job by myself.

There'll be a large barge-like vessel with a sail drifting off the Île St-Louis on the Seine in the middle of Paris. They plan to use small boats with engines to ferry the Slovaks aboard the Yvette, the barge. Then their idea is to sail it up the river to the port at its mouth. There they'll transfer their inhuman cargo to a larger shipping vessel, take them to an isolated part of the British coast. I'll see they never leave Paris alive.'

He sat behind the wheel, waited until the autoroute was quiet, drove back on to it and headed at speed for Paris.

They had entered the Paris suburbs when Tweed made a suggestion.

'Philip, I could phone Loriot, Chief of the DST. He's an old friend. Tell him what is happening, where to go.'

'No!' Philip spoke over his shoulder. 'By now he'll have heard about the explosion at that bridge near Aix. And all the mangled bodies in the fields and floating down that river. He'll check all the hotels for names.'

'We had false passports,' Tweed objected. 'I told you that earlier.'

'Makes no difference.' Philip was authoritative. 'He'll be concentrating on short-stay visitors. He'll ask for their descriptions. Some of those concierges are observant. Now you'll have an hour to amuse yourselves – I'll drop you near the Place Vendôme and the Ritz. Then take a cab to the Gare du Nord. You'll arrive in time to catch the Eurostar. I don't think Noel will use it. He'll fly back – as he came in . . .'

Near the Place Vendôme Philip practically pushed out Tweed, who wanted to thank him for all he'd done. Standing on the pavement Tweed called up to Philip behind the wheel, who still had the engine running.

'Take good care of yourself. Call me – more frequently.'

'When I've something to report. Look after yourself, Paula.'

The automatic door closed and they were left standing as the carrier drove east. Towards the Île St-Louis.

They walked along the Rue St-Honoré, the main street with its fabulously expensive shops. It was early afternoon and the sky was full of menacing clouds drifting very low.

Tweed and Paula walked ahead with Newman and Harry bringing up the rear. They were still performing their role as guards. Tweed took them into a cafe where they consumed coffee and delicious cakes. Paula was ravenous.

'I'll leave you for a couple of minutes,' Newman

said, standing up. 'We passed a shop selling the most glamorous scarves. I'll get one for Roma.'

'Getting serious, are we?' Paula teased him.

'She's nice and very intelligent. Be back in minutes.'

They were leaving the cafe to wait for Newman. Paula went out first, paused to glance in both directions. She backed into the cafe, bumping into Tweed, pushing him back. Grabbing his arm she returned them to their table, which was at the side of the cafe with a view of the door.

'What was that about?' Tweed demanded.

'Radek. He's coming this way down the street.'

'Are you sure?'

'Yes, I bloody well am. I studied his photo. See him in a minute. Let's pray he doesn't come in here. We've given up our weapons . . .'

Harry sprang up from the table, concealing a leather-covered sap. He walked swiftly across to a table on the far side, ordered coffee, insisted on paying for it. They were the only occupants of the cafe. The waitress placed coffee in front of Harry, smiled at the tip, went out of sight through a door at the back.

Radek, wearing a dark coat, a black hat, wandered in. As he walked straight to their table the sneer on his Slavic features was prominent beneath his curved moustache. One hand reached inside his coat and he took off his hat with the other. He bowed briefly to Paula.

'You will tell me, Mr Tweed, where the others are and what they are doing otherwise I shall shoot Miss Grey.'

He spoke very rapidly, excellent English but with an accent. For once in his life Tweed was uncertain. He opened his mouth to say something, anything to delay the killer. That was the moment when Harry appeared behind the Slovak and hammered his sap hard on the back of his hatless head.

Radek's eyes opened very wide, then he collapsed backwards. Harry caught him, lowered him to the floor as the waitress appeared again. Paula stood up, spoke quickly to her in French.

'This poor gentleman has collapsed. Could be a heart attack. Call an ambulance. We have to go but we'll be back.'

As they hurried out of the cafe the waitress rushed to the phone.

Outside Newman appeared, carrying a beautifully wrapped package. He stared at their obvious haste. Paula hailed an oncoming cab.

'Gare du Nord, please,' said Tweed, handing the driver a large tip. 'And hurry, or we're going to miss our train.'

Paula repeated the request in French, seeing the driver's stare of incomprehension. They piled into the back, Tweed and Paula occupying the main seat while Harry and Newman used the jump seats. They were moving.

At the Gare du Nord, Tweed found an empty coach. The Eurostar was on the verge of leaving. They had just settled in their seats when it glided out of the terminus.

Tweed told Newman what had happened. Newman stood up and carefully placed his wrapped gift with their small bags. He didn't comment until he sat down.

'How the devil did Radek reach Paris so quickly?'

'By busting the speed limits on the autoroute, would be my guess,' Tweed told him. 'When we were parked in the lay-by while Philip collected our weapons I noticed a car going over the limit. Two people inside – the driver and one passenger. Too quick to identify anyone.'

'Did you kill Radek?' Newman asked Harry.

'Definitely not. That would have brought the police. He will be out for about an hour and then recover – with the mother and father of all headaches.'

'What puzzles me,' said Paula, 'is how he spotted me, knew who I was.'

'We've taken photos of people,' Tweed reminded her. 'So why shouldn't someone from the Cabal have

214

done the same thing? Then Noel, the hyper-efficient Noel, takes the prints with him.'

No one said any more until they emerged from the tunnel into Kent. Paula peered out of the window, heaved a great sigh.

Unlike in Paris, the sun was shining brilliantly out of a duck-egg-blue sky. Not a cloud in sight. She savoured the green fields which, early, were beginning to sprout, the orchards coated in a green fuzz.

'I'm glad to get out of France,' she said. 'So glad to get back to England and peace.'

'Don't count on peace,' Tweed warned. 'We have a savage murder to investigate and a battle to crush the merger of all the security services.'

'Do shut up,' Newman told him. 'She's had a rough ride. Your problem is you never appreciate the finer things of life.'

'Sorry. You're right, Bob. Paula has had a nerve-racking trip most of the way. I do realize that.'

'I just want to get home, to have hours of sleep in my own bed. In the morning I'll be a hellcat,' Paula added.

21

Tweed walked into an atmosphere of crisis.

He took off his coat, settled down in his chair, looked round his office. Monica, grim-faced, got up to come over to him. Pete Nield was standing up, arms folded, no sign of a smile. Marler stood against the wall, fiddling with his cigarette holder, which was empty. He stared at Tweed.

Paula, who had been going to leave, sat down at her desk. Newman waited by the door, scanning expressions. It was Tweed who broke the ice.

'Well, what happened in my absence? You all look as though a bomb has gone off.'

'It has, in a manner of speaking,' Monica said, standing stiffly in front of his desk. 'First, General Macomber phoned, told me that under no circumstances must Tweed go anywhere alone. He added he'd just seen the Cabal. Then Benton Macomber bulldozed his way in. Asked to see you urgently. I said you weren't available. "Is he abroad?" Benton asked. I said I'd no idea where you were. He said you must call him the moment you returned, then pushed off. Pete,' she went on, turning to Nield, 'maybe you'd like to describe your experience.'

'Sinister,' Nield began. 'Early this afternoon I saw a large white van stopped across the road. Had TV painted on its side. They were using cameras to photograph this building. So I went out, crossed the main road in front of the van. It started moving, nearly mowed me down. I skipped on to the pavement and it stopped. I opened the passenger door. The thug beside the driver swore at me. I demanded to know what the hell they were doing, who they were. The passenger tried to kick me in the face. I grabbed his leg, hauled him out, repeated my questions. The driver produced an automatic, pointed it at me, ordered me to let go of his mate. I did so. The van drove off.'

'Intimidation,' said Tweed. 'So if they're playing rough we must respond at once. Marler, work out a plan.'

'I already have done. I'll need Harry's help. Now . . .'

Both men left the office. Tweed, his manner calm, took out a pen and a pad, began doodling. Those remaining waited for his next words.

'Interesting that Benton asked if I was abroad. He

knew I was. Was checking your reaction, Monica. You did well.'

'How could he know?' Paula wondered aloud.

'Radek. He'd report our presence to Noel, wherever he was keeping out of sight of violence. Noel would then phone the information to the Cabal. Benton came in about five o'clock this afternoon?' he asked Monica.

'Not far off that.'

'We'd be on Eurostar. Noel probably flew back ahead of us. With Radek. Which reminds me.' He took out a photo Philip had handed him, gave it to Monica. 'Take that downstairs. Ask them to make five copies. Urgent. Then everyone has a copy.'

'Horrible-looking brute,' Monica commented.

'The devil himself,' chimed in Paula. 'Radek.'

'You think he's over here already?' Newman suggested.

'Sure of it. He'd fly back with Noel. We have two choice killers to watch out for. Fitch, now Radek.' He looked at Paula. 'You go back home, escorted by Newman. You won't mind if he sleeps in your spare bedroom tonight?'

'I'd appreciate it, when I do go. I'm wide awake now we have all this to deal with. I find it strange that General Macomber should warn us.'

'Could be he doesn't like the Cabal. Or it could be part of the campaign of intimidation.'

'You can't suspect the General,' she protested.

'I suspect everyone until we've smashed the Cabal. Why, I wonder, did he visit the Cabal when he's supposed to detest his offspring? I sense everyone is lying.'

'Can I tell you about my encounter with my informant yesterday?' Nield enquired.

'Encounter?' Tweed queried. 'Yes, go ahead.'

'I wasn't happy, so I called her and suggested we had dinner. She accepted immediately, said she was worried. This is how it went . . .'

Nield had arrived promptly at Coral's apartment. When she opened the door she was dressed to kill. Her flaming red hair was piled on top of her head, and she wore a short close-fitting white dress, accentuating her excellent figure.

'Come in and have a drink first, Pete,' she invited him with a glowing smile.

'Unfortunately we haven't time,' he replied, thinking quickly. 'I've booked a table at that restaurant just down the road. If we don't grab it now they'll give it to someone else.'

'OK. Let me get my coat.'

'What are you worried about?' he asked as they walked down the street.

'It can wait until we've had a drink. I need one. Brandy.'

Seated at a corner table, well away from any of the crowd already creating a babble of voices mingled with the clink of glasses, they were able to talk unheard.

'This is good,' she said as she consumed her starter, a mix of sliced melon, oranges and bananas, generously flavoured with brandy. 'My favourite tipple, brandy,' she told him.

'What is worrying you?' he had asked again.

'The Parrot. She asked me out to lunch today, took me to a very posh restaurant. I saw the bill later. Sky high.'

'I thought you were enemies. That's what you said last time we talked.'

'I know, Pete. I thought so too. Now she's all over me. I can't do anything wrong at work. During lunch she said one of the Cabal was after her. Wouldn't say which one. She's not prepared to play ball with him – so she's worried they'll manoeuvre her out of her job.'

'They?'

'The Cabal. They support each other. They're planning something aggressive against Tweed's outfit. Thought you ought to know.'

'But how do you know this? They're in a separate room.'

'I know.' She fluttered her eyes at him. 'You'll think I'm wicked. The hinges between our large room and the Cabal's HQ have been oiled, but the door doesn't shut properly if someone isn't careful. When the Parrot is away I creep over, open it just a bit more and listen to what they're saying.'

'Dangerous.'

'I'm very careful. I have a file tucked under my arm. There is a filing cabinet close to that door in our room.'

'Going back to what you said earlier,' Pete said, pausing while the waiter served their main course, 'you referred to some aggressive action planned against Tweed. Any details?'

'Only that Noel, who was away, planned it. Benton said he hoped Noel wouldn't go mad. Then I sidled back to my desk. Just in time. One of them closed the door.'

'Noel was away. Where?'

'No idea . . .'

They chatted about other things until they'd finished the meal. When they left the restaurant, Nield walked her to the entrance to her flat. She took out her keys, opened the door, tucked her arm in his. She turned to face him, her eyebrows raised, invited him in for a quiet drink.

'I'd love to,' he lied, 'but before I came over I was dealing with another problem and they will want to hear about it back at Park Crescent. Certain phone calls have to be made this evening. Maybe another time?'

She made a moue as he kissed her on both cheeks. Not best pleased. She said good night, walked in and closed the door in his face.

22

'So,' Nield concluded his narrative, 'I escaped without being compromised. Coral looked furious.'

'I don't believe one word of what that woman says,' decided Paula. 'Why is she twisting and turning the situation in that building?'

'It's possible that she's acting on instructions from one of the Cabal,' Tweed mused. 'But I doubt it.'

'Which one?' Paula asked.

'I have no idea. I rather doubt my theory. Can't think of what she's up to.'

'Maybe she's barmy,' Nield suggested. 'It was someone out of their mind who committed that horrible Viola murder.'

'She's too small to have done it,' Nield said.

'It's like a mosaic,' Tweed ruminated. 'Every piece fits in somewhere. But we're missing the main picture.'

'Oh Lord!' Newman burst out. 'I'm missing one

expensive present. I've left the scarf for Roma on the rack on the Eurostar.'

'No you haven't,' Paula told him. She opened her hold-all on the floor beside her, produced the wrapped scarf, handed it to Newman. 'I always check nothing's been left when I leave a plane or a train.'

'I can't thank you enough,' Newman responded, the relief showing in his face. 'I do feel better now.'

'Romance for Roma,' Paula chaffed him.

'And while you two are blathering,' Tweed said grimly, 'I'm wondering what Marler and Harry are up to.'

Wearing masks over their faces, Marler and Harry were showing infinite patience as they waited. Harry was leaning against the wall on one side of the metal door guarding the entrance to Special Branch HQ. Marler had adopted the same position on the other side.

They had positioned themselves so they were invisible to the slow swivel of the security cameras on the wall above them. Every now and again Harry stretched his legs up and down to fight off cramp. Marler remained still as a statue. He checked his watch. They'd kept up their vigil for over an hour. Patience was a virtue.

The side street was so dark, so ill-lit, that anyone passing down Whitehall who glanced their way would not see their faces, let alone their masks. Marler raised a hand holding one of the grenades. He had heard something. Harry pulled a face. He didn't believe Marler had heard a thing.

The steel door rose slowly without warning, sliding up and over into its slot. Marler risked peering inside. The slow escalator was on the move. Nelson was standing still, letting the escalator do the work.

A few steps behind him Benton, clad in a shaggy coat, was studying a report. Behind him Noel was standing quite still. So Noel was back from France. Which meant Radek was in town.

As the step Nelson stood on neared the bottom Marler nodded to Harry. They acted as one. Marler's first tear-gas grenade landed on Nelson's step, burst, sending up a great cloud of the gas. At the same moment Harry had thrown another higher up, a perfect throw, hitting Benton's tread. Another great cloud of gas erupted.

Nelson was choking, his eyes hurting as he wobbled, not sure what to do next. Marler lobbed his second grenade high up, actually hitting Noel on the knee, where it burst. All three men were choking, coughing, wobbling all over the place. The Parrot appeared at the top, stared in disbelief, caught a whiff of the gas, ran back into the office to call an ambulance. Marler and Harry, masks off, were gone.

★

Tweed was talking to Nield when Marler and Harry returned to the office. He thought Harry looked pleased with himself while Marler's expression was his normal blank.

'Pete,' Tweed continued, 'what game do you think Coral Flenton is playing?'

'No idea. Except she is playing some game. I'd sooner not go near her again.'

'Then I'll go tomorrow,' Paula piped up. 'I got on well with her and we agreed to meet again soon. Because I'm a woman she'll find it harder to manipulate me.'

'Good idea,' agreed Tweed. 'Now Marler, Harry, what have you been up to?'

Marler, in a few words, explained what they had done at the Cabal's HQ. 'Teach them to send a fake TV van to try and photograph this place.'

'Think I'll have a bit of fun,' Tweed said. 'Monica, can you get their number? I'll take over immediately.'

'May I speak to Miss Partridge?' Tweed asked when he took over the line. 'That is Miss Partridge speaking? Good. Tweed here. I gather Benton Macomber wanted me to contact him.'

'They're ill,' she blurted out. 'In hospital.'

'Nothing serious, I hope? Expected back maybe tomorrow? I know there have been a lot of cases of food poisoning.'

'Yes, there have,' she said, having recovered her wits.

'Well, give them all my regards and wishes for a speedy recovery. Don't eat in any strange restaurants.'

'I cook my own meals at home,' she responded sharply.

'I don't think I know where you live.'

'Hammersmith. In a big flat I bought ages ago.' A pause. 'Maybe you'd come over and see me for supper one day. My address is . . .'

Tweed scribbled down her address, phone number, mobile number.

'I shall look forward to that,' he told her. 'Maybe we could meet soon.'

'Soon as you like,' she replied in a seductive tone he didn't know she was capable of. 'Thanks for calling. See you . . .'

'You must be smitten,' Paula joked.

'I'd like to smite her. But she's a piece of the mosaic we are assembling. Away from the Cabal she may let her guard down.'

'She'll tell them.'

'You know, I don't think she will,' Tweed replied. 'Now it's time Newman took you home. I saw you yawn. You must be exhausted.'

'Bed would be nice.'

Newman drove off first and Paula followed him. The traffic was lighter and as he moved up Brompton Road he slowed almost to a crawl. She wondered why. Then he parked, turned and gestured for her to join him.

'Something wrong?' she enquired as she settled beside him.

'Couldn't be more wrong.'

'What is it?'

'See that battered old Ford outside the entrance to your yard? Two men in front, the driver gesturing towards your place to his companion. Recognize anyone?'

'Oh God! Not the driver, but his passenger is Radek.'

'And the driver is Fitch. Inside that car is the most deadly killing machine in town. They're checking your place. Aren't you glad Tweed told me to look after you? I could kill them both,' he went on. On his lap was a Smith & Wesson. 'Perfect opportunity.'

'Don't.' She placed her hand on his. 'It would be murder. I don't think the police would take into account what they are.'

'This isn't my normal revolver,' he argued. 'It's one Harry gave me. Never been used before. Serial number filed off. No check on the bullets would be found in the records . . .'

'Don't!' she repeated more emphatically. 'I'd like to kill them myself but it's too dangerous. And it's just outside my flat. I'd be the first one the police grill.'

The argument was settled as the Ford drove off down the Fulham Road. Newman waited to give them time to get well clear, then drove on, crossed the road into the yard, parked the car out of sight at the back of the building. Paula, who had returned to her car, followed him.

'I won't use the spare bedroom tonight,' Newman decided as she fiddled with her door keys. 'I'll sleep on the couch in the living room, then I can see and hear anyone coming.'

'I'll make up the couch into a bed,' she promised him. 'It has one of these pull-out beds underneath it. I'll make you comfortable.'

'I know you will. And I'll have my normal revolver handy. No, I don't want anything to eat. Just a carafe of water.'

In the living room overlooking the street she fussed with pillows and sheets and blankets. Then she gave a great yawn as she said good night. In her bedroom she forced herself to take a quick shower, dried, flopped into bed and was fast asleep the moment her head hit the pillow.

In the morning, when it was still dark, Paula was up first. She found Newman still awake. She went to close the curtains.

'Don't do that,' he warned. 'I need a view of the street. You look a million dollars,' he remarked as he put on his shoes and windcheater. 'I take it you slept well.'

'It was glorious. I didn't dream once. Breakfast now, then back to the office, I expect. I'm wondering how Radek got here so quickly.'

'Simple. Radek flies over from Paris with Noel. Then Noel drives him in the car he's left at airport parking to Fitch's hangout.'

'Which is where?' she asked as she skilfully broke eggs over a pan in the compact kitchen leading off the living room. 'I hope you're hungry.'

'Could eat a horse,' Newman said.

'Sorry, not on the menu. You were saying?'

'Harry knows he has a warehouse in the East End. He's never been inside but a pal has, described it. Fitch sleeps in a small messy room. The main feature is a vast room which has nothing in it. The floor is the old planks. Noel will know the place.'

'Why Noel?'

'Because he's the Planner. Fitch is just the type of scum Noel would use for dirty jobs. I've got Noel, with his public-school accent, weighed up.'

'Sit down. Eat . . .'

At Nelson's insistence, against the doctor's wishes, the three men were released from hospital after promising to drink plenty of water. They were walking down the exit stairs, watched by the doctor, when Nelson stumbled, grabbed hold of the banister.

'I expect to see you back here soon,' the doctor warned.

'We're businessmen,' Nelson shouted. 'Not doctors who piddle around for a few hours a day.'

'Not another word,' Benton told him in his quiet voice.

The limo Nelson had called for on his mobile waited for them outside. A uniformed chauffeur opened the doors. They had just got in when Nelson gave an abrupt instruction to the driver.

'We're in a hurry to get to our building. No crawling.'

Near Trafalgar Street the limo was stopped in a solid motionless wedge of traffic. Noel glanced out of the window, saw a newspaper stall. He opened his door, dived out. Behind the wheel the chauffeur raised his eyes to heaven. He could have started moving while Noel was half out of the car. At the newspaper stall Noel asked for the latest edition of the *Daily Nation*, paid, dived back into the limo, began studying the paper.

'Expecting good news?' Benton asked caustically.

'You never know . . .'

He broke off, swearing silently to himself, using the foulest language.

Newman drove off from her flat first. Paula's car was close behind him. They were nearly at Park Crescent when she honked her horn. Newman glanced in his rear-view mirror, saw her parked, running into a newspaper shop. She came out quickly with the *Daily Nation*, the latest edition, which the shop's owner told her had just arrived.

She dropped it on the seat, honked again and they drove on to Park Crescent. As soon as she sat at her desk Paula began studying the paper, concentrating on Drew Franklin's column. She smiled, waved her hand in the air in a victory gesture.

'So what is so exciting?' Tweed asked.

'Three cheers for Philip Cardon. Harry, that barge thing off the Île St-Louis. You were going to help Philip do something. What was it?'

'Sounded a tricky idea to me. Philip was giving me a frogman's suit while he put on his own. Then we were going to wait until all twenty-five Slovaks from the second coach had been ferried aboard in small boats from a ramp on the Île. Waited a bit longer while they were hidden in the hold. I'd have had two limpet mines with magnetic attachments, Philip one. We'd then have swum out from the same ramp, unseen underwater. I had to attach two of the mines either side of the prow while Philip attached his on the stern. Then we'd have swum to the opposite shore. Philip had a small powerful radio. When he pressed the button the mines would have detonated. Why are you asking?'

'Mind if I see that newspaper?' Tweed asked.

Paula ran across. She had folded the paper to the front page. Drew Franklin's report was very prominent.

IMMIGRANT SABOTEURS
KILLED ON SEINE

A cunning plan to smuggle Slovak saboteurs into Britain was foiled yesterday evening in Paris. The ship bound for Britain was stationary opposite the Île St-Louis when a huge explosion took out the entire bottom of the ship, which sank quickly. The French police report they are still searching the Seine for bodies.

'So Philip did it by himself,' Tweed commented. 'I really will have to send him more funds. That eliminates the rest of Radek's army of killers, remembering the explosion on the bridge outside Aix. No one like Philip.'

Inside the Cabal's HQ, Noel's expression was murderous. He met the Parrot, who made the mistake of speaking to him.

'You're looking so much better. I was really worried what that tear gas would do to you. You're looking great.'

'Am I?' He raged. 'Well if so it's nothing to do with

seeing you of all people as soon as we arrive. Cow!'

'What did you call me?' she shrieked.

'Cow! Cow! Cow! Get your legs moving. We want a gallon of coffee.'

He was menacing. His hands were clenched into fists. He was waving them at her. Hell, she thought, he's going to hit me. She slipped into the next room, slammed the door behind her. Nelson was glaring when Noel sat down at the three-sided table. His voice was a deep rumble.

'That, Noel, in case you've forgotten, is a key member of our team. She deals with all the paperwork.'

'No, she doesn't,' Noel rapped back. 'She takes it next door and dumps it on Coral Flenton.'

'Are you contradicting me?' Nelson asked, leaning forward, his eyes glittering viciously. 'You're not totally indispensable, you know.'

'Lost my cool,' Noel said, recovering control. 'Apologies to you, to both of you. Just back from France. I guess I'm tired.'

'So how did it go in France?' Nelson asked, sneering.

'Partly OK, partly not. You can't win everything.'

'And would this,' Benton asked gently, 'be some of the partly not?'

He pushed across the table the Drew Franklin column he'd cut out of the paper. Noel read it again, as though for the first time. He nodded.

'Someone else handled that. They were going to be the core of our special squad.' He smiled engagingly. 'The OK part is Radek is over here. He's brilliant. Tough as granite but with a subtle brain.'

'You'd better exercise tight control over him,' Benton suggested. 'I've heard of his reputation.'

'Situations on the Continent are different from over here.'

Noel had regained his confidence. Time to assert his position. He smiled at the other two. Then he spoke emphatically to get his message across.

'I should have said things used to be different on the Continent. Look at what happened last night. To all of us, including you, Benton. We were leaving the building when we were savagely attacked with tear-gas bombs, which put us in hospital. Who do you think was responsible? Tweed, of course. So now we pay back. Ruin Tweed's reputation for ever. Then deal rather more brutally with the rest of his team. Put them out of action. At the least into hospital for a long time. Maybe more if they fight back. Agreed?'

'I think you're right,' said Nelson. 'Go ahead.'

23

Tweed was known in security circles for his remarkable intuition, his ability to foresee what the enemy's next move would be. He had just listened to Marler's tear-gas exploit with Harry. Later Marler had checked the hospitals, had found the whole Cabal was undergoing medical treatment.

'The battle between us and the enemy will accelerate. I'm sure they won't take what they suffered lying down. We must prepare for a no-holds-barred counter-attack. So it's vital we strike first. I want those three compromised so they're thrown out of their positions. Marler, Newman, work out a strategy. I'm still trying to track down who slaughtered Viola.'

'I suggest,' said Paula, 'that I visit Coral this evening, turn her inside out. A woman with another woman can often do that better than a man. No criticism of you, Pete.'

'Do it,' agreed Tweed. 'Try to find out more about

Viola. What we need is information.'

'What about me?' asked Nield.

'And me?' growled Harry.

'I want you both to guard Paula. Keep in the background so Coral never sees you. I have a feeling Paula could become a major target.'

'So could you,' Harry growled again.

Paula jumped up, operated a lever. Outside the large windows steel blinds were lowered at a slanting angle. They had been designed to ward off explosive grenades.

'Now we're safer,' she said.

'I should have thought of that before,' admitted Newman. 'I also think George downstairs should be armed. Heaven knows he can handle a gun. He was in the infantry.'

'Agreed,' said Tweed. 'Now I'm going to contact Benton. I'm curious as to why he wanted to see me while I was away.'

An hour later Noel, his head covered with an old peaked cap, his clothes shabby, his shoes down at heel, was inside the warehouse. He stood in the large empty room with Fitch and Radek.

'It's open warfare against Tweed and his whole team,' he said, using language he'd have toned down back in Whitehall. 'The key figures are Tweed and his tart, Paula.'

'Kill them?' suggested Fitch.

'I have a better idea,' interjected Radek. His accent was pronounced, his command of English perfect. 'We drive both out of their minds. They end up insane permanently. That will scare the rest of the team stiff. They'll be leaderless.'

'An original idea,' Noel agreed with a sadistic smile. 'I like it. But how are you going to do that?'

Radek opened the large case he had brought with him. He took out a number of viewing screens, four projectors. He attached a screen with nails to each of the four wooden walls. His eyes gleamed as he turned round.

'This way whichever way they look they can't avoid what will appear. We need iron rings inserted into the floor. Tweed and this Paula will be tied to the rings. It should take an hour or so before they go out of their minds.'

'I still don't see it,' protested Noel.

'You will. You may feel queasy after only a short demonstration but that will wear off. Better take these earplugs or you'll go deaf.'

He set up the projectors so that each screen had one projected on it. Then he lifted out another machine, laid it on the floor behind them. They watched as he inserted film then, lighting a torch, switched off the overhead lights.

Noel was beginning to get nervous. What fiendish

apparatus was Radek setting up? Radek noticed his nervousness when he suddenly swung the powerful torch beam straight into Noel's face.

'Turn that bloody thing away from me,' shouted Noel.

Radek grinned. He loved to see a man breaking down. It was one of the pleasures of life. He shone the beam on the projectors, bent down, pressed four buttons, switched off his torch. He stood up to enjoy himself, slipping the earplugs in place.

Each of the four screens began showing moving pictures. Noel gazed, eyes glued to what was showing. Up in the mountains somewhere. Snow on the ground. Thick wooden posts with a man tied to each, wearing hardly any clothes. By each post a man holding a huge axe began swinging it. Noel stared, his face taut.

The first post attracted his attention. The man swinging the axe brought it down in a sweep, sliced off a foot above the ankle. Blood spurted. The axe was raised and brought down again. The second foot was severed. The prisoner's mouth was wide open, doubtless in an unheard scream of terror. The axe was hoisted again, brought down on the prisoner's right shoulder, severing half the shoulder and the arm.

Noel forced himself to glance at another screen. A similar scene, but the axe held by another man descended on top of the prisoner's head, splitting the skull in two down to the neck.

Radek felt for the knob on the other machine, turned it on, his grin even more sadistic. Fitch had earlier inserted his earplugs. Noel had omitted to do this. A diabolical sound filled the warehouse room.

Desperately Noel jammed the plugs into his ears, fumbling one, so he was still subjected to the noise from hell. He rammed the second earplug in place, heaved out a deep breath.

The room had now gone crazy. The bestial pictures. The penetrating screech, rising and falling non-stop. Noel could hear it even with the plugs in place. He looked at Fitch, seated on the floor, staring at one screen, then another.

Noel saw no point in staying in the warehouse any longer. He knew now how Radek was going to operate on Tweed and on Paula. He shouted at Radek to switch on some light. The Slovak turned on his torch, aimed it at the door he guessed Noel would head for, which he did.

Radek was amused as Noel walked quickly, opened the door, disappeared, pulling the door shut behind himself. Not a man for the High Tatra, Radek said to himself. He saw no point in telling Noel he had given him less effective earplugs than those he'd handed to the motionless Fitch. He leant down, pressed the buttons. The screens went blank.

'Think what one hour of this would do to Tweed and Paula,' he told Fitch, who had removed his plugs. 'Two once normal people, now insane. Spending the rest of their lives in an asylum.'

24

'Do sit down, Benton,' Tweed greeted his visitor. 'Would you like a cup of coffee or tea?'

'Coffee would be very acceptable, thank you,' Benton replied.

He had phoned Benton at his home in Hampstead, inviting him over. The Cabal member had accepted the invitation at once.

Only Paula and Monica were also present. Tweed had thought his visitor might talk more frankly if the other members of his team were absent. There was a pause and Tweed studied his guest.

Shorter than Nelson, Benton was in his early forties Tweed guessed, as he had when he had visited the Cabal at their HQ with Paula. Now he had a better chance of weighing up the man's appearance and personality. Round-headed, he had a bald patch on top of his head. His small eyes were greenish and shrewd under heavy lids. He wore a conservative grey suit which did not flaunt expense. His hands were folded in his lap. He gave Tweed the impression of someone with perfect self-control. Monica brought in coffee and Benton took it black, thanking her.

'I am sorry I was not available when you phoned, asking to come and see me,' Tweed said amiably. 'What is worrying you?'

'You are perceptive,' Benton observed in his quiet voice. 'May I ask, have you sent your report to the PM?'

'Not yet. It may come from my Director, Howard. He has just returned from a visit abroad.'

'I see.' Benton sipped at his coffee, then turned to look at Paula. 'I'm losing my manners. My apologies for not acknowledging your presence when I arrived.'

'That's all right,' Paula replied with a smile. 'Welcome.'

'I am worried,' Benton said, turning back to Tweed, 'at the near state of war which has broken out between our two departments. It's unseemly, dangerous.'

'Mainly operated by Horlick, your half-brother?' said Tweed, using shock tactics.

'Oh, so you know about Noel.' Benton chuckled, glanced over again at Paula. 'I'm impressed by your sources of information. I shouldn't be. Your reputation is well known. Noel is the youngest of us, sometimes a bit of a wild lad.'

'Wild enough to screw a cat's neck through a

hundred and eighty degrees?' asked Paula quietly, following Tweed's lead with shock tactics.

'May I ask how you know about that?' Benton asked, his manner now disturbed.

'Someone took a photograph of the pillar at the entrance to your father's mansion,' Tweed fibbed. 'Someone else here in London told us about the mysterious incident,' he went on.

'Mysterious is the word,' Benton said quickly. 'We never did identify the culprit.'

'Here is a draft of my report for Mr Howard,' Tweed went on, producing a thick typed sheaf from a drawer. 'It is only a draft, subject to toning down,' he emphasized as he handed it to Benton.

His guest took out a pair of rimless spectacles, began to study the report. Paula noticed that the glasses transformed his whole appearance, gave him a sinister look.

'That's a copy, but I must keep it,' Tweed continued.

Benton read the report slowly. Then he stared at Tweed. 'I would certainly hope this is toned down.'

'We'll have to see.'

Paula noticed Benton, thrown off-stride, was slowly turning the thick sheaf into a roll. Absentmindedly he squeezed the roll with both hands. Paula felt a wave of shock pass over her. The motion of twisting the report reminded her of how someone would screw a cat's neck. As though the thought had been transmitted telepathically, Benton suddenly turned again to look straight at her. His gaze from behind the rimless glasses was disturbing. Dr Jekyll and Mr Hyde flashed into her mind.

'Oh dear, I'm sorry,' Benton said, turning back to Tweed. 'I was thinking and I've spoilt your copy.' He began unrolling the report, used thick fingers to smooth it out before passing it across the desk.

'Doesn't matter,' Tweed said. 'It's only a copy. So how do you propose to calm down the tense state of affairs growing worse almost by the hour?'

'How do *you* propose to do that?' Benton rapped back.

'Touché!' Tweed threw both hands into the air. 'We are going round in circles. You could talk to your colleagues.'

'Oh, I most certainly will.' He removed his glasses. 'May I assume you will do the same thing?'

'Depends on any further developments.'

'What does that mean?' enquired Benton, finishing his coffee. He turned in his chair to address Monica. 'That coffee was the best I've drunk for a while. My thanks.'

'It means that there must be no further attempts to attack my staff.'

He stopped speaking as an object hurled from the outside struck one of the metal blinds Paula had lowered. The object bounced off, fell into the street and exploded. Paula jumped up, peered out of the window just in time to see a man in a dark overcoat diving inside a Ford which took off immediately, racing into the main street, fortunately empty of traffic for a brief moment.

'Grenade.' Tweed stood up. 'That's what I'm talking about.'

'Lucky no one was on the pavement in the Crescent,' Paula snapped. 'They'd have been killed.'

'Surely,' Benton began, standing up, 'you don't think that had anything to do with us.'

'I think,' Tweed replied grimly, 'you had best go back to your HQ and have a long talk with your colleagues. By the way, did either Nelson or Noel know you were coming here?'

'No, they were both out . . .' Benton hesitated as though he'd made a mistake. The implication was that the grenade would not have been thrown if they had known Benton was going to be in the office. 'I did mention earlier that I was coming to see you,' Benton added quickly.

'When was "earlier"?' Tweed demanded, keeping up the pressure.

'I really think I'd better go now.' He paused. 'Truce?' He held out his hand to Tweed who appeared not to notice it as he slipped from behind his desk and opened the door for Benton to leave.

25

In the evening Paula was on her way to meet Coral
Flenton. She had phoned first and Coral had
sounded delighted she was coming. Tweed had
planned protection for her and she had accepted the
idea without a murmur. The grenade hurled at the
steel blind had shaken her. The protection was heavy.

'We are facing ruthless men capable of anything,'
Tweed had warned. 'The interview with Benton did
nothing to reassure me . . .'

It was a murky evening as Paula drove slowly into
Covent Garden. The dark was intensified by a low
ceiling of black clouds. Close behind her Newman
drove in his car with Nield in his car behind him. A
motorcyclist purred past them. In the saddle was
Harry, who pulled up a few yards beyond the
entrance to Coral's apartment.

Paula saw that the space she'd used on her previous
visit was empty. She turned into it, got out, locked the

car, inserted coins into the meter. By now both Nield and Newman had found parking spaces. They had planned in advance where each of them would wait. Newman bought a cup of coffee and a newspaper he'd pretend to read opposite Coral's entrance. Recalling the photo sent to them by persons unknown of the scene outside Viola's flat, he was disturbed to see the lighted frosted-glass window.

As soon as Paula pressed the bell the door was opened and Coral stood there, smiling. As she stepped inside Coral threw both arms round her visitor, hugged her. Paula used her foot to kick the door shut behind her.

'I am so relieved to see you,' Coral said as she led the way down a long hall and up a flight of stairs. They went into the living room, modestly but tastefully furnished.

'Has something happened to disturb you?' Paula enquired as she sat on a sofa.

'I suppose it has. I don't know where the hell I am.'

Coral picked up a glass and drank. Paula sniffed brandy. Then she saw the bottle perched on a small table near the sofa. She asked for wine when Coral offered brandy.

'What's the problem?' Paula asked after sipping her wine.

'The Parrot. I don't know where the devil I am with her. For weeks she's been on my back, now she's so friendly. She takes me out for a posh meal – I may have mentioned that before – she even suggested that we stand shoulder to shoulder to outwit the three bullies in the next room. I'm treading warily. She has a terrible temper. And I'm due for promotion into another department. I don't want the Parrot to turn nasty again, to find some excuse for throwing me out. I need the money.'

'Anything else on your mind? Although what you've told me is enough.'

'I keep thinking of poor Viola. I told you we knew each other at school. I read the description of what happened to her and keep thinking of it. Bad dreams. I wonder how Marina, her twin sister, is feeling.'

'Marina?' Paula repeated. 'I didn't know about her. A twin sister. Did they get on well together?'

'They did not.' Coral paused, refilled her glass. 'You see, they both behaved in the same way.' She hesitated.

'You mean with men?' suggested Paula.

'Yes, I do. It sounds awful but they were competitive.'

'In what way?'

'In price. What they charged for their services, if you see what I mean.' She had another drink. 'At least, Marina was. Viola wasn't. What they charge a man for you know what.'

'I see.' Paula took another small sip. This was a

new development no one had mentioned before. 'Where does Marina live, then?'

'She has a luxurious pad in a street off Mayfair. Do you want the address?'

'If you don't mind . . .'

She studied Coral while she was scribbling on a pad. Her movements were jerky. Nerves? It could be the brandy but Paula doubted it. Coral was informally dressed in denims and a white blouse buttoned to the neck. Coral handed her the sheet she had torn off the pad. Paula noticed the writing was neat but jerky. She folded the note, put it inside her hold-all in a zip-up pocket.

'Thank you.'

'It has her address, her phone number, her mobile number.'

'I suppose Viola gave you this information,' she said gently.

'That's right. I was having a drink with her one evening in her Fox Street flat. She asked whether I'd consider going to see Marina. To try and patch up the relationship. I didn't go, didn't like the idea.'

'Probably very wise. Are you hungry? I think I am.'

Paula had decided it was time to go to the restaurant before Coral used the brandy bottle again. They had reached the front door when Paula noticed the simple lock.

'Covent Garden is getting all sorts of people

floating round it these days. I'd feel happier if you installed better locks. Maybe a Banham and a Chubb.'

'How nice of you to think of my safety . . .'

'Do any of those three men come on to you?' Paula asked before they went outside.

'No trouble from Nelson. Sometimes I don't like the way Benton looks at me when he's wearing those rimless specs. The one I have to fend off is Noel, but I can handle him. I'm afraid I'm not really dressed for dinner.'

Paula looked at her. Coral had her glorious crown of red hair piled up on top. She gave Coral a quick squeeze as she spoke.

'You look gorgeous. And I'm not exactly dressed for the Ritz. Neither will some of the other women be fit for a fashion parade!'

Once outside, she was immediately aware of the chill, but Coral had slipped on a jacket. Paula glanced around casually. No sign of her 'protectors' but she knew they would be there.

'Marina? A twin sister?' The surprise was evident in Tweed's voice.

Paula had just returned very late from her visit to Coral. The only other occupants in the office were Marler and Monica.

'And where are the three I sent to watch over you?' Tweed demanded fiercely.

'Not to worry,' replied Paula, perched on the edge of his desk. 'Newman escorted me here, saw me safely inside, then said he was going back to his car. I think he's gone back to join Pete and Harry. I suspect they're staying for some time, watching the entrance to Coral's flat, now I've gone. Which I think is smart. Maybe someone else watched me leave.'

'In that case they are smart. They're acting on the advice I've hammered into everybody. Think for yourselves. Now tell me about your evening.'

'Before I start, here are Marina's details. Address and so on.'

Tweed handed the folded sheet to Monica, asked her to record it. She opened the sheet, looked at it, returned it to Tweed.

'I've memorized it. I'll transfer it to the key address book.'

Paula had a lot to say. She recalled every word of her conversation with Coral, adding her own thoughts as she continued. She was aware that, behind her, Monica was using her hundred-and-thirty-words-a-minute shorthand to take down every detail.

As she'd expected, Tweed became a Buddha, sitting motionless, his eyes never leaving hers. His powers of concentration were legendary. She waved a hand as she concluded.

'Now you have the lot. Interesting?'

'And I've got the lot,' Monica called out. 'I'll type

you a report. How many copies?'

'Five, please,' Tweed told her. 'A copy for each member of the team. It's so important everyone has the data in this situation. Paula, interesting? I think it was vital you decided to go and see Coral. Significant is the word.'

'Why?' Paula asked.

'Because the Parrot is playing a devious game. Also because now we know of the existence of Marina. I shall have to go and see her.'

'Want me to come with you?' Paula suggested ironically. 'To protect you?'

'So far I've been pretty good at protecting myself against alluring and predatory women. And thank you, Paula, for doing such a professional job. Now I'm going to do something I should have done earlier, but we've been chock-a-block.'

'What's that?'

'I intend,' he said after checking his watch again, 'to visit the scene of the crime in Fox Street. If I go now I should arrive at roughly the time Saafeld said the hideous crime was committed.'

'I'm coming with you, of course,' said Marler.

'I agree,' Tweed said reluctantly.

He could hardly have refused. Not when he was hammering on about everyone's safety. He stood up and Paula slipped off the edge of his desk. He took hold of her shoulders and again his voice was fierce.

'You are not allowed to leave this building until someone – Newman, Pete or Harry – has got back. They will escort you home, will check out every corner in your flat before you enter it, then they will sleep on that sofa in the living room, or in the spare bedroom . . .'

'Oh, for Heaven's sake,' Monica burst out. 'They'd do that anyway. Are you suffering from paranoia?'

Tweed made no reply, but grabbed his coat, and put it on as he went down the stairs followed by Marler. Outside the night was fresh and colder. Tweed opened the car, slipped in behind the wheel as Marler dived into the rear.

The passenger door next to Tweed was opened, and Paula was on the seat next to him as he switched on the engine. She slammed her door shut. Tweed opened his mouth but she beat him to it.

'No argument. You've said before I take over if you're out of action. On top of that I'm well guarded with the two of you. And, on top of that, we're visiting the flat of a poor woman – woman – who was foully murdered. I'm a woman. I could spot something a man could miss.'

Tweed, driving away from Park Crescent, had opened and closed his mouth twice. Like a fish, Marler thought, watching him in the rear-view mirror. Tweed's mind was revolving as he drove on, heading towards Covent Garden.

Paranoia, Monica had said. Could she be right? Was he in danger of overdoing his warnings? Paula had done a good job, extracting information from Coral, and some of it might eventually lead them to the psychopathic murderer.

'You've got a point,' he ultimately admitted.

Paula showed no elation, no hint of triumph. She was gazing out as they neared their destination. Fox Street, a name which would go down in the history of criminology.

No one was about at this depressing hour. The car wobbled over cobbles. They had entered Fox Street. Tweed slowed the car to a crawl. It was a narrow street, with poor illumination from ancient lamps protruding from walls on metal arms.

'Nearly there,' Paula said. 'Within yards . . .'

She had been checking the house numbers, which were lit up by lights behind them. Tweed parked on the pavement. They could now see the notorious house, police tape still strung across it. As they got out the door opened, Marler had his gun in his hand.

'It's Chief Inspector Hammer,' Tweed warned.

The burly policeman, huddled up in an overcoat, stood hands in his pockets. Mistake, in this area, Tweed thought. If Hammer was attacked he'd never get his automatic out in time. He went up to Hammer, who was staring at the three of them without pleasure.

'Bit late on the case, aren't you? Place has been given a real search. Nothing.'

'I'm getting a sense of what the atmosphere was like when it happened. Not exactly bustling with people. And, in case it has slipped your memory, I am the chief investigator.'

'What's the girl messing about at?' Hammer asked rudely.

'The girl is a woman. She appears to be checking the street in case something was dropped by the murderer. Did you people do that?'

'Waste of time. Front door was closed when we arrived. Which suggests she knew the killer. Doesn't it?'

'Possibly. On the other hand if she was expecting him – or her – she could have come down to let him in. You hadn't thought of that – or had you?'

Hammer grunted. He was ignoring Tweed, watching Paula as she searched the cobbled street with her torch. She bent down as her beam reflected off something. A diamond ring was slotted inside a crack in the cobbles. She put on latex gloves, picked it up.

'Nothing that matters, I'm sure,' Hammer said aggressively.

Paula walked back to Tweed, showed him the ring by the light of her torch. Tweed recognized it. Viola had worn the ring on the third finger of her right hand when they'd dined together at Mungano's. During their visit to Saafeld at his mortuary he had noticed a mark on the finger where she had worn the ring. The killer must have wrenched it off the severed hand. He must have dropped it when leaving the building.

Hammer grunted again, stalked off towards his car parked in the shadows. Tweed took out a transparent evidence envelope, dropped the ring inside and placed it inside his pocket.

'Could that be important?' Paula asked. 'So much for the chief inspector's careful search. It's eerie round here,' she added. 'It rather frightens me.'

'Then I suggest we go inside this house of horror. I've got the front-door key from Hammer. A plodder, not the most distinguished chief inspector I've known . . .'

They entered. Paula noticed the lock was a Banham. Not easy for anyone to pick. Tweed felt around, switched on the light as Marler closed the door. They were in a long wide hall with tasteful paper on the wall. Ahead of them a staircase rose, built of mahogany with matching banisters. On the first-floor landing Tweed, latex gloves on his hands, opened a door to his right.

'The bedroom,' Marler said. 'Where it happened,' he added quietly. He found a switch and lights came on all over a spacious tastefully furnished room.

Paula's eyes instinctively went to the tall frosted-glass window overlooking the street. There were few signs of blood and she guessed one of Saafeld's technicians had scraped it for DNA samples. A waste of time. Commander Buchanan had told Saafeld the blood was all Viola's.

A double bed stood in the centre of the room. A white sheet covered the entire bed. Paula lifted a corner. Underneath was only the mattress. The sheets and blankets had been taken away for examination. No sign of blood on the mattress, but that wasn't surprising. On the floor on the far side of the bed a chalk mark outlined where Viola's body had been killed and cut up. Faint brown stains where the residue of her blood seeped into the wooden floor. Paula continued moving slowly round the room.

'This is probably useless,' Tweed remarked. 'It will have been searched by experts.'

'I never trusted experts,' Marler said, standing by the closed door.

Tweed was opening drawers, closing them. Paula stood still, clasping her own latex-gloved hands. Where would a woman hide something? She lifted up the lid of a musical box. It began to play a romantic tune, which disturbed her. How many times had Viola sat listening to its melody? She found it very sad.

Inside the box was a selection of expensive jewellery. She emptied it out into one hand, placed it on top of the dressing table where the box had rested.

Tweed looked at it as she made her comment.

'Well, the motive certainly wasn't robbery. Not that we ever thought it was. This is very expensive jewellery.'

'Shouldn't have been left here,' he said, and turned away to continue his search.

The base the jewels had rested on was a thick blue cushion. Paula extracted a nail file from her shoulder bag. She pressed the tip gently down the side of the cushion, eased it up. Underneath was a folded sheet of paper. She opened it, read the wording inside.

Marina. Call her and try and make it up. There followed the address and phone numbers Coral Flenton had provided. She showed it to Tweed. He pressed his lips together as he studied it.

'We've found something the police missed,' he told Marler.

'I told you I mistrusted so-called experts.'

Tweed showed him the note in neat handwriting. Marler raised an eyebrow.

'It's a fresh lead,' said Tweed. 'I'm going over to see her when we leave here.'

'At this hour?' said Marler.

'I think, like Viola, Marina is a night bird. Surprise can throw people.'

'Then we're coming with you,' Marler told him. 'Not going to have you wandering round on your own at this hour.'

'All right. But you must both keep out of sight. She won't say a word if she's overwhelmed with three people. Let's get moving.'

26

Paula found it eerie being driven through Mayfair at this hour: not a soul about. There was an unsettling silence when Tweed turned down a cul-de-sac. He parked by the kerb and they got out together. The heavy silence seemed to press down on them.

Marina's flat was situated in one of the old terraced houses lining both sides of the street. The atmosphere reminded Paula of a stage setting for a menacing play. Tweed had gone up the steps, was about to press the button which had a card alongside inscribed Marina Vander-Browne, when Marler tugged his sleeve.

'Front door is open,' he whispered. It was the sort of street where you automatically whispered.

Beyond the heavy front door was a narrow hall, an equally narrow staircase leading upwards.

Tweed whispered: 'Follow me. According to the card she's on the third floor.'

They began to climb up three staircases covered

with a red carpet. When they reached the third floor Tweed looked up. Above them was another floor. Marler gave Tweed a strange-looking whistle, inserted an earplug with a wire disappearing inside his coat.

'Paula and I will wait here, out of sight. Any trouble, you blow it. She won't hear it but I will.'

Tweed moved close to the speakphone outside a heavy door. He pressed the bell. Waited. Nothing. He pressed it again. At head height the door had a closed flap over a Judas window. It opened suddenly. A woman's face was staring at him as he held up his folder.

'Investigating the murder of Viola,' he said tersely. 'Could I come in and have a word with you?'

'At this hour?' Through the bars over the opening he could see she was fully dressed. Smoke was drifting up from a cigarette. 'Who are you, anyway?'

The voice was cut-glass. She repeated her question, this time less politely.

'It says who I am on the folder you can see. SIS. I am Tweed.'

'Oh, him. Bloody good job I stay up late. Don't get up very early in the morning. Can't burn the candle at both ends.'

As she was talking he heard keys turning in three locks, then the clanging removal of four chains. The place was a fortress. Eventually she opened the door and he slipped inside. He was relieved when she turned only one key, leaving it in the lock.

'Better come in and join me with a drink,' she suggested as she stared him up and down. 'And you may smoke.'

Tweed was intrigued to see how much like Viola Marina looked. The resemblance was striking – she too had thick blonde hair, though hers was trimmed shorter – but there was a hardness Viola had lacked.

She wore a short white dress which hugged her excellent figure. The eyes were again blue but hers were cold. Leading him into a flamboyantly furnished living room, she sat on a very long wide sofa, patted the place where Tweed should sit close to her. He chose a chair further away from her. She crossed her legs, began swinging her right leg. On a glass-topped table before her was what Tweed would have called a complete bar, laden with bottles and glasses.

'Drink.' It was almost a command accompanied by a flashing smile. 'Scotch on the rocks, gin, brandy? Come on, I can't call out the lot.'

'I don't drink on duty.'

'On duty! You come to see me of all people at this hour on duty? Come off it.'

The leg was still slowly swinging up and down. Tweed had trouble not glancing at it. In her brazen way she was as attractive as poor Viola had been. He decided he'd preferred her twin sister.

'On official duty,' he emphasized.

'Oh, I see. You don't do it when you're official. Well at this hour you're off duty. Want to see the bedroom?'

'No thanks. It's comfortable in here.'

'Then we could use the sofa. It's wide and long enough. I should know by now.'

'Miss Vander-Browne . . .' His voice now had an edge to it. 'I would have thought it would have been a shock when you heard the horrific way your sister had died.'

'I'm sure she asked for it.'

Tweed drew in a breath. The sheer cold-bloodedness astonished even him with all his experience. His voice became tougher.

'After being raped. By a man – or a woman. Her legs were chopped off at the knees, her arms at the shoulder, then her head . . .'

'Oh, do stop it. You're spoiling what could be a pleasant night for you. Take your mind off it.' She became coy, which was even more sickening. 'I assume you have five hundred pounds on you? The fee always comes first.'

'Had you heard from your late sister recently?' he demanded.

'Why would she be in touch?'

'Because I have evidence she had been hoping to make it up with you.'

She hesitated for the first time. She poured herself

a fresh drink, swallowed half of the glass's contents. Then she lit a cigarette with a steady hand. A granite heart, Tweed thought. But for the first time he saw a sign of nervousness.

'She did call you, didn't she?' he persisted abruptly.

'Yes, she did. About ten days ago. All lovey-dovey. Couldn't we meet and talk things over? I said "What for?" and slammed the phone down on her.'

'That was so very nice of you, in view of what's taken place since. Did you both have any of the same clients?'

'We might have done. I'm not sure.'

'I need some names.'

'What sort of names, for Christ's sake?'

'Mutual clients' names.'

'Tweed, I've just told you I don't know. She might have told one of them my name, hoping for a big fat commission.'

Tweed drank some of the wine she'd poured for him. He needed it to take the foul taste out of his mouth.

'You were sisters,' he continued grimly. 'What was she like?'

'The oh-so-bright one,' she said sarcastically. 'Came down from Oxford with a double first. I left Cambridge with nothing. Except useful contacts with men which have been profitable up to the present. All men are alike – which is something I did learn at Cambridge . . .'

'Wrong!' Tweed snapped. 'Some men are, I agree, but many are not fodder for your night activities. Why do you need the money?'

'That's a damned personal question.' She reared up, then pulled down her dress tighter over her chest, in case he hadn't noticed her assets. 'All right,' she continued viciously, 'we both had a rich uncle who left us each a legacy. Enough to live a normal life but not enough to buy things at Escada. I like to buy good clothes. They make all the difference when I entertain the occasional rich man.'

'Occasional?'

'Viola gave me the idea.'

Tweed lost his temper. 'You filthy liar. I've a good mind to take you down to the Yard for a proper interrogation.'

'I do have friends there.' She reached out a hand towards him. He evaded it. His normal controlled temper returned. He spoke softly.

'You have absolutely no regrets as to how your sister died?'

'None at all. Why should I? It eliminates some of the competition.'

Again Tweed was stunned by the cold-bloodedness of this woman. She was watching him, hoping to revel in his shock. His expression remained normal, neutral. He took out a pad and his pen. She frowned, then tucked both legs under herself, swivelled round so she was facing him with an inviting smile.

'I need your full name, telephone number, mobile number. I'm waiting.'

She frowned, probably annoyed that he had not reacted to a pose which had trapped other men. Without speaking she reached over to a small gold box, took out a printed card with a red rim round it, handed it across to him. He was careful to take hold of it by the edge. It was carrying her fingerprints. He stood up.

'I shall probably see you again.'

'Of course you will.' She gave him a lascivious smile. 'I know you will. When you think about me.' She jumped up. 'Back in a sec. Must rush to the loo.'

As soon as she was gone Tweed poured the rest of his wine into a large plant pot nearby. Taking out a handkerchief, he dipped it in her glass, slipped on a latex glove, used the handkerchief to wipe off his fingerprints. He was very quick. When she returned she'd changed her outfit. She was now clad in a transparent nightdress, belted at the waist, the hem ending above her knees.

He headed for the door, concealed the latex glove with his back to her, turned the key, slipped the glove into his pocket after pulling open the door. Marina called out something to him but he was outside on the

landing, heading down the first flight of stairs. He
paused, looked up.

'Be very careful who you let into your apartment.
Don't forget what happened to Viola . . .'

In looking up as she slammed the door he saw
Paula and Marler peering down from the fourth floor.
They joined him as he unlocked the car, slipped
behind the wheel. He looked up at the building.

'Tart can't see us,' Paula told him. 'The only
window overlooking the street has frosted glass. I
gather you didn't enjoy the interview.'

'Cold-blooded little snake.'

Tweed was crawling so as not to wake up sleeping
people. As he turned into the main street he saw an
old shabbily dressed woman lifting her head out of a
large rubbish bin she had been exploring. He pulled
in at the kerb, got out, his voice friendly.

'Doubt if you'll find anything worthwhile in there.'

'Never can tell, sir. Me mate once found a real
pearl necklace. Took it to the police,' she went on in
her heavy Cockney accent. 'I'd 'a done the same.
Takin' stuff like that can get you inta the police
station if you tries to 'ang on an' sell it to an 'andler.
You bin up to see Lady Muck? You'se smart, takin' a
woman and a man with you. For an 'our with a man
what's loaded she wants a fortune. And 'er so high-
and-mighty.'

'You've seen men go up to see her?' Tweed enquired.

'Loads of 'em. When it comes to those not so well off she's mean as muck. So, Lady Muck.'

'Sounds as though you've met her.'

'I 'ave. She comes out one evenin' and I'm skint. Asks her for something to buy meself a meal. Know what she says?'

'Tell me, please.'

'"You should do an honest day's work like other people." I nearly laughed in her face. Honest? When you knows 'ow she makes 'er livin'? Make you want to spit.'

'So you see who goes in there sometimes?'

'If I's workin' this big bin, I do. One man came out pulling up his trousers. Couldn't get 'em round 'is waist. I heard something plop. Called out to 'im, "Think you'se just dropped something, sir." He just rushes off to 'is car 'idden up an alley. So I walks over and you'll not believe what I found on pavement.'

'What was that?' Tweed asked with a smile.

'A wallet. Kind a man keeps in his back trouser pocket. Inside was three hundred nicker. I belt down the street, waved it at him as he drives towards me. Bastard never stops, damn near drives over me. I thought, right, mate. So I keeps the three hundred nicker. Was I wrong, sir?'

'I think you were very sensible. Do you often see the men who visit the lady?'

'Lady? Got that wrong, didn' you? Yes, if it's this time o' night I've seen a few. Chap who dropped his wallet was a short, fat little man.'

'I'd like to ask you a question, if I may.' Tweed took out the photos of the Cabal that Marler had taken in Whitehall. 'Recognize any of these men?'

She produced an ancient pair of spectacles. One of the arms was bent. To see the photos she had to cock her head sideways. She took her time with each photo.

'No, not 'im. Not 'im either.' She paused. 'Bingo. I know this one 'as visited 'er. Sure as I'm standing 'ere.'

She handed the photos back to Tweed. He turned round, stared down the street they had just left. Black hole of Calcutta except for the street lamp opposite Marina's entrance. He turned back to the Cockney woman who had put away her glasses.

'Are you sure you could see clearly at this distance? I do want you to be sure, please.'

'Got long sight without me specs, ain't I? Street lamp down there 'elps a lot. It was 'im.'

'I'm very much obliged for you talking to us.' Tweed took out his wallet, handed her a ten-pound note. 'Get yourself a decent meal. Not your usual places.'

'Gawd bless you, sir. I'm skint. Honest I am. Don't know what to say.'

'Don't say anything. May I ask you your name, in case I'm in the area and want to ask you something?'

'Why not? Annie 'Iggins. That's me. You take care, sir.'

Tweed was silent as he drove them back to Paula's flat. He waited while Marler, with Paula's key, checked the place out. He returned in a few minutes.

'All clear. That sofa in the living room looks inviting. So I'll park myself on it while Paula gets a good sleep.'

Paula got out of the car. She did not close the door. She leant in and stared at Tweed.

'That's right. Keep us all in suspense. Who did Annie Higgins identify as the visitor to Marina?'

'Noel Macomber.'

27

Tweed was driving back to Park Crescent when the mobile phone Paula had left on the seat beside him started buzzing. He cursed, and pulled in. Paula must have been very tired to forget it. He answered.

'Yes?'

'You have a visitor. She's very anxious to talk to you . . .'

The line went dead. Tweed was puzzled. She? He couldn't imagine which woman it might be. So many were cluttering up his investigation. Coral Flenton, Marina Vander-Browne, the Parrot. He sat still for a moment, switched off the mobile. At this hour? He checked his watch: 2 a.m. Only one way to find out.

His mind churned as he completed his journey. This was the most difficult case he'd ever tackled, even including those when he was at the Yard. He just had no idea who was the chief suspect.

Parking his car outside the Crescent, he pressed

the bell in the agreed sequence, walked inside when George unlocked and opened the door. He took off his coat as he darted up the stairs. He felt very alert. Opening his office door he found two people inside.

Monica working her computer. The Parrot seated in a chair facing his desk, a cup of coffee close to her. She swung round, gave him a warm smile. He could still see she was worried, even frightened. As she had been on her first visit to him which seemed ages ago.

'I do hope you'll excuse my calling at this barbaric hour,' she began in a soft husky voice, 'but I needed a safe refuge. Someone in a car was stalking me on my way home to Hammersmith. No one else was about . . .'

She trailed off as Tweed nodded, settled behind his desk which meant he was facing her directly.

'Whereabouts were you, and what was the make of the car?' he asked, his manner businesslike.

'It was in Whitehall that I first saw it. I didn't think a lot of it until it kept following my route, so I veered off here hoping someone would still be in the office. As to make, I'm hopeless on car makes.'

'What made you sure he was stalking you?'

'He had his headlights on full beam and drove close behind me. At times I was almost blinded by the lights in my rear-view mirror.'

'Was it Nelson, Benton or Noel?'

'I've really no idea. Don't even know it was a man. I just couldn't see the driver. May I take off my coat? It's warm in here.'

'Go ahead.'

At that moment Howard, Tweed's Director, opened the door. In his early fifties, Howard was as always wearing an expensive Chester Barrie suit, grey with thin stripes, pristine white shirt, and elegant Valentino tie. His shirt cuffs were shot from beyond the sleeves, decorated with gold cufflinks.

His large clean-shaven face had a pink complexion. His voice, like Marler's, was upper-crust. He exuded authority. When he saw Tweed's guest he paused, looked at Tweed, then at the Parrot.

'Sorry if I've interrupted something. At this hour I'd have expected to find no one here except Monica.'

'Howard, Director of the SIS,' Tweed introduced. 'This is Miss Partridge, who came to tell me of a development.'

The Parrot was still gazing at Howard. Tweed had the odd sense of reading her thoughts: Would this be a good catch? Probably loaded with money. Wonder if he's married?

Stop it, he told himself. Your imagination is running riot. She continued gazing at Howard with a ravishing smile. He nodded to her, then turned to Monica as he made his request.

'Could you let me have the first twenty pages of the

report? I need to double-check something.'

Quick-witted, Monica collected twenty pages and handed it to him. He thanked her, then left. Howard already had the draft of the whole report in his office. He had used that as an excuse to get out of the office while Tweed dealt with his visitor.

'I think your Director is a most impressive man,' the Parrot remarked.

During this interlude the Parrot had taken off her coat. She was wearing a blue dress. It was supported by thin blue straps slung from her shoulders, leaving her arms completely bare. She lifted one hand to push back a lock of her thick brown hair from her face.

'Now I'm scared stiff about driving home. Would it be asking you too much to escort me to my place in Hammersmith? I know it's rather a distance but at this hour of the night – in view of my recent experience.'

'Of course not.' Tweed stood up, relieved at the prospect of getting rid of her. 'You drive your own car and I'll follow close behind in mine.'

'I cannot tell you how grateful I am . . .'

Her bare arms stretched out as though she was determined to hug him. He ignored them, went across to Monica after asking the Parrot for her address. She gave him a plain white card. No red or gold rims. With it in his hands he nipped across behind her back to Monica, dropped the card on her desk. She picked it up, took only seconds to scrutinize the details, handed it back to Tweed.

When the Parrot stood up he had her coat in his hands. He helped her on with it, avoiding touching her bare arms.

'Your coat too,' said Monica, jumping up and taking it off the hanger she had placed it on when he arrived.

'Back within less than an hour,' Tweed said, holding open the door for his guest.

The streets were deserted as the two cars drove through the middle of the night. Reaching Hammersmith the Parrot overtook Tweed's car to lead him down a narrow side street with a wall of terraced houses on either side. Tweed had already seen a familiar car in his rear-view mirror.

The Parrot parked. Tweed parked behind her and got out to see her safely into her home. The security on the front door was poor. An ordinary lock and nothing else. The Parrot spoke as she inserted her key.

'You'll come inside so I can thank you with a drink. I will not take no for an answer.'

At that moment a third car jerked to a stop behind Tweed's. Paula jumped out, followed by Marler. She called out in a cheerful voice.

'Hello there, Miss Partridge. You're out late. But

so are we. There's a restaurant not far away we like. We were driving off when we spotted Tweed's car.'

'She's just invited us in for a drink,' Tweed said, smiling.

'I'll have coffee, I'm driving,' Marler drawled.

'A glass of Chardonnay would be super,' bubbled Paula.

The Parrot's expression was a picture. She made a great effort to convert annoyance and rage into a feeble smile as she opened the door.

'You're most welcome,' she said through gritted teeth.

Inside there was a narrow hall, doors leading off at the sides. The Parrot headed at a brisk trot up the stairs at the end, the treads carpeted with a red material. At the top she continued her trot along a landing to another door. Beyond it was a surprisingly large living room.

Paula glanced round. The furniture was not antique but was restful and modern with a collection of sofas and chairs and cupboards. Paula grabbed Tweed's arm, guided him to a sofa. They both sat. Even here Marler chose to stand in a corner against a wall.

The Parrot disappeared into the kitchen and Paula followed her. Money had gone into equipping her kitchen. Everything was brand new and expensive. The Parrot was taking out bottles and glasses from a cupboard when she noticed Paula.

'Thought I'd give you a hand,' Paula said with a smile.

'Not necessary.' Her tone was abrupt. 'Go back and do make yourself comfortable. I can cope with this little lot.'

Paula returned to her seat on the sofa, soon followed by the Parrot with a silver tray of drinks. She distributed them, sat down with a sigh and relaxed. She reached for her glass, looked round at her guests.

'What shall we drink to?'

'A swift solution to the appalling murder of Viola,' Tweed suggested, raising his glass.

'That's a macabre toast,' the Parrot commented, 'but if you want that I'll go along with it.'

Paula noticed her glass trembled briefly as she raised it to her full lips. She was drinking neat Scotch. Tweed spoke again as he placed his glass on a glass-topped table.

'Miss Partridge, what is it like working with the three Macombers? They strike me as men with very different characters – even if they are brothers.'

'Oh.' The Parrot waved a hand airily. 'I get by. With any job at my level there is bound to be the odd problem.'

'What sort of problems would they be?'

'Present company excluded –' she glanced at Marler, who seemed to bother her standing on his own – 'but men are subject to wildly varying moods.'

'I agree,' Tweed pressed on, 'but so are women. There is a myth that men and women differ enormously from each other. I don't think they do. They often have similar worries and uncertainties.'

Tweed went on talking as Paula jumped up and swiftly headed for the kitchen. She called out over her shoulder.

'Excuse me, but I've lost one of my earrings. I heard it drop on the floor when I was in the kitchen.'

Earlier, arriving in the hall, she had detached one earring, slipping it into the pocket of her windcheater. She listened, could hear Tweed talking, then the Parrot answering.

She set to work quickly, looking for a meat cleaver. All the drawers slid open silently. Then she came to one which was locked. Why? She'd ignored the cupboards, an unlikely place to put a cleaver. Taking the earring out of her pocket, she quickly attached it to her ear.

Paula had the Parrot as one of her prime suspects. When she had her long meal with Coral Flenton her companion had told her she'd once caught the Parrot in a passionate embrace with one of the Macombers. Paula had asked her which one but Coral had shaken her head, said it was more than her job was worth.

Paula was re-entering the living room when she encountered the Parrot coming to see what she was up to. She gazed at Paula and then half-smiled.

'I see you have both on now. So you found it?'

'Yes, thank Heaven, it was difficult to see. It had slid close to one of the cupboard bases.'

As they returned to the living room Tweed stood up. Marler headed for the door to the landing.

'I have enjoyed our chat,' Tweed said.

'I want to thank you so much for escorting me safely home.' The Parrot was rushing towards Tweed when she knocked over a heavy revolving table crammed with books in shelves. She bent down, lifted it effortlessly, carried it across the room, trotting swiftly before she dumped it. She then rushed back to Tweed, hugged him, kissed him on both cheeks.

'I want you to know how much I appreciate what you did,' she told him.

Marler led the way downstairs, followed by Tweed and Paula, with the Parrot bringing up the rear. As they walked down the hall their hostess tapped a closed door.

'My bedroom. The window overlooks the street, so early in the morning I can sit up in bed and watch people going to work early.'

'It has a lock, I presume,' said Tweed, pausing. 'A really good lock.'

'Oh, I sleep with it partly open. I must have fresh air.'

They left the flat, walking into dark stillness without a sound. Tweed caught Paula's arm, took her to the passenger seat of his own car. Marler nipped along to the car in which he'd driven Paula.

They were moving through still deserted streets towards Paula's flat when she told Tweed about the reason for her supposed missing earring.

'Why would she have one drawer locked?' she asked.

'For a dozen reasons – sharp knives out of reach of a visiting child, who might wander in there exploring, anything. How come you turned up with Marler? You wouldn't know her address.'

'Yes, we did. Marler phoned Monica about something and she told him where you had gone with the Parrot, gave him the address.'

'So you came running to my rescue? Was that it?'

'No. It wasn't. We didn't like the idea of your driving back on your own. Simple.'

Tweed dropped Paula outside her flat as Marler pulled up behind him. He drove off, ignoring Marler who came to his open window suggesting he spent the night in Paula's spare bedroom.

His mind was churning as he drove slowly. It was the time of night when drunk drivers happily assumed there would be no one else on the road. His mind was still churning as he parked his car in the nearby mews, only a short walk from his house.

His mind was churning on the thought of the Parrot sleeping in that downstairs bedroom over-looking the street. With the window open.

28

Tweed was early at the office. He hadn't slept much, but was exceptionally alert. As he greeted George and started running up the staircase George called up to him.

'Gentleman waiting for you . . .'

'Who?'

'Didn't give a name. Not the sort of chap you bandy words with. Said he'd an appointment with you.'

Tweed walked into his office. Monica raised her hands in a gesture of helplessness. Seated in the chair facing his desk was General Lucius Macomber, very erect and dressed in a smart business suit.

'Didn't expect you,' Tweed said, taking off his coat, which Monica caught. 'You're an early bird, General.'

'Been like that all my life. Just got back from a meeting with my three cursed offspring.'

'They were early too,' Tweed said in surprise,

sitting in his desk chair, facing his visitor.

'Had to be. I phoned them. Told them to be at their station an hour ago. They were, of course.'

'I hope you enjoyed your visit.'

'I did. They didn't.' The General bared his teeth in a grim smile. 'I did all the talking. They listened. Kept quiet. Which is the way it should be.'

'May I ask what you told them?'

'You can. You're a bright chap, Tweed. Know what's going on. So do I. Told them they were a bunch of lunatics. Merging the security forces into one big dinosaur. They didn't like what I said.' He paused as he let out a barking guffaw of amusement. 'You agree with me.'

'I think it's madness.'

'Good chap. Between us we'll stop them. No doubt about it.'

He slapped the palm of his hand so hard on the desk Monica jumped behind him. He turned round, gazed at her. 'That woke you up, didn't it? You look like an asset.' He turned back to Tweed, switched the subject.

'Things are hotting up on Black Island. The locals are in a state over those buildings sprouting up at the western tip. No good just being in a state. Do something about it, is my motto. They were up in arms about the oil refinery when it was built. Expect you saw it while you were down there.'

'No, I didn't.'

'The tide must have been high. The fellow who ferries you across guides his barge in an arc to the east. You wouldn't see it. If he takes you over at low tide he goes straight across to Lydford. You'll damned well see the monstrosity then.'

'I'll look out for it next time I'm down there.'

'Nice to chat with you.' The General stood up. 'Must go. Time waits for no man, and all that. Got equipment to buy.'

'Will you be in town long?'

'No. Three or four days. Must get a bit of relaxation while I'm up here.' He stretched out a hand. 'We're in this together. Right?'

'Right,' said Tweed as he stood, shook the extended hand.

'I'm off.' He turned to Monica with a smile. 'Don't you let this taskmaster run you into the ground. You know what the late President Reagan once said?'

'No, sir. I'm afraid I don't.'

'"They say hard work never killed anyone, but why take the risk?" Great man, Ronald Reagan.'

Then the General was gone. Like a hurricane arriving and departing. Tweed sat still for several minutes, then spoke to Monica.

'Did he leave an address where we could get hold of him?'

'No.' Monica spread her hands again in the helpless motion. 'I did ask him that when he'd stormed in. He just turned round, smiled, said, "No, you can't."'

'I wonder what he meant by getting a bit of relaxation?'

Tweed looked disturbed as he asked the question. He was gazing out of the window, as he did when he contemplated something dangerous.

Shortly afterwards Tweed asked his second question as Marler arrived, followed by Newman and Harry with Pete Nield.

'I wonder what sort of equipment he plans on buying while he's up here.'

'Who was up here?' Marler asked.

Tweed gave a résumé of his conversation with the General. It didn't take him very long.

'What was his real reason for coming?' Paula mused, sitting at her desk.

'I'm not sure,' Tweed told her. 'His mind moves like lightning. He's got the energy of three young men. There was a whiff of scandal about him, as I recall it, after the end of the Gulf War. A captain he'd had to discipline told a reporter the General had ordered his men to shoot down a bunch of Arabs who came over a ridge with their hands up.'

'Did he?' Paula asked.

'Yes. Fortunately a TV reporter attached to the army had been filming everything at the time. The film clearly supported what the General said had happened. A line of Arabs had crossed a ridge just as the war started, hands held up. They were followed almost at once by two more lines of Arab troops, all carrying automatic weapons. It was a trap. If the General's troops had moved forward to take charge of the Arabs "surrendering" they'd have been mown down by the second and third lines. And they had more coming behind them. So the General was a hero, as he should have been. Trouble was the first reports had already appeared in the press. People remember the so-called bad things, forget the truth which later comes to light.'

'The General is smart,' Marler commented. 'And virile.'

'What was that word you used?' snapped Tweed, jumping to his feet.

'Virile.'

'The same word Frank, the keeper of the Crooked Village on Black Island, used.'

Tweed wandered over to the window. He stood staring into the distance. Monica knew he was disturbed again.

In the Fulham Road, on the opposite side to Paula's flat and a distance back, an old Ford was parked. Inside and behind the wheel Fitch had glasses glued to his eyes when, earlier, Paula had left with Marler.

'It's her,' he said to Radek, seated by his side.

'I can see that,' Radek growled, 'and without peering through binoculars. She's well guarded, was when she came back early this morning. We'll have to wait.'

'For what?' Fitch demanded aggressively.

'For when she returns home alone – or, better still, with Tweed. Then we can grab both of them.'

'Could take for ever.'

'I've waited in the same spot for three weeks to kill a man. Patience is the key. Or we could start a fire or a riot in the East End. That might send most of the team away from her.'

'Tricky. That schmuck Harry lives somewhere down there. He might catch on. So how are you going to start a fire?'

'Take in concealed beer bottles filled with petrol. Order drinks, sit in a dark corner. Spread the petrol on the floor. Use a cigarette lighter and clear out in the panic. The Pig's Nest would be a good place.'

'It might just work,' Fitch said. 'Needs thinking about.'

Harry had disappeared from Park Crescent without saying a word to anybody. No one worried. Harry was independent at times in the decisions he took. He returned in the early afternoon, carrying his 'tool-kit' bag.

'May we ask where you have been?' Tweed enquired gently.

'You may. While you lot have been sitting on your backsides, chewing the fat, I've dealt with something you asked me to do when I could. I've just driven to Peckham Mallet. Found the place on the map. Paula told me earlier how to find it.'

'And?' Tweed persisted as Harry drank from a bottle of water Paula gave him.

'That truck you saw parked in a field,' he said to Tweed. 'It's still there. No one about. Not even the guard. I checked in the quarry where you'd hidden him after Paula hit him on the nose.'

'He's not still there?' she said anxiously, wondering if she'd hit him too hard, maybe killed him.

'No, he wasn't. And I could see his footsteps in the chalk where he'd hauled himself out of it. Now, that truck.'

'What was inside it?' she asked, so relieved at hearing the guard had to be alive and well.

'A small load of Semtex, attached to wires leading to the detonator box. So I fiddled with the wiring. When it was attached to the detonator the clock was at zero. Now it's at sixty seconds. I also found a map showing the way to Richmond Park.'

'Oh, my God!' exclaimed Newman. 'Exploded there it would cause a mass slaughter.'

'No, it wouldn't,' Harry contradicted him. 'The

route marked led to a side entrance a long way from the river. Hardly anybody uses that entrance. I checked on my way back. Not a soul about.'

'Well, what will happen when the driver arrives to position it?'

'He'll get in, start the engine. The vibrations will set off the clock, then the detonator. I doubt if he'll have even moved forward before the whole caboose explodes harmlessly in the field. End of truck, end of driver.'

'Well, that's one worry off our minds,' Tweed commented. 'So many thanks to you, Harry.'

'All part of the job.'

A moment later George appeared. He was holding an envelope sent by registered post. He took it over to Paula. 'For you,' he said and left the office quickly to return to his post.

'I recognize the handwriting,' Paula said. 'It's from Coral . . .'

'Stop!' Tweed had jumped to his feet. 'Don't open that. Take it downstairs and have it X-rayed.'

'I think that's carrying security a bit far,' she grumbled, but she left them with the package to consult a boffin. She was back quickly. 'It's OK. The X-ray showed a key and a folded sheet of paper. If you don't mind, I would like to open it.'

Dear Paula – Got something to tell you. I'm so excited! Can you pop over one evening? Soon! Love, Coral.

She was taking it over to show Tweed when Newman snatched it off her to her intense annoyance. He read it, gave it back to her.

'Do you make a habit of reading people's personal correspondence?' she snapped.

'I do in the present dangerous situation.'

She glared at him, then gave Tweed the letter as Newman completed his comment.

'Sounds as though she'd just got a new boyfriend.'

'I agree,' said Tweed, returning the letter to Paula. 'Might be nice to call on her when you can.'

'When I can,' she said, returning to her desk. 'Nice to know she trusts me.' She held up the front-door key. 'But it will have to wait a few days. I've got my own report you asked me to type for Howard and a dozen other things in my lap.'

The door opened and Howard himself walked in. Normally amiable, his expression was grim. He chose his favourite chair, assumed his usual seated stance, sprawling one leg over an arm of the chair. Tweed waited for him to say something.

'I've read your proposed report on present happenings for the PM, Tweed. The situation is even worse than I had realized. I hope you don't mind, but I have strengthened certain passages.'

'I thought you'd tone them down.'

'We've got to shock him into action with the Cabinet – with the truth. I would like to wait a few days before I submit it, subject to your approval. It will give me time to talk to certain important MPs and key civil servants. Then we drop this bomb in the PM's lap – after the ground has been prepared.'

'I leave the timing to you.'

Howard, who would have been useless handling Tweed's work, was a clever diplomat when it came to dealing with the Whitehall jungle. He dealt with people Tweed had no desire to meet. Howard was pompous, but he dealt with pompous people. He studied Tweed.

'You've got so much on your plate yet you look so fresh. This crazy idea of merging all security services. Then you are investigating a particularly brutal murder. It's a lot.'

'I'm coping,' Tweed said.

'I wish to thank all of you,' Howard said, standing up. 'I do know you employ your many skills to support Mr Tweed. And a key element in any problem is always you, Paula. My thanks.'

On which note he left. Paula was taken aback. Never before had Howard been so nice to the staff. It was a sign that he appreciated the tension they were all working under.

'I'm going down to Whitehall,' Marler announced. 'To keep an eye on that Cabal. See you . . .'

'And I'm off to my patch,' Harry said, jumping up. 'Something's happening in the East End. Back sometime.'

'Paula,' said Nield, 'would you mind if I go and see Coral? Can I tell her your package has arrived safely? That you'll be coming to see her but you're overwhelmed just now?'

'Wish you would. Saves me a phone call, maybe several before I get her when she comes back from work.'

'On my way.'

The phone rang shortly after Nield had left. Monica answered, pulled a face as she looked at Tweed.

'We've got Commander Buchanan downstairs. Wants to see you yesterday.'

'I suppose I'd better see him.'

Tweed had stood up behind his desk to greet his old friend. Buchanan, wearing uniform, shoved open the door roughly, came in with an expression like thunder.

'Welcome, Roy,' Tweed said with a smile. 'Do sit down. Now, what is the problem?'

'You are.'

'Tell me about it, Roy,' Tweed replied calmly, sitting down.

'Chief Inspector Hammer wants a statement from you. Including your movements on the night of the murder of Viola Vander-Browne. He knows you dined with her at Mungano's that night. Then she drove home alone. No trace of you afterwards. So no alibi.'

'Because I have no alibi,' Tweed informed him quietly.

'Well, you're Hammer's chief suspect,' barked Buchanan.

'Commander,' Paula called out, 'do you mind keeping your voice down.'

'Interrupting your concentration, am I?' Buchanan shot back as he turned to look at her.

'Yes, you are,' she replied.

'Sorry, I didn't intend to do that.'

Buchanan had calmed down a bit due to Paula's intervention. Tweed waited, hands clasped on his desk.

'I visited you on the day after that horrible murder, said I'd come back the next day. You weren't here. No one would say where you'd gone. Now, what about that statement?' Buchanan asked more quietly.

'I'm the chief investigator. There will be no statement.'

'Oh, dear.' The Commander took off his peaked cap, mopped his damp forehead. 'Maybe I overshot the mark a bit. There has been a new terrorist alert and we're working without any hope of sleep.'

'We have known each other many years, Roy,' Tweed reminded him.

'I know, but Chief Inspector Hammer—'

'Bloody Hammerhead,' Paula said to herself.

'What was that?' Buchanan demanded, turning again to her.

'Nothing.'

He was giving her a hard look. She stared straight back, a certain look in her eyes. He dropped his gaze first, then stood up, the cap in his hand.

'Well, I've done all I can,' he snapped.

'Many years,' Tweed repeated.

Buchanan opened his mouth as though to apologize but nothing came out. He disappeared.

'What do you think of that?' Monica asked indignantly.

'He's exhausted,' Paula said. 'He had a gaunt look. I doubt he's had sleep for several days.'

'Nor has Tweed on many occasions,' Monica persisted, 'but he's never lost his self-control. Maybe we can get a bit of peace and quiet now for the rest of the day and evening.'

She turned out to be quite wrong.

It was much later when the phone rang. Monica answered, called out to Tweed.

'Professor Saafeld on the line.'

'Yes,' said Tweed after picking up his extension.

'There's been another one.'

'I see.' Tweed paused. 'Who? Where?'

'A Marina Vander-Browne. I can give you the address.'

'I know it. Not the same modus operandi?'

'Exactly the same. Suggest you don't bring Paula. It seems even more hideous somehow.'

'I'll come now.'

29

They were driving in the dark again, through the same deserted streets. Paula had expected more traffic and she found it puzzling. She looked at Tweed.

'What time is it?'

'About 2 a.m.'

'It can't be that late.'

'It is. You've been working nonstop. So have I. Time has passed without our noticing it. I'm glad I persuaded Monica to leave early just for once.'

'Maybe that old lady, the bin scrounger Annie Higgins, will be about. She could have seen something.'

'No sign of her,' Tweed replied as he parked in the main street. He thought it unwise to drive down the side street where Marina had lived.

'Why are we getting out here?' Paula asked.

'Because we were here last night.'

They walked rapidly down the murky street, tall

terraced buildings on both sides, a single street lamp outside the block where Marina lived. Had lived.

'Was it like the Viola killing?' Paula asked.

'According to Saafeld. We'll know when we get inside.'

A police tape was strung across the entrance, each end tied to a railing. Outside it stood a uniformed policeman, watching them coming. He held up a hand. Tweed and Paula held up their identity folders, the policeman lifted the tape.

'Third floor,' he said.

'Thank you.' Tweed just stopped himself saying, 'We know.'

He went inside, started climbing the first flight very slowly. His head was looking down. Paula became irked. At this pace they would never get there.

'Why are we crawling?' she wanted to know.

'It was raining last night. Tonight too. So an intruder would have left footprints on these treads. You look, too.'

'I should have thought of that myself.'

'Did you notice,' he asked as he continued his slow climb, 'that on the ground floor in the entrance hall there was an alcove without a window?'

'Yes, I did notice that.'

'It could have been vital to the killer. Wait until we've asked Saafeld a few questions.'

They continued their snail-like climb until they

were close to the third floor. Tweed had found no trace of footprints and he remarked on this fact to Paula.

'It could be significant. Very.'

'In what way?'

'Wait until we've seen Saafeld. I've devoted a lot of thought to the first crime. Imagining myself as the killer, how I'd go about it. Quiet now . . .'

Another police tape across the entrance to Marina's flat, with a uniformed policeman guarding it. They both showed their folders. The policeman did not lift the tape so Tweed lifted it himself. He came face to face with Saafeld, who frowned when he saw Paula. She spoke up firmly.

'I saw the other one. I've been inside your place. I'm getting used to it.'

'I thought I was.' Saafeld smiled. 'All right. Follow me. Bedroom down the corridor.' He tapped a closed door. 'In there the living room. Now. Here we are.'

He led the way through an open door. The bedroom was large. Paula didn't like the furniture. Too suggestive of what it was often used for. A very large bed had curtains hanging from brass rails. A canopy covered it just below the ceiling. There was a huge long, wide sofa piled up with cushions, and a large dressing table with three tall mirrors swivelled at a peculiar angle so they could be seen from the bed. The ceiling above the sofa was covered with a large mirror.

It was what lay on the bed which made her compress her lips. As with Viola, Marina's severed head was placed a few inches above her butchered neck. Again, the arms had been severed just below the elbows, the legs detached below the knees. Everything was placed to make Marina look like a huge doll torn to pieces.

Tweed turned to Chief Inspector Hammer who had joined the group – himself, Paula and Saafeld. Hammer seemed not in the least disturbed by the macabre arrangement.

'Chief Inspector,' Tweed said quietly, 'would you mind leaving us alone.'

'What for?' Hammer demanded belligerently.

'Because I have asked you to.'

'I'll go and check the living room.'

'I suggest, Chief Inspector, that you go downstairs and check the street carefully. The murderer might have dropped something.'

'If you insist.'

With a furious expression, Hammer left. They heard him clumping quickly down the stairs. Tweed closed the door, turned to Saafeld.

'From the chalk lines I see on the other side of the bed I assume the murderer used the same technique as with Viola.'

'I think so. He threw her naked body on the floor, gave the back of her head a hard bang to disable her.

Then he raped her – or she did,' he added glancing at Paula. 'No semen we could ever use for DNA, and she was interfered with using a device sometimes employed by women.'

'You think she was alive when he raped her?' Paula asked.

'I think it's likely she was.' He produced a transparent evidence envelope from his bag, held it up. 'This is the gag that was across her mouth when I arrived. But in that case what could be the motive?'

'Jealousy,' Paula replied.

'You could be right.' He put the evidence envelope back in his bag. 'Again he severed the arteries but this time the jet of blood released hit the mirrors, not the window.'

Paula looked again at what she'd noticed earlier. Each of the mirrors was drenched in blood. Saafeld saw where she was looking.

'Samples of the blood have already been taken. I doubt they will help. It will all be Marina's, so no DNA of the murderer.'

'What puzzles me,' said Tweed, although he thought he knew the answer, 'is that the murderer's clothes must have been soaked in blood. He couldn't just walk out in that state.'

'I suspect,' Saafeld said quietly, 'that as before he wore a surgeon's outfit. White coat, cap, gloves, and a face mask, with large glasses to protect his eyes. He later took them all off, stuffed them into a bag, maybe a large briefcase, and walked out wearing a business suit. As soon as he could he'd burn the lot. What he did with the meat cleaver – that was the murder weapon, I believe, in both cases – I don't know.'

'Suggests someone involved with the medical profession?' Tweed enquired.

'Not necessarily. That's the sort of equipment you can buy at any hospital-supply outlet. He probably visited several, buying one thing here, another thing somewhere else.'

'But he couldn't walk in on his victim dressed like that,' Paula objected.

'He probably arrived downstairs,' Tweed suggested, 'then called up to each victim, "Be up to see you in a minute." Then he'd change into his killing gear downstairs before he came up.'

'That's how I see it,' Saafeld agreed.

'And again no sign of forced entry?' Tweed enquired.

'None at all. Which means the victim knew her murderer – was expecting him,' Saafeld emphasized.

'So he'd used the speakphone to gain entry,' Paula remarked. 'Then he probably changed into his killing gear – to borrow your phrase, Professor – in the alcove just inside the front door. We ought to search that thoroughly.'

'It's been done,' Saafeld told her. 'I sent Hammer

down with a policeman he called an expert searcher. Firkins, I think was his name. They found nothing.'

'Hammer might miss something,' Tweed observed. 'Firkins wouldn't. I know him and he's very good.'

'They must have been related,' Saafeld speculated. 'The same name, and oddly enough very similar in appearance.'

'They were twin sisters,' Paula informed him. 'We only learned that recently.' She made herself stare at the head again. Almost a replica of Viola but even in death the face was harder.

'Roughly what time did this happen?' Tweed asked.

'Rigor mortis hasn't set in yet. Just an educated guess but somewhere between midnight and 2 a.m. Subject to more accuracy after my post-mortem. This really worries me,' Saafeld said, turning to Tweed, who had never heard him say anything like this before.

'Why?'

'I told you about blood storm. The creature committing these crimes is likely to get the urge to strike again soon now. You see, Viola was murdered about ten days ago. The intervals between his overwhelming desire to kill again will lessen considerably. His next urge to kill and mutilate could be as little as three or four days from now. It's an accelerating process.'

'Who found her?' Tweed wondered.

'A Mrs Gaskin, a real nosey-parker who came in late, lives on the fourth floor. The TV was on full blast.'

'Which would drown Marina's screams as he applied the gag. He probably turned the volume up.'

'Exactly.' Saafeld turned to Tweed. 'Paula catches on very quickly. Well, this woman heard the TV going full blast when she reached the third floor. The door to Marina's flat was open, so she came in to protest that she couldn't sleep. Walked straight in here. She gabbles. Her son is a clerk at Scotland Yard, so she called in, spoke by chance to Chief Inspector Hammer. He had the sense to call me before he rushed over.'

'What happened to this woman?' Paula asked.

'She was still here when I arrived. In the living room. She was having an attack of hysteria, gabbling nonstop. I phoned a private hospital, told them to put her in a private room with a tough nurse. Ambulance arrived quickly, took her away. I thought you'd want to decide the timing when the news is released. This card gives you the hospital's address.'

'Thank you. And now I think we'd better go.'

'I agree. All the police technicians have been and gone. I'm waiting for an ambulance with a special stretcher. I do need this poor woman to be taken to my place with exactly the same arrangement she is in now.'

'Arrangement,' Paula repeated on their way down the three flights. 'Horrible word.'

They reached the ground floor and Paula asked Tweed to wait a moment. Using latex gloves and a powerful torch she went inside the alcove. Tweed stood waiting, hoping she'd hurry up. It was a waste of time.

When Paula emerged after only minutes she was holding something in her gloved hand. She showed it to Tweed. It was a locket. She shone her torch on it as she opened it. On each side was a miniature photo of a woman. Viola on the left, Marina on the right.

'I found it at the entrance to a mousehole, half inside. The murderer must have dropped it when he was changing his gear back to what he was wearing underneath.'

'I wonder how he got hold of that?'

'He stole it. As a trophy. Of his exploits. The bastard.'

They were driving back to Paula's flat in silence. Tweed eventually spoke what was on his mind.

'So, according to Saafeld we may have only three or four days to identify the murderer before another woman is found slaughtered. We'd better get a move on.'

30

They drove back at modest speed to Paula's flat. The streets were silent. A light drizzle had begun to fall. Tweed was tired out, a rare state. Paula lifted a hand to hide a yawn. She too was on her last legs. It had been a long day with the grim climax in Marina's flat.

Driving along the Fulham Road, Tweed turned in to the yard, stopped outside her entrance at the front. He got out to check the inside of her place, left the key in the ignition, something he'd never normally have done. She followed him.

There were no lights in the flat below hers, which was occupied by a woman Paula had assumed had gone abroad. She was usually a night bird with her lights ablaze. She suddenly sensed someone was behind her, caught a faint whiff of chloroform. She sucked in a deep breath, held it. A cloth soaked in the liquid was pressed over her face as another arm wrapped itself round her.

Tweed was aware of nothing. A chloroform cloth was pressed over his face and he took in the full dose, sagging as burly arms caught him. They were dragged round the back, shoved into the rear of a car.

Paula had absorbed a little of the chloroform, enough to put her out of action for a short time. One man leaned in, dragged the hands of Tweed's slumped form, pulled them round his back, clamped on plastic handcuffs.

Paula, now vaguely aware of what was happening, held her hands a few inches apart, in her lap. Plastic handcuffs clamped her wrists together. She was more aware of what was happening now. Two men's voices.

'Get in Tweed's car,' said Radek. 'The friggin' fool has left keys in the ignition. Hide it where ours is parked.'

God! she thought. Fitch and Radek.

'No!' snarled Fitch. 'We leave our own car round the back. It's stolen, so are the plates. It is a Ford – like Tweed's. Take hours for anyone to think it's odd.'

'Why haul the bodies from one car to another? Get behind the wheel, Fitch, and we'll move off now.'

'Guess you could be right. I'll drive. Throw that blanket over 'em. Patrol cars drift round this time of night. Then we head straight for the warehouse . . .'

*

At one stage during the drive, which seemed to Paula to go on for ever, they stopped briefly in the East End while Radek dumped both treated cloths in a rubbish bin, then moved on.

At one convenient moment Paula stretched her cuffed hands under the blanket to check Tweed's neck pulse. It was beating regularly. He was just unconscious. Eventually the car stopped, waited while Fitch checked no one was in the area. Returning to the car, he gave the order.

'Padlock undone, doors open. Radek, you take Tweed up over your shoulder, I'll take his bedmate,' he said coarsely.

Paula was thrown over Fitch's shoulder, was carried behind Tweed up wide wooden steps, into a large room. Fitch paused to turn on a wall switch. Dim light flooded every corner of the bare room, emanating from lamps attached to the walls.

'What about the car?' Radek wanted to know.

'Forget it. Everyone round 'ere knows I drive Fords, that I'm always changing them. Position them.'

Fitch dumped Paula's limp form on the floor. She could feel all her senses returning suddenly. Radek dropped Tweed without ceremony on the wooden floor. He stood up, walked over to Paula.

'I'll check her for weapons. You do Tweed.'

'No mucking about with her,' Fitch warned,

walking nearby to Tweed. 'I know you with wimmin, so watch it.'

Paula stayed slumped as Radek began to check her. His hands explored the upper parts of her body first, pressing into her chest, over the rest of her body slowly, enjoying his work. Paula had dressed quickly. The slim leg holster holding her Beretta was, unusually, strapped to the inside of the leg. Eventually he started running his hands slowly down the outside of her legs from thigh to ankle. She spat savagely in his face. He jumped.

'This one's awake,' he called out, then slapped her very hard across the face, so hard her head jerked sideways.

He stood up, spat back at her, so furious that he didn't continue his search any further. Fitch had found Tweed's holstered Walther under his arm. He threw it across the room. It landed close to the wall.

'You won't ever be needin' that again, mate,' he told him with a grin.

Tweed's eyes were now open, staring up at Fitch who, despite his ruthlessness, didn't like the look.

'That's right,' he sneered. 'Keep the eyes open. So you can watch the picture show.'

Paula, sitting up now, pretending to sway, watched as Radek bent over the four projectors, aimed at different angles. Looked like the sort of thing you might see in a Hollywood studio. Then she saw four screens, one attached to each wall. What the hell was all this?

'You can manage on your own now,' Radek said, making it a statement. 'I am off to find some beer. Not as good as you get in Bratislava, but good enough. OK?'

'Shove off,' Fitch said rudely.

He was bent over a handle in the floor close to Tweed. He lifted a large round wooden lid, shoved it to one side on the floor. Faintly Paula heard the distant sound of rushing water a long way down in the exposed hole. She didn't like the sound of that.

'What the hell do you want that for?' Radek demanded.

'In case one of them isn't driven barmy for good they'll go down the chute. When you knows me better, Radek, you'll knows I thinks of everything. Now switch on the machines, then piss off and drown yourself in beer.'

Paula saw Fitch fix in earplugs. She was more puzzled than ever. Out of the corner of her eye she saw Radek bend over his apparatus.

'You can stay and watch if you want to,' Fitch bawled out.

'Seen them often enough. Get this lot started and I'm off looking for beer.'

He pressed levers on the projectors, adjusted the focus as pictures began to appear on all four screens.

Vile pictures, Paula thought. Tweed had managed to sit up on the floor, his handcuffs behind his back, making him a prisoner.

Radek turned to the other machine, pulled a switch halfway down. A terrible ear-splitting screech filled the warehouse. Nerves on edge, Paula stretched her hands as wide as she could inside her lap. The pictures turned her stomach. A cow tethered in a field. A man with a huge axe appeared, raised it, chopped off the cow's head. Blood welled out, the poor creature's legs jumped madly, even though headless. Then it flopped. A fresh picture on another screen. A peasant woman, tied to a block of stone. A short fat man appeared, also carrying a huge axe. He rested it gently on the woman's exposed neck. Her mouth was wide open, presumably screaming. The fat man raised the axe, brought it down with a tremendous swipe, took her head right off the neck. It rolled on the ground. He kicked it towards the screen. It vanished. Paula glanced at all the screens. On each some hideous massacre was taking place. She forced down a feeling of sickness. Three women tied to a huge rock were approached by three men carrying axes. Execution was going to be synchronized.

Paula sucked in her breath as she saw their stomachs were bare. The target for the axes. Fitch walked past her, then bent down to be close to her ear.

'Not loud enough. I'se turning up the sound.'

Still close to her ear he giggled. Giggled again. That was what did it.

He pressed the switch lower and the walls seemed to tremble under the diabolical blast of sound. The assault on her ear drums. He bent down again, giggled in her ear. He walked away from her to sit on the cheap wooden chair he'd sat on near Tweed, his back to her. She turned sideways, forced her right hand down inside her leg despite the pain of the cuffs, grabbed the Beretta out of its holster.

She aimed at Fitch's back. First bullet in his shoulder. Fired again. Second bullet in the centre of the back, close to the spine. Swinging round she emptied her gun at the projector, the sound system. The pictures died. An uncanny silence.

It all happened so quickly. She swung round. Tweed had heaved his whole body against the chair, toppling chair and Fitch over sideways. The thug slid to the edge of the chute, legs vanishing inside it, hands desperately clinging to the lip of the hole.

Tweed forced himself upright. Stiffening his legs, he stood above Fitch's terrified face as Paula staggered alongside him. Fitch was screaming. Nothing like the screams the poor women in the film must have uttered, Paula thought.

'Help me! Please! Help me,' Fitch gasped.

Tweed raised one foot. Stamped it down hard on

one of the hands supporting him. The other hand let go. Fitch was plunging down the circular metallic chute, both hands flat against the metal, desperately hoping for support. There was none. They heard a faint gurgle as he sank below the torrent of water surging towards the Thames. Then only rushing water.

31

Tweed drove back with Paula to her apartment. He had told her he would sleep on her sofa in her living room and, relieved, she had thanked him. Both were suffering a reaction but there was something else that had to be done. To safeguard her, Tweed took Paula with him.

Arriving back at her place, they both wore gloves before climbing into the Ford that Fitch had left parked behind the house. Luckily Fitch had left the ignition key on the front seat, ready to come back and make a quick getaway. Again, luckily, on first leaving the warehouse, they had found the ignition key to Tweed's car left in the same place. Fitch had not wanted to waste any time at either end.

Tweed drove Fitch's car while Paula drove his, keeping close behind him. Tweed found a deserted side street in the East End, left the Ford there, moved behind the wheel of his own car and drove it back to the concealed area behind her flat. Earlier they had freed each other from the handcuffs.

After all this they were very tired. Tweed had a brief snack Paula prepared him before she went to her bedroom. She should sleep like a babe, he felt sure as he perched on the sofa with coffee, his Walther on the cushion by his side.

Any fear that he might drop off to sleep disappeared as he took out his cartridge-paper notebook. In it he listed every single person connected with the murder case – and anyone else who had been involved in their enquiries.

It was a murky dawn when Paula, to his surprise, came in fully dressed.

'Didn't expect you for ages,' he greeted her.

'Had a strange dream. Don't know why. I was alone in the office when the door opened. A man came in, gripped a meat cleaver. As he came towards me I was scared stiff. His weird eyes staring at me through those weird glasses. I tried to scream and nothing came out. Then I woke up.'

'Who was it?'

'Benton Macomber. In those funny glasses.'

Tweed did not have to check his list to know that among his long list of suspects was Benton Macomber. He told her dreams were a poor substitute for fact and she agreed. Then she said she'd made breakfast because afterwards she was going off to see someone.

'Who might that be? It will be very early.'

'Coral Flenton. I know she gets up at unearthly early hours. I'll probably be just in time to share a cup of coffee with her.'

Later Tweed drove Paula down to Covent Garden so she could see Coral. He was careful to park in a slot before he reached her flat entrance, but at a point where he could see it. Paula had entered the place a few minutes before Tweed saw someone.

The Parrot, wearing a long coat with her hair obscured by a wide-brimmed hat, suddenly appeared and stopped on the other side of the street opposite the entrance. She opened a newspaper, pretended to read it. It was obvious to Tweed she was watching Coral's entrance. Why?

Inside, when Coral, fully dressed, had let Paula in, she had showed pleasure at the arrival of her visitor. In the living room she had offered coffee, which Paula had accepted.

'What about breakfast?' Coral asked.

'I've had some. What about yourself?'

'Finished it half an hour ago. It really is lovely to see you. Did you get my note?'

'I was just going to thank you for it,' Paula replied, seated in an armchair opposite her hostess. 'You sounded so excited. A new boyfriend? Or shouldn't I ask?'

'It's a secret. I've changed my mind about telling you. I'm sorry, but I'll let you know if it works out. Now I'll show you the rest of my safe harbour.'

Across the hall was a door leading into a fairly large bedroom. A double bed with a headboard occupied the bulk of the space. The floor was polished wood with a rug on each side where you would step out in the morning. A tasteful dressing table was perched against the far wall.

'Check the closets,' Coral urged. 'I should say wardrobes but you'll see why I used the American term.'

Paula opened one of the two double doors, which had to be pulled hard to overcome a tendency to stick. She was surprised. The depth and width of the 'closet' was spacious. She walked inside, like entering a small room. Three coats suspended on hangers caught her attention. One a camel hair, another a smart evening coat, the third a smart raincoat. Coral chuckled and gently pushed the door almost closed. A light came on inside. Coral opened the door.

'The wiring's set up the wrong way. The light should come on when you open it. I'm getting it fixed.'

'Nice coats,' Paula remarked as she stepped out.

'Expensive.'

'The new boyfriend?' Paula chaffed her.

'Not yet! My aunt married a rich man a few

months ago and generously sent me a very fat cheque. I blew it on those coats.'

'You're on top of the world, then.'

'Not entirely.' Coral's expression changed.

'Why? Is anything the matter?'

'I'm bothered about a man who stalks me. I'm walking along a street and I know he's behind me. I look back and he's gone. It's bothersome.'

'Description?'

'I never see him. I just know he's there. Must sound a bit silly. Maybe I've got too much imagination. Women do sometimes get this idea in their head.' She laughed. 'It probably comes down to vanity.'

Paula studied her. The Parrot was an attractive woman but older. That could upset some women. Coral was younger and a stunner. About five feet three inches tall, she was slim and her red hair piled on top of her head was seductive. Her features were perfectly moulded: a fine forehead, her eyes large above a perfect nose and a full mouth. Yes, some older women could come to hate her.

'Do you know anything about the Parrot's earlier life?'

'She grew up in the Midlands, in some place called Walkhampton. A small industrial town, I gather. She was educated in a prep school and then passed into a grammar. She left Walkhampton when she was twenty, came down here, whipped through the civil service exam. Her parents died in a car crash soon after she'd arrived down here. After passing top in the exam she set to work – she's said this to me – to push her way up quickly, shoving other people out of the way.'

'But now she's turned friendly with you?' Paula suggested.

'She did. I told you about that. Now she's turned really nasty again. She humiliates me.' Coral mimicked the Parrot's way of speaking fast. '"Miss Flenton, I gave you these pencils to be sharpened. They've still got thick ends. I need them with needle points. Try again. Can't you do even a simple job like that properly? Your problem is you're lazy. Spend half your time thinking about men, I suspect. Men are for when you've left the building. That is, if you can find one. Well, don't just listen to me. Sharpen those damned pencils." She's started finding fault with everything,' Coral concluded.

'Goes up and down a bit, doesn't she?'

'A friend of mine in the next department thinks she's manic. Bit strong, I thought. I suppose she based her idea on the Parrot's wild mood swings. Sorry to drop all this stuff on you. Next time we won't mention my job.'

'I'd better go now,' said Paula, standing up. 'Actually, you are always interesting. I'll come again if it suits you.'

'Please! And don't forget you've got my spare front-door key so you can come in when you want and wait for me to leave work.'

Outside, hunched down in his car, Tweed watched the door open. Paula and Coral hugged each other. Then Paula, head down in thought, walked slowly towards him.

The moment the two women appeared the Parrot took off, striding briskly in the opposite direction. Tweed opened the passenger car door and Paula slipped inside. She reported every word which had been exchanged, described the layout of Coral's flat. Tweed waited until she had finished, talking quickly, before he told her about the Parrot's vigil.

'I can't make head nor tail of that,' Paula commented.

'I can,' Tweed said as he began to drive. 'The fact that she walked off as soon as the two of you appeared tells me a lot.'

'Such as?'

'She was expecting a man to come out, a man who'd spent the night with Coral.'

'Who?'

'I just wish I knew. It doesn't help me to solve those two murders with these women at each other's throats.' He frowned. 'Or maybe it does.'

*

The Cabal were assembled round their strange three-sided table. Nelson kept moving his blotter, rearranging his pens, which showed nervousness unusual for him. The other two waited until he spoke.

'I think we've got to do something damned quickly to make those few wobbly Cabinet ministers support our draft bill to merge the security services.'

'Maybe it's time to frighten them,' Noel suggested. 'If an explosion – terrorists, of course – took place in London, that would do it.'

'In London? Where in London?' Nelson's expression was appalled. 'We must not risk any casualties.'

'In Richmond Park.'

'You must be mad,' sneered Benton, glaring through his glasses.

'Mad as a hatter,' roared Nelson.

'My intermediary,' Noel began in his soft voice, 'has found a part of Richmond Park a long way from the river. There is an entrance never used at this time of the year, on the outskirts. The only casualty, if any, will be a tree or two. It will be thought by the police the driver was taking it by a roundabout route to the populous area of the park but the bomb exploded prematurely. Panic, but no one even injured.'

'You have complete confidence in this intermediary?' demanded Nelson.

'Complete.'

It was a tactic of Noel's to invent so-called intermediaries, so no one in the room knew he was making the contacts himself.

'What do you think?' Nelson asked.

'We do need something to wake those ministers up now,' Benton suggested.

'I suppose we do.' Nelson's large fleshy face was a picture of uncertainty. 'If we all vote in favour we'll do it,' he decided.

They all lifted a left hand. Noel stood up, careful not to smile. 'Then I'd better go outside and make a phone call.'

Tweed and Paula arrived at Park Crescent to find the whole team in the office. Marler was stuffing his flying gear into a large bag, first trying on his flying helmet to make sure it fitted comfortably.

'What's going on?' Tweed asked as Monica took his overcoat.

It was Harry who answered. He wore his camouflage jacket. He was tucking away grenades, one into each pocket.

'Marler and I have decided we'd better check up on that truck, make sure it's still there. Marler is flying me down there. He says you told him there was a landing place on top of the big hill.'

'Mountain High,' Tweed recalled. 'I want everything tricky dealt with. And fast.'

'Then if the truck's still there with no one about I

could blow the thing up myself,' Harry offered.

'Do it. Paula and I cleaned up one dangerous aspect in the early morning. I presume you all know there's been another horrific murder. Another woman. Same beastly method.'

'It's in the late edition of the *Daily Nation*,' Newman said. 'Drew Franklin's column. He really does have a marvellous network of contacts.'

'And off the record,' Tweed snapped, 'I imagine a chief inspector's wallet is fat with another two hundred pounds. Can I see the report?'

'We're off,' Marler said, leaving with Harry as Tweed read:

SECOND VANDER-BROWNE HORROR MURDER

Another House of Death now exists in London. The brutally mutilated body of Marina Vander-Browne was discovered at her Mayfair address early this morning, similar to how her sister, Viola, was cut to pieces only a week ago. Chief Inspector Hammer said they were making progress with their investigation.

'Making progress backwards,' Tweed snorted, handing the newspaper back to Newman.

He stood up, swept his gaze round the remaining

members of his team. From his expression they knew something grim was coming.

'You should all know that Professor Saafeld believes this fiend – man or woman – may strike again during the next few days.' The timbre of his voice was deep. 'Saafeld calls it blood storm. The killer gets a surge of desire to murder and as this surge accelerates, the time gap between his slaughters decreases. We have only days to identify who it is. I want to know as much as we can extract from all the members of the Cabal, as one approach. Newman, you will do your best link up with Noel, to grill him. Nield, your target is Benton. Paula, you interview the Parrot.'

'Can I wait a few hours to do that?' Paula requested. 'I've somewhere I want to go before I see her.'

'Agreed,' Tweed said abruptly. 'I will take on Nelson, but that may have to wait until the end of the day. Howard wants me to go through the report for the PM with him. The timing of showing him that document is vital. Marler and Harry will be given their assignments when they return from Peckham Mallet. Then I may have to make a quick trip to interview General Macomber. I will be back late this afternoon.'

'You're going down there alone?' Paula asked anxiously.

'Yes. No argument. The General is up to something. Here is a tip which might help you all. We are looking for someone – again man or woman – who is capable of the most sadistic cruelty.'

'Who screwed the cat's neck through a hundred and eighty degrees all those years ago,' Paula suggested.

'Possibly. Remember, we have perhaps only two days to prevent a third horror.'

In the afternoon Tweed was driving towards Tolhaven and the ferry to Black Island when Marler and Harry returned to the office from their trip. But they had flown there together with Marler as pilot of his light aircraft and Harry trembling beside him.

'I could do with a tot of brandy,' Harry gasped.

He was making an effort to walk steadily. Monica jumped up, opened a cupboard, grabbed a bottle of brandy and a glass. She poured a stiff tot. He swallowed half of it, heaved a sigh of relief. He swallowed the rest, stood up straight from the hunched position Monica had noticed when he had entered the office.

Marler, a sardonic smile on his face, had followed him in.

Harry assumed his favourite position, seated cross-legged on the floor. Marler walked past him, stood against the wall, put a cigarette in his ivory holder, lit it.

'We've had a bit of an adventure,' he drawled.

'A bloody nightmare,' snapped Harry.

'I'll tell you what happened,' Marler began. 'Monica, you might take this down. As a statement for Tweed . . .'

32

Marler drove them to a private airfield outside London where his light aircraft was housed. The owner ordered his team to trundle the machine on to the runway.

Marler was handing a helmet equipped with earphones to Harry. He explained this was so they could communicate with each other clearly in midair. Reluctantly Harry donned the helmet.

Dazed with apprehension, Harry, who hated flying, found himself seated next to Marler as the plane took off, climbed. It was a brilliantly sunny day, warmish for April. Not a cloud in the sky.

'Wobbles about a lot,' Harry complained.

'Actually, old chap, we are flying very steadily. Look out at the scenery. Marvellous view.'

'Is it?'

Harry stubbornly stared straight ahead as Marler studied the map, checking the route to Mountain High near Peckham Mallet. Near General Macomber's cottage. He glanced at Harry's ashen face.

'Shouldn't take long to get there.'

'Seems like forever already.'

'Relax. I once flew this plane down to Provence in the south of France.'

'Thank Gawd I wasn't with you.'

'Harry, take this with that bottle of water I gave you. It's a Dramamine pill. Paula swears by them when she's flying over the Atlantic. An eleven-hour flight to San Francisco.'

'She takes one?' Harry stared dubiously at the small yellow tablet. Marler waited until he had swallowed it before he replied.

'Actually, she doesn't. But she persuades Tweed to take one if he's flying or on a sea crossing.'

'Does it work for her – him?'

'Yes, it does. Every time.'

'Well, it's not working for me.'

'Give it a few minutes to get into your system.'

Harry sat very still, grimly silent. Marler was looking down, admiring the beautiful countryside, clear as crystal in the sunlight. Rolling downs like frozen green waves, dense evergreen forests, cars looking like tiny models crawling along motorways. They had crossed from Surrey into Sussex.

'May be a bit of turbulence ahead,' Marler warned.

'What's turbulence?'

'Plane might rock a bit from side to side, up and down.'

'Take me home.'

'We always complete our missions,' Marler said sternly.

'Do these things ever crash?' Harry whispered.

'Not with me as pilot.'

The plane suddenly swayed from side to side. Then it dropped, climbed again. Marler again glanced at Harry. He had a dozy expression, was now looking out and down. The plane was now flying on an even keel.

'Bit bumpy there for a moment,' Harry commented.

Glancing once more at Harry, Marler noticed the colour was coming back into his face. The Dramamine had worked. Harry was taking an interest in his surroundings. He pointed ahead.

'What's that big hill ahead? An alp?'

'You only get those in Switzerland. That's Mountain High . . .'

'I can see a large truck in an empty field. That could be it. A man's walking towards it. Keep this thing steady.'

Harry took out his powerful binoculars, focused them. He could see the burly figure in denims and a windcheater quite clearly. Could see the man's ugly face under a peaked cap. He swore colourfully.

'What's the matter?' Marler asked.

'See that chap heading for the truck? That's Mugger Morgan. A real villain. Been hauled up for two killings, which he did. Got off on a technicality. Friend of Fitch. He's looking up at us.'

'Have to trick him. We're joy-riders. Brace yourself.'

Marler looped the loop. Harry found himself staring at the sky, then the earth above him. He yelled in terror.

'It's OK,' Marler called back.

He looped the loop a second time. Harry was staring up at earth again. They were crashing. He knew they were crashing. The plane levelled out, the view became normal. Harry let go of the breath he had been holding.

'What the hell did you do that for?'

'To fool Mugger Morgan. He'll think we're mad joy-riders.'

'Mad is the word!'

'Keep an eye on him. What's he doing now?'

'Stopped looking at us. He's climbing into the cab. He's going to drive the truck off. We're well away from him.'

They both looked down at the truck, which appeared very small from their height. There was no one else about anywhere.

The truck moved forward perhaps ten feet, then

the explosives detonated. The entire vehicle lifted off the field. There was a blinding flash, a distant boom. The roof shot skywards, split in two. The truck's sides blasted outwards. The cab where Mugger Morgan had sat disintegrated. A small crater appeared in the field. Fragments descended to the field as debris fell inside the crater.

Inside the Park Crescent office Marler concluded his report to Monica at about the time Tweed parked his car outside Tolhaven.

It was a different ferryman who took him across to Black Island in a calm sea. It was also a different route from the one to the east he had travelled with the team. So he saw the ugly globe-shaped structures of the oil refinery near the western tip of the island.

He was totally unprepared for what happened when he had walked past the village of Lydford.

33

Instead of turning left towards General Macomber's house and the Crooked Village, Tweed turned right, walking along the track towards where the brutal prison was being built by the Slovaks. A glimpse through the trees showed him eight of the prison buildings had been erected. He was appalled.

A glimpse to his right through a gap in the forest showed him the oil refinery. He stopped. He pressed his binoculars to his eyes. A tall slim man, clad in a camouflage outfit, including a cap, was detaching a rubber hose from an outlet. His hand, covered in a fireproof glove, checked to make sure the tap had turned off the outlet. Over his shoulder was slung a shotgun. The camouflaged figure began walking towards Tweed.

A few feet from where he stood Tweed saw a thick rubber hose turning away, heading towards the prison. A shaft of sunlight shone on its oily surface.

Tweed smelt petrol. He stepped well back away from it.

The figure was close now, moving briskly. The shotgun was now in the figure's hands, aimed towards Tweed. He grabbed the Walther from its holster, aimed it at the approaching figure as it came close.

'General,' Tweed snapped, 'if we shoot each other I can't see it will help either of us.'

'You are right,' General Macomber replied, lowering the weapon. 'Your timing is bad, but perfect.'

'Perfect?'

'From your point of view.'

'I've just come over by the ferry.'

'Which has a different ferry master. Perfect.'

'Why?'

'Because he won't recognize you when you go back. It leaves for the mainland in ten minutes. Then leave for London. By then you'll have seen the fireworks.'

'Fireworks?'

'That diabolical prison must go. I have also cancelled the monthly allowance to my three evil offspring. Are you ready, sir?'

'Ready for what?'

'The fireworks.'

Saying which, the General took out a cigarette lighter, bent down, lit it, and with a quick movement let the flame touch the edge of the pipe which disappeared towards the prison. The flame flared along the outside of the pipe into the distance. The General stood up, stepped back close to Tweed, put the lighter in his pocket.

'When it reaches the prison the pipe is full of petrol inside,' he explained. 'I once served a short spell with the Royal Engineers.'

Tweed was almost hypnotized, watching the low line of fire sweeping towards the prison. The General checked his watch.

'You have five minutes to catch the ferry. Wait just a little longer.'

'The Slovaks don't have explosives, do they?'

'I did notice they are careless about storing grenades.'

'In which case . . .'

'They will explode.'

'I suppose the Slovaks who built this place will be away at lunch?'

'They have taken to eating lunch inside the prison. About now.'

'So . . .'

'They will be on the premises.'

'You don't like the Slovaks?'

'Not the ones from the Tatra mountains. In Bratislava I once met several I liked.'

Tweed was watching the progress of the flaring

pipe. It was getting close to the prison buildings. No sign of guards. They were getting careless.

'The grenades may injure a few,' Tweed remarked.

'Oh, there's something else,' the General said casually. 'I've explored the place in the night. The Slovaks sleep inside an encampment some distance away. I found a store of bricks of Semtex.'

'My God!'

'I think you should catch that ferry now. You were never here. I was taking a nap in my house. Good luck with finding that murdering animal. I'm sure you will. The fire has reached the section of pipe filled with petrol. Go now.'

Tweed saw the distant pipe flare up into a huge column of flame. It had reached the inside of the prison complex. He hurried back to the ferry. The barge was just leaving. Scrambling aboard the stern, Tweed went to the prow so he could get off quickly. Soon they were in mid-channel.

He looked back. Well beyond the oil-refinery complex the world was on fire. Great tongues of flames shot skywards. Black Island became Red Island. The ferryman, at the stern, stared in disbelief as the inferno increased in intensity. Then the devastating explosion roared and Tweed knew the fire had reached the Semtex.

Large sheets of steel were hurled upwards as the explosion destroyed the hideous prison. And the

Slovaks who had erected it, Tweed thought. Was it his imagination – or did he see half a body tossed up, a burning body, before it fell back out of sight?

'Stupid foreigners!' the ferryman shouted.

Tweed shrugged, gave no reply as the barge slid in to the mainland dock. He stepped down and hurried towards Tolhaven. Since he'd taken the precaution of buying a return ticket he was able to leave the ferry immediately.

Tolhaven's main street was, as usual, deserted. When he had reached his car parked outside the town he took off the beret he had worn. Amazing how such a simple article changed the appearance of a man who never normally wore any kind of hat.

He paused at the crest of a hill, looked back. The western tip of Black Island beyond the refinery was a curtain of flame.

As he headed back for Park Crescent Tweed mentally crossed off General Macomber from his list of murder suspects.

34

While Tweed was on his way to Tolhaven, Newman was obeying his order to interview Noel Macomber. He phoned Noel first.

'Robert Newman, SIS, here. I think we should meet urgently.'

'Why?' the soft voice whispered.

'To discuss a peaceful solution.'

'I see,' after a long pause. He'd consulted his colleagues. 'Where? When?' he enquired.

'Now. I could arrive at your building at twelve. You know a discreet bar near you?'

'Yes. I'll leave our HQ at twelve.'

So it came about that Newman found himself seated with Noel in the leather-walled alcove of an exclusive bar in Victoria Street. They faced each other. Noel had occupied the seat inside the alcove, his back to the wall as he swirled his second glass of Scotch.

When he first saw him descend the steps of the HQ building Newman was startled. Noel wore a smart white suit, a pink shirt, a colourful cravat and two-toned shoes. Now, in the quiet bar each was waiting for the other to speak first.

Newman had studied the face of his opponent. It was peculiar. Triangular in shape with the apex the pointed jaw. Yet there was a certain handsomeness many women would find attractive. The almost lidless eyes were yellow and rarely moved. Newman decided it was time to move in for the kill.

'Where were you on these nights?' he asked, pushing forward a sheet of paper with the two murder dates. 'Between the hours of 11 p.m. and 3 a.m.?'

'Funny way to start discussing a peaceful solution.'

'Tweed has a long list of suspects. We eliminate you and move on to the next name. Logical.'

'You really expect me to recall where I was on two out-of-the-blue dates?'

'Yes. Because in both cases – Viola and Marina – the crimes were splashed all over the following morning's papers.'

'Point,' Noel agreed. 'On each night I was drunk and went to my flat at ten o'clock to sleep it off.'

'Anyone to confirm that?'

'Not those nights.' Noel grinned wolfishly. 'I didn't have a girl with me in bed. Too drunk.'

'Did you know either woman?'

'I visited Marina about a month ago at midnight.' A second wolfish grin. 'She only worked in the early hours, if you catch my meaning.'

'And Viola?'

'Didn't know she existed until I read the paper about her unfortunate experience.'

'It was more than unfortunate for her.'

'I suppose it was.' Noel emptied his glass, called for a refill, raised his thin eyebrows at Newman, who shook his head. He was on his first Scotch still. 'Newman, can you keep a secret until late this afternoon?'

'I suppose so.'

'Nelson is being appointed to the Cabinet. As Minister for Internal Security. A new post.' Noel raised his thin brows which exposed all his yellowish eyes. Disconcerting. 'You won't, then, be rushing to phone your chum, Drew Franklin?'

'Hardly, since he isn't my chum. Regarding a peaceful solution. Wouldn't the first step be to dismantle the awful prison system being erected on Black Island?'

'Damn it!' Noel exploded, his face turning red. 'You're conspiring to wreck a system it has taken us months to plan.'

He jumped up to leave, but not before he had swallowed his third full glass of Scotch. 'Now Nelson will be in the Cabinet this afternoon I'll be able to have you as the first one thrown into the prison on Black Island. As a social saboteur.'

He dived out of the alcove, rushed for the door, very fleet of foot, Newman noticed. Then he rushed back, threw a twenty-pound note on the table, rushed again through the bar and in doing so nearly knocked over a waiter before disappearing full tilt into the street.

'He must be annoyed at something,' Newman said with a smile to the stunned waiter as he also walked slowly out of the bar.

It was a very thoughtful Newman who made his way back up Whitehall to where he had parked his car.

35

Nield, waiting in Whitehall near the Cabal's HQ, was taken aback at Benton Macomber's reaction to his approach. He had expected hostility initially. He walked up to Benton as he descended the steps into the side street.

'Benton Macomber, sir?'

'That's right. What can I do for you?'

'I'm Pete Nield of the SIS,' he said, showing his folder. 'I would appreciate a few words with you. I'm investigating the murders of Viola and Marina Vander-Browne.'

Benton would be in his late forties, Nield estimated. He was well built, with unusually wide shoulders which gave him a hunched appearance. His clean-shaven face was bony, the observant eyes greenish, his complexion rugged with a reddish tinge, the mouth full-lipped and sensual. He exuded an air of suppressed energy.

'I'm just going for a quick lunch,' he explained.

'Just a sandwich and a drink at an up-market wine bar at this end of Victoria Street. Why don't you join me? Later it gets busy but it will be quiet now.'

Benton walked with long strides and Nield, being shorter, had to hurry to keep up with him. He's a very fit man, Nield thought as they turned into the wine bar. Neither said another word until they were seated at a table and Benton had ordered for them both after consulting Nield.

Both drank Scotch. Benton sipped his glass, pushed it away. He smiled pleasantly at Nield.

'I drink moderately, unlike Nelson. Doesn't seem to affect his ability to think and act. What is this?' He glanced at the sheet with the dates of both murders, pushed it back.

'I thought those dates might be significant.'

'The first date is when Viola Vander-Browne was savaged and murdered. The second is when her sister, Marina, was killed.'

Nield was taken aback. Benton was so different from what he had expected. It was more like talking to a favourite uncle. He pressed on.

'Where were you on those particular nights between the hours of 11 a.m. and 3 a.m.? You have a remarkable memory,' he added.

'A phenomenal memory. Born with it, or inherited it. Who knows? But specific hours on two different nights? That's pushing it a bit. Wait a minute.'

Benton took out a pocket diary. He then extracted a pair of rimless glasses from a case, put them on. The transformation rattled Nield's nerves. Benton glanced at Nield, then looked at his diary before staring at Nield. The rimless glasses had converted Benton into something sinister. The greenish eyes pierced Nield's. Sinister was not a strong enough word.

'The night Viola died I was with a girl, Patsy, in a flat I rent in a mews off Mayfair. She left at 10.30 p.m. She'd exhausted me,' he remarked with a strange smile. 'I went to bed, slept until morning. Not much of an alibi, Mr Nield.'

'What about the second date?' Nield persisted.

'Spent the whole evening and night in my Mayfair flat. Alone. No alibi at all.' He took off his glasses and again looked normal. 'I'd appreciate it if you'd not mention Patsy, at least by name, if at all. I'm just about to divorce my wife, who is visiting her boy-friend in Canada.'

'I'll forget Patsy — unless it becomes essential to name her. I have to ask you these questions because you're one of a number of names on Tweed's list of suspects.'

'Then you'll have to tell Tweed to leave my name on it.' Benton smiled pleasantly, sipped a little more of his Scotch.

Nield drank the rest of his Scotch. He still had in

his mind the evil vision of Benton wearing his rimless glasses. Which was the real man?

'Who do you think killed those women?' Benton asked suddenly.

Nield was briefly stunned by the sheer bravado of the question. Benton must have guessed the whole Cabal was on the list of suspects. He rallied swiftly, gazing straight at Benton.

'Someone powerful. Someone who lives in London. Someone who will be identified by Tweed within the next twenty-four hours.'

'I see.' Benton paused. Now he was stunned. 'You are very confident . . .'

'Someone,' Nield continued his counter-attack, 'who left a clue at one of the crime scenes.'

Benton called for the bill, paid it quickly, stood up, his expression grim. His mouth was turned down at the corners, all traces of the benevolent uncle absent. Without a word he strode out of the winebar, moving rapidly.

Nield sat smiling. He ordered another sandwich. He had broken through the wall of bland innocence the Cabal presented to the world.

36

Paula, returned from her visit outside the capital, parked her car in a spot just vacated by a businessman wearing a dull black suit, the 'uniform' these days of men who worked in the City.

She walked into the side street, trotted behind Benton, who seemed in a great hurry. He said something into the speakphone, the great door slid upwards, she followed him on to the escalator. He was so absorbed by something on his mind he never noticed her. Clasped under her arm she had two carefully folded copies of different editions of the *Daily Nation*.

She walked into the Cabal's private room behind Benton. Two people were sitting at the triangular table. Nelson and Noel. Nelson jumped up when he saw her.

'You can't come in here,' he snapped.

'I've come to congratulate you,' she said merrily, waving the huge headline on the special edition.

NELSON MACOMBER MINISTER OF INTERNAL SECURITY

'And,' she continued, still walking towards the door into the next room, 'Miss Partridge has something to tell me.'

She had entered the next room, closed the door behind her, before Nelson, who had jumped up, could reach her. Inside, Coral Flenton was standing up, a wide smile on her face as she waved her hands in the air, then did a little dance.

'It's a wonderful world,' she sang, mimicking Louis Armstrong as she went on dancing.

The Parrot stood a distance away from her, strong arms folded under her chest. Her expression was murderous. She suddenly became aware of Paula and her expression became grimmer. She swung back towards Coral.

'Shut your face!' she screamed. 'Stop that awful row or I'll shut it for you!'

'There's a witness if you attack me.' Coral nodded towards Paula and picked up a heavy ruler. On her desk was the *Daily Nation*, folded to the headline announcing the new Cabinet appointment.

'I'll throttle you!' the Parrot screamed again at Coral.

'No, you won't,' a quiet commanding voice said.

Nelson had appeared from the next room. Obviously he had heard the Parrot screaming. The large man walked quickly across the room. The Parrot froze. Nelson gave the order as he passed her.

'You wait exactly where you are until I get back.'

He continued walking until he reached Paula, who had moved to the other side of Coral's desk. His manner was calm but determined. He gripped Paula's right arm, kept walking.

'This is no place for you, Miss Grey. I'm asking you to leave by the back entrance. Don't come here again.'

Still gripping her arm tightly he walked her towards a door in the rear wall. He used his other hand to press down a safety lever. He was opening the steel door when Paula reacted.

'Take your hand off me. You're hurting me.'

He kept hold of her as the door swung open. She used the tip of her left shoe to kick him hard on the shin. He grimaced, gave a grunt of pain, let go of her arm and she walked out on to a platform at the top of a flight of metal steps leading down into the street.

'Miss Grey,' Nelson called down, his tone now friendly.

'What is it?' she called back, glaring.

'In my anxiety to calm things down I gripped the wrong woman's arm. I apologize if I hurt you. Unintentional.'

He was smiling warmly. He even saluted her to emphasize his change of mood. Still pausing, she glared at him again, refusing to let him off the hook.

'Maybe you'd better learn to control your temper before you park your seat in your Cabinet chair.'

She continued descending the steps, did not look back again. So she missed the blaze of annoyance which appeared in his large blue eyes. She did hear the slam of the metal door shutting as she leaned against a wall to adjust her shoes. She had chosen the wrong footwear and had walked a lot when she'd reached her destination well outside London.

More comfortable now, she walked left along the alley, her sense of direction taking her to the end of the side street which led to Whitehall. She stopped for a moment when she saw who was walking towards the entrance to the HQ. Tweed.

37

'What are you doing here?' Paula asked.

'I told you earlier. I want a word with Nelson Macomber.'

He stopped speaking as the steel door swung upwards and out of sight. Wearing a dark suit with a flower in the buttonhole, Nelson stepped into the street. At the top of the escalator Paula saw a crowd of staff, all clapping their hands. Beaming, Nelson turned to wave to them, then turned to Tweed.

'Heard your voice on the speakphone. I was just coming down. I'm on my way there.'

He gestured to the end of the alley. Parked by a Whitehall kerb was a long black limousine. A uniformed chauffeur stood at attention.

'So congratulations are in order,' Tweed said.

'My dear Tweed . . .' Nelson threw both arms round him, hugged. 'I am so looking forward to working with you.' He beamed at Paula. 'And, of course, with your attractive and hyper-efficient Paula.'

She stepped back, worried that he was going to hug her. He was a big man and the thought of those strong arms squeezing the breath out of her did not appeal.

'Well,' Tweed said amiably, 'you've got one of the two sensational headlines all to yourself.'

He produced a folded newspaper from under his arm, still gripping a second newspaper under the same arm. He opened it to show the headline announcing the Cabinet appointment. Nelson took it and studied it as though seeing it for the first time.

'Overdone it a bit, haven't they?' he said with a complacent smile.

'Oh, I don't know,' Tweed remarked. 'Pity it's swamped by the next edition they rushed out at breakneck speed.'

He took the second newspaper from under his arm. Again it was folded to the even larger glaring headline with the story below written by Drew Franklin.

BLACK ISLAND TORTURE PRISON EXPLODES IN FLAMES

Paula peeked over Tweed's shoulder as he handed it to Nelson, then studied the newly appointed minister's expression. All the joy in Nelson's face vanished like a mark wiped off a window. He stood motionless as he read the detailed text. One sentence referred to 'the body parts of the Slovak builders flying into the air . . .' Another referred to 'the hideous KGB-like torture chamber ready for so-called "social saboteurs". That is, ready for anyone speaking out against the government . . .'

'This is blatant nonsense,' Nelson squeaked.

'He has printed photos to illustrate his text,' Tweed remarked.

'This is your work,' Nelson snarled.

'Don't be silly . . . Minister. Drew Franklin has contacts everywhere.'

'My car awaits,' Nelson said, drawing himself up. 'You can keep that filthy rag.'

He still kept under his arm the 'filthy rag' of the *Daily Nation* reporting his accession to the Cabinet. Before he reached the limousine they heard him swearing at the chauffeur.

'In future I'll expect the damned rear door open as soon as you see me coming . . .'

'And we'll get back to Park Crescent,' Tweed said quietly, 'so I can hear how everyone got on with their interviews.'

'And I've been to Walkhampton in the Midlands where the Parrot spent her childhood and teenage years,' Paula told him.

'Tell me when we're all together to listen.'

They were driving back to Park Crescent slowly –

through all the traffic in the world, so it seemed to Paula. She kept quiet. She could almost hear Tweed thinking intensively.

'I'm hoping,' he said eventually, 'that someone who has been interviewed slipped up. But don't bet on it.' He sighed. 'If Saafeld is right there is so little time left.'

The whole team was waiting when they arrived. Marler had decided to give Tweed a brief verbal version of his flight with Harry to Peckham Mallet. Monica looked annoyed since she had already typed the report of what had happened. Tweed looked relieved when Marler concluded.

'So the bomb detonated in the field. Good work, Harry. I am glad one problem has been solved. Now, I'll listen to the interviews you had with different members of the Cabal.'

He appeared to be listening intently, his eyes never leaving those of the person speaking. Yet Paula had the impression half his mind was elsewhere. The interview he showed the greatest interest in was Nield's.

'Benton is a strange man,' he commented.

'Something else on your mind?' asked Paula.

'Yes. Everyone has done well. But I'm no nearer to pinpointing who might be the murderer. I'm now going to suggest a quite different approach, since time is getting desperately short.' He paused. 'Forget the identity of the murderer. Instead, who is likely to be the next victim?'

He had startled everyone. They looked at each other, then stared at Tweed. Even Paula couldn't see where he was going.

'Before we get involved in something else,' Paula spoke up, 'I forgot to tell you what I found out about the Parrot in Walkhampton. She wasn't popular even as a small girl. The reason? She was so bright, and knew it, that she tended to dominate everyone. After prep school she went to a grammar – and was always top of the class. Oh, and her father had a shop. He was a butcher.'

'A butcher!' Newman exclaimed.

'The next victim,' Tweed repeated emphatically. 'If we know who the next victim is, we can stake out her home and wait for the murderer to appear with all his – or her – equipment in a large carrier or briefcase . . .'

'I see your point,' said Paula. 'A different approach. I just wonder who the next victim is.'

'The Parrot, of course,' Tweed affirmed. 'She works next to the room where the Cabal meets. She is the one person most likely to have overheard their plans. She is dangerous to the Cabal. If killed in the same way as Viola and Marina no one will connect it with her knowledge of the Cabal.'

'I do believe you're right,' exclaimed Newman.

'On top of which,' Tweed plunged on, 'we are familiar with where she lives. Her place in the side street in Hammersmith. We disguise ourselves to fit in with the scenery. We use mobiles to keep in touch with each other.'

'I've got a great idea,' piped up Harry. 'What time do we get there?'

'Before 10 p.m,' Tweed replied.

'Then,' Harry continued, 'I've time to get in touch with a pal who runs a cab. He owes me. He'd loan it to me so I could drive round the area as a cabbie. Maybe even take you one by one at intervals as a passenger.'

'That,' agreed Tweed, 'is a great idea.'

'I could be a street cleaner,' Newman said. 'They often work at night. The pavements are so crowded in the daytime now.'

Paula yawned openly for the second time. She looked at Tweed, who had been watching her. She stood up as though to stretch aching limbs.

'Will there be enough of you without me?' She suppressed another yawn. 'I nearly walked myself into the ground in that dreary city.'

'You can't go home,' Newman protested.

'I know. No one to protect me. Which is why I'll stay here with Monica until you get back.'

'Agreed,' said Tweed. 'Monica can go now to the deli with Newman. Get you both something to eat.'

'Thanks.'
Paula sat down, slumped in her chair, closed her eyes. She knew that this time Tweed had got it wrong.

38

'The Minister, Nelson Macomber, is downstairs and would like to see you.'

Tweed concealed his surprise. The rest of the team, except for Paula, had at Tweed's suggestion gone out to have a good supper. It was going to be a long night, staking out the Parrot's flat.

'Tell the Minister I welcome his visit and I'm at his disposal.'

Tweed had stood up. He walked to open the door to welcome his visitor. It was 8.30 p.m. and dark outside. Monica gave the message to George and then darted to the window, pulled back a curtain. Parked outside their entrance was a large black limousine with the uniformed chauffeur standing on the pavement. Tweed had opened the door and they heard the heavy tread of their visitor coming swiftly up.

'Welcome, Minister,' Tweed said with a smile, holding out his hand.

Nelson grasped it, beaming with the famous smile always present when press photographers were anywhere near him. At her corner desk Paula stood up, a file under her arm.

'I will leave the two of you to your discussions,' she said.

'No! No! Please do stay.' Nelson released Tweed's hand, used his own to wave her back. 'You are one of the two most important people in this organization. So you, also, will want to hear why I am here.'

Nelson had changed into a new blue suit with thin pinstripes. He looked larger than ever and sat in the chair facing Tweed's desk as his host sat in his swivel chair. He politely refused offers of coffee, tea or anything else to drink, then smiled at Tweed.

'Since my appointment you are the first person I am calling on, Mr Tweed.'

'I appreciate that, Minister.'

Paula thought she had never seen Tweed calmer or more relaxed. He sat, both elbows on his desk, his hands perched under his chin. His eyes never left those of his visitor.

'Nelson, please, since we shall all be working together.' He glanced at Paula who nodded, without smiling. 'Now let us dive straight into the core of the problem. Britain's moral structure has collapsed. Anything goes. On the TV we see filthy films showing explicit sex with no holds barred. Granted, many are shown late at night, but not always. Even late at night, at any hour, this filth must be controlled, banned. How many children under, say, twelve, are secretly watching this dirt while their parents are out at some wild party? Do you agree so far?'

'Of course I do,' Tweed said.

'This immoral poison is infiltrating the whole country. In London, after dark, it is not difficult to see couplings taking place against a wall. It is Sodom and Gomorrah in the open.' His voice rose to a powerful timbre. 'Decent women can no longer walk home in safety – even in daylight. Certain judges impose light sentences when a man before them is convicted of rape. Those judges must be removed and replaced by judges of sterner stuff. Are my views upsetting you, sir?'

'So far, not in the least. I agree with what you are saying,' Tweed replied.

'Child-molesters are convicted, put in prison, released when some psychiatrist pronounces them "safe". Within weeks, even days, the freed man commits the same foul crime again. Having deviated once they should be kept behind bars for many years, maybe for ever.'

'How do you propose to eliminate the moral rot?' Tweed enquired.

'One method, by training hundreds of selected men and women to patrol the streets on foot. To show a strong presence everywhere. At night. In daytime. Many will have to be trained in moral sense. We must change the entire moral atmosphere of this country to one of decency. New people must be appointed to control TV programmes. It will be a tremendous task but we must hammer away until we are no longer a cesspit. Still with me, sir?'

'Completely, so far. What about the proposed new system of the State Security?'

Nothing in Tweed's manner changed. Nothing suggested he was waiting at the peak of alertness for the reply.

'We went over the top on that one,' Nelson told him. 'We are toning it down. We may even drop the whole idea.'

'What about Noel?' Tweed persisted.

'Good point. He'll drop into line. If he doesn't we can get rid of him.'

Nelson stood up after checking his watch. He shook hands with Paula.

'I'm afraid I'm late for a boring meeting but one I must attend. Thank you for listening to me. We must keep in close touch.'

Then he was gone.

'Well, Paula, what did you think of that?'

'I was partly taken aback. He expressed some views which you hold strongly. But he's a politician. I just don't know.'

She had just finished speaking when the door opened and the team, led by Newman holding a large white cardboard container, flooded into the room.

'Time to go to Hammersmith,' Newman warned. 'We've had our meal. Here's yours. I'll drive and you can eat in the car. Sandwiches, a lot of fruit, a flask of coffee. OK?'

'Very,' said Tweed. 'And many thanks.'

'Well,' Newman said cheerfully, 'with a bit of luck we'll solve the last problem tonight and trap the murderer.'

'There is one other problem,' Tweed corrected him. 'Radek, the chief Slovak. I've been in touch with Interpol. Radek is wanted in four countries in Europe for assassinations. He is dangerous. He prides himself on always earning the huge fees he's paid. He's never failed yet.'

'He's probably skipped off abroad by now.'

'I think not,' Tweed told him grimly. 'And I am his target. I'm convinced he's in London, waiting for his opportunity.'

'We'll keep our eyes open, then. We're ready when you are.'

'I'm the cabbie,' Harry said. 'Cab's outside. And you'll be my passenger.'

'I expect you'll charge me a fortune,' Tweed joked to lighten the tense atmosphere building up inside his office. 'Start going down now.'

'Don't forget your dinner box,' Newman said as he left the office followed by Harry and Marler.

Under her desk Paula crossed her fingers, hoping she was right in secretly disagreeing with Tweed's decision.

As Newman left the building, entering the Crescent, he saw, parked by the kerb a few yards to his right, a motorcyclist, equipped in full gear, bent over his machine. The motorcyclist lifted his head, raised his helmet a few inches to call out.

'I do hope you will not mind my parking here while I see what is wrong with my machine. It is dangerous to park on the main route.'

'That's OK,' Newman called back. 'Hope you fix it soon.'

The motorcyclist waved a hand in acknowledgement, lowered his helmet and went on fiddling with the engine.

Newman walked to his car while Harry climbed into his cab. It was dark and cold, a typical April night. The only illumination was a street lamp midway between the entrance to the SIS entrance and the motorcyclist.

Newman settled in his car behind the wheel. His car was parked sideways on to the entrance and when he lowered his window he had a good view of Nield descending the steps carrying, as were the others, his 'tool-kit' bag stored with weapons. In his wing mirror Newman could also see the motorcyclist still toiling over his machine. Now they were only waiting for Tweed.

'. . . dangerous to park on the main route.' Surely most people would use the word 'road'? He had his Smith & Wesson in his lap as he checked it swiftly as he always did before action. Tweed appeared, carrying his dinner box, walking carefully down the steps.

Newman caught the movement out of the corner of his eye.

The motorcyclist throwing his helmet over the back of his head.

Straightening up, legs apart.

Both arms extended, both hands gripping a gun.

Aimed at Tweed.

Newman's own hand, gripping the Smith & Wesson, was pointed out of the open window. He pressed the trigger. The motorcyclist's hands dropped. He staggered for a moment, then fell over backwards, his sprawled body still on the pavement.

Tweed, a Walther in his right hand, the dinner box clutched under his left arm, ran to the body, reached it a second before Newman. Still pointing his Walther, he bent down, checked the neck pulse, then stood up.

'Dead as the proverbial dodo. Thank you, Bob. For saving my life. I was careless. I did see him, had my Walther out. Two seconds late. It's Radek.'

George had come rushing out from his guard post, holding a gun. Instinctively, Tweed glanced up. He saw Paula's anxious face peering down at them. He grinned, waved a hand cheerfully. Then he gave terse instructions to George.

'Contact Commander Buchanan. Tell him someone tried to shoot me as I left the building, but Newman, who was outside, fired first, killed the assassin. Named Radek. Don't tell Chief Inspector Hammer anything. It must be Buchanan . . .'

'Are you all right?'

It was Paula who had practically thrown herself down the staircase and was shivering. Not from the cold. He repeated to her his instructions, adding something.

'Get a sheet of canvas to cover Radek's body. Be careful not to move it. Tell Buchanan when he gets here I had to leave in an emergency on my murder investigation. You don't know where. I must go now. See you . . .'

She left George to cover the body, told him to stand in the open door's shadow to watch over the corpse. Rushing back upstairs, she called Buchanan, reached him immediately on his mobile.

'Understood, Paula. I'm in the East End. I'm leaving now.'

Paula grabbed her windcheater, gave Monica a

brief report on what had happened. She had put on the windcheater and explained quickly.

'I'm off to join the others and Newman has waited for me,' she lied.

Checking her watch, she saw she was late. She hurtled down the stairs. She paused in the empty hall to check the loaded Browning was OK, then checked the Beretta in her leg holster. Outside she paused to tell George she was on her way to join the others, then rushed to her car, dived behind the wheel. At that time of night there were no crowds in Park Crescent rushing out to see what had happened – they had all gone home. She started the engine and drove off as fast as she dared through fairly deserted streets to her destination.

Covent Garden.

39

It was after 9 p.m. when Paula parked in the street where Coral lived. The street lamps at intervals created a pleasant glow in the moonless dark. A few couples strolled slowly, stopping to chat, to engage in an embrace.

On the first floor above the entrance to the flat a window of frosted glass was illuminated by a pink lamp inside. It was almost red and Paula suppressed a shudder. With the key Coral had given her she opened the front door. There was a groan from the hinges which startled her. She went inside the wide hall which was also lit by a ceiling lamp.

She closed the door slowly and avoided it groaning a second time. She was very late and wondered whether Coral was taking a bath behind the frosted-glass window. Her rubber-soled shoes made no sound as she ascended the stairs at the end of the hall.

The door to the living room was open. Paula

glanced inside, then entered the bedroom where the door was also wide open. The double bed was a very low affair, only a few inches off the floor. The floor was wooden, covered here and there with rugs.

She moved cautiously, very quietly. In the far wall a glass door was slid half-open. She could now hear the shower going full blast. Under the cover of the noise she walked quickly to the second closet which contained Coral's coats. She didn't think Coral would open this closet unless she was going out. Which seemed unlikely – there was a bottle of champagne in an ice bucket, two glasses on a table.

She opened the closet door slowly. It stuck at first, then gave way with a loud creak. She glanced at the bathroom but the noise of the shower had muffled the noise. Beyond a glazed door she had a glimpse of Coral's figure. She looked away quickly.

She had stepped inside the roomy closet, pushing coats aside, when the shower was turned off. She heard Coral talking on a mobile, her voice soft, excited.

'Hi, there. Great to hear your voice. What was that?'

Presumably the caller had said something, then Coral replied.

'Sure I'll be ready for you then.' She giggled. 'In fact I'm ready for you now.'

Again, presumably, a response from the caller.

'No, I'm not. Don't be naughty . . .'

Another pause while the caller said something.

'Didn't say I loved you. Liked you a lot, I said.'

Another pause.

'That's all right. Get here when you can.' Another giggle. 'I'm not going anywhere. Bye.'

Paula, behind the coats, tensed. If she came into this closet . . . Unlikely with only three coats for outside wear, but still . . .

She remembered seeing a neatly folded pile of underwear on a chair in the bedroom. Also a dress had been folded carefully over the back of another chair.

The closet door looked heavy but the next thing she heard distinctly was the clink of a glass. Coral was not dressing for her visitor. Instead she was sitting down to drink champagne. Wearing nothing.

Paula wished she'd taken off her windcheater – it was warm inside the closet. She decided she dare not risk it. She might make a noise, hit one of the coats hanging from the brass rails.

She settled down to wait.

40

Seated in the passenger seat at the rear of the cab, Tweed was checking maps of the area round where the Parrot lived. He was busily changing several of the positions Newman had suggested for the watchers.

'Told 'im you'd muck about with the sentry posts, Guv,' Harry called back.

'How close are we now?' Tweed called back.

'Five minutes away at the most. Then we're outside the side street where the Parrot 'ibernates. We're in 'Ammersmith already.'

'I want you to cruise round very slowly so I can check up on the team.'

'Parrot's pad is in sight now.'

Tweed peered out. The Parrot's first-floor flat was on the corner of the main street and the side street. It had two windows on the main street side. They were a blaze of lights. He could also for a moment see the windows overlooking the side street. Again the lights behind them were on. The Parrot was at home.

He saw a decrepit-looking individual sweeping the pavement with a broom. The sweeper was tall, wearing an Australian-style hat with the brim pulled well down. He suddenly realized it was Newman.

Harry crawled so slowly past the end of the side street he was almost stationary. Tweed spotted a down-and-out leaning against a wall opposite the entrance to the Parrot's flat. A beer bottle, held by the neck, was dangling from his left hand.

'That's Pete Nield,' Harry told him.

'And Marler?' Tweed queried.

'Never spot him. Why do you think we call him the Invisible Man?'

'I want to know now where Marler is,' Tweed demanded. 'That is an order, Harry.'

'OK. He's merged in the shadows of the house next door to the entrance to the Parrot's place. No one can enter that building without Marler being within feet of them. So how far do you think an intruder – or a visitor – can get?'

'Thank you, Harry. This means the Parrot's place is sealed off. Which is what I wanted. Now cruise slowly back and forth as though looking for a customer. I'm slumped down out of sight. I'll appear if someone tries to hire you.'

'They won't. I've got the light off, showing I'm busy. I suggest you relax and eat your meal.'

Tweed slowly ate his meal, drank from his water bottle as he kept an eye on the silent streets and thought.

He was going over in detail the reports the team had given him about their interviews. Somewhere there was a clue. No one under pressure of interrogation was able to avoid making a slip at some time.

Then he had an idea. He asked Harry to lend him his mobile, then to turn on the overhead light. From his top pocket Tweed extracted the card General Macomber had tucked into it. He rang the General's phone number. A woman, sounding like a housekeeper, answered quickly.

'General Macomber's residence. Who is this?'

'Tweed of the SIS. I'm sure the General has told you I met him this morning . . .'

'Yes, sir, he did. I know who you are.'

'Then could I please have a word with the General?'

'I'm afraid not. He left early this afternoon for London. He wasn't able to say when he would be back.'

'Thank you. I may call you tomorrow. Good night.'

Tweed was disturbed. What could the General be doing now, prowling round London? Where? Why?

He had dismissed him from his mind after the explosions on Black Island which had destroyed the prisons. Had he misjudged the General?

Benton. He was a strange character. Difficult to understand. Apparently the peacemaker in the Cabal. Apparently? Yet he had revealed an evil temper when ending Nield's interview with him.

Noel. Violent in many ways. The Planner of the whole grim system. Was his mind unbalanced? If so, to what degree?

Nelson. To some extent appeared to have similar views to himself on the present state of Britain. He was controlled and clever. During his recent visit to Park Crescent had he been throwing a smokescreen in Tweed's eyes? To keep him quiet?

The Parrot. Harry was now taking the cab back to the area of her flat. All those lights in her windows began to bother Tweed. Had they been switched on automatically by timers? Was the Parrot actually inside her flat?

At the back of his mind he was being irritated by the playing of a pop song. Louis Armstrong. 'What A Wonderful World.' What a wonderful world . . .

There flashed back into his restless mind Paula's description of the scene in the room next to the Cabal's HQ. The newspaper folded to the glaring headline on Coral's desk. Her dancing, singing 'What a wonderful world'. The Parrot screaming at her to shut up . . .

'Harry!' he called out. 'Give me back the mobile.'

He pressed the numbers which would put him through to Monica at Park Crescent.

'Put Paula on the line immediately.'

'She's not here.'

'What?' Tweed went cold.

'Quite a long time ago,' Monica explained, 'she left to join you and the team. But there was something odd about what she did . . .'

'For Heaven's sake, what was odd?'

'I watched her drive off from the window. I'd expected her to turn left towards Baker Street but instead she turned right to the east. I couldn't understand why she'd—'

'Thank you. I must go now.'

Inside the cab Tweed sat stunned, fearful. But only for a few seconds. From memory he pressed numbers as fast as he could, giving each member of his team the desperately urgent order.

'Emergency! Forget the present assignment. Head as fast as you can, full speed. Emergency! Head for Covent Garden.'

41

Inside the closet at Coral's flat Paula was feeling the strain of her vigil. Coral's visitor had still not made an appearance. Paula had remained standing up and still for ages.

She dared not check her watch in case any movement caught one of the coats and dragged it along the rail. She dared not sit down for the same reason, so she remained standing like a statue. Her legs were aching from staying in the same position for so long. At least she wore sensible shoes with rubber soles, so occasionally and with great care she eased her feet inside them.

In the bedroom Coral had not helped when she had put on a CD of Louis Armstrong's 'What A Wonderful World' on repeat. By now Paula was sick of the melody, sick of Louis Armstrong, whom at one time she had liked. There was the occasional clink of a glass and Paula assumed Coral was drinking more of her champagne. The sound made Paula feel thirstier and thirstier. It was getting intolerably warm inside the closet.

The one plus for Paula was she able to sip water from the bottle she had brought with her. By choosing the times when the CD was playing she hadn't the worry that her swallowing the water would be heard.

Another problem was she felt it vital to hold the butt of her Browning in her right hand. Her hand kept getting clammy and this problem had to be dealt with. Trying to aim and fire a handgun with a slippery palm was not a good idea. So, at increasing intervals, she tucked the gun inside her windcheater pocket and with her left hand used a handkerchief to dry the palm. Every time she took this essential precaution she was worried the automatic would slip out of the pocket and crash on the wooden floor.

The endless waiting was pure hell. Paula wished she had thought to balance her aching back against the rear wall. She dared not move now. Those bloody coats. Knowing the time would have helped psychologically, knowing how long she had been inside her self-imposed cell. She had lost all track of time. She could have been in the closet for two hours, an hour, even for only half an hour. She just had no idea.

To counter the heat, to keep her mind alert, she dug her nails into the palm of her left hand. She was beginning to hate the lights which had come on, stayed on, when she had first entered the closet. Would it have been more comfortable to stand in the dark? She couldn't make up her mind. She knew now how punishing it must be in prison when inmates were thrown into solitary with lights on to keep them awake.

She had just once more wiped the palm of her right hand dry, then carefully grasped the Browning, when she heard a muffled voice in the hall.

She couldn't hear what it said, whether it was a man's or a woman's. But she heard clearly Coral's response when she stopped the CD.

'Welcome. I know it's been raining. Take off your wet stuff. Hang it on the hooks in the wall down there. No hurry. You'll find a towel on one hook so you can dry yourself.'

She could hear Coral moving about. The click-clack of spiked heels on the floor. She might have nothing else on but she was wearing shoes. Very sexy, Paula thought savagely.

Very slowly and cautiously she moved closer to the shut door of the closet. She was convinced there might not be much time to save Coral if the murderer had arrived. She might have very little time to react. On the other hand she must not appear too quickly. If she did so whoever would be coming up the stairs might, unseen, have time to dart down into the hall, through the open door, vanish in the streets. She remembered that both Viola's and Marina's front doors had been found left open.

There was the sound of heavy feet padding up the stairs. Saafeld had said something about the murderer wearing canvas shoes, large size, probably padded inside with cloth to give the impression of a killer with large feet, in case the feet stepped in blood, left marks . . .

'Like to start with a drink?'

Paula had heard Coral filling glasses with champagne. She would be waiting with a glass in each hand . . .

'Oh, my God! No! No! No!'

Coral shrieking as the padding steps reached the bedroom.

Shrieking with pure terror.

Paula pushed at the closet door. Oh, God, it was sticking. The click-clack of Coral's shoes rushing to the far side of the low bed. Paula used her shoulder, the full power of her body against the door. It flew outwards. She nearly lost her balance, recovered. She heard the thud of Coral being pushed over backwards, sprawling, the back of her head striking the wooden floor.

Paula nearly went into shock when she saw the white apparition. A long surgeon's gown, surgeon's cap over the whole head, surgeon's mask from the bridge of the nose downwards, enormous goggles, dead eyes staring through them at her, in the right hand a large meat cleaver. Lord, it had been quick. Over Coral's mouth a scarf tied as a gag. Coral's eyes open.

The white apparition saw Paula, darted quickly round the bed towards her, meat cleaver raised high to strike, to slice down the middle of her skull. She held her ground, Browning held steady, both hands gripping it. She fired once, twice. It was still coming. Maybe had body armour. She elevated the angle of the muzzle, fired three times at the head. It stopped, stood still for seconds, fell towards her, cleaver still in its hand as the body crashed to the floor.

The cleaver blade thudded an inch into the floor. People rushed into the room. Tweed first, then Buchanan and the team, headed by Newman.

Paula was still standing, the muzzle of her Browning now shuddering. Gently, Tweed removed the weapon from her and dropped it into an evidence bag.

Stooping down, he used a latex-gloved hand to wrench off the mask and the goggles in one careful movement. The head and face of Nelson Macomber stared up, lifeless, its complexion red as the setting sun after a summer's day.

Paula ran to the far side of the bed where Coral was stirring. She grabbed a dressing-gown off a chair, helped Coral to her feet, helped her to don the dressing-gown, removed the gag. Despite protests she guided her out of the bedroom, into the living room and closed the door. She handed Coral some under-wear, then outer clothes. She stopped Coral reaching for a full glass of champagne.

'Plenty of water first. Then coffee . . .'

Epilogue

Four weeks later

Tweed was in his office with Paula and Bob Newman. A general election had taken place. There was an air of relief at Park Crescent. The government had fallen, the opposition had taken over power.

'What was the main reason for their defeat?' Paula wondered.

'This.'

Tweed held up a month-old copy of the *Daily Nation*. The headline above the first of many stories by Drew Franklin was enormous.

NEWLY APPOINTED CABINET MINISTER MASS MURDERER

Below it the text described vividly the scene in Coral Flenton's flat when Paula had shot Nelson

Macomber dead as he was about to carve Coral up. This attempt was linked with the horrific killings of Viola and Marina Vander-Browne. A police report from Commander Buchanan left little doubt Nelson Macomber was the murderer of both women.

'And this,' said Tweed, holding up another copy of the paper printed two days later.

NELSON MACOMBER'S 'CABAL' PLANNED PRISON STATE, GB

The text described in detail the prisons built on Black Island with photos of the torture chamber. The smuggling in of the Tatra mountains Slovaks was also described, illustrated with a photograph of their brutal chief, Radek.

A few days later the same paper, with Drew Franklin's by-line, printed the devastating report Tweed's Director, Howard, had handed to the now resigned Prime Minister. Also there was a copy of the draft bill proposing the creation of State Security. A draft which had been destroyed.

'I do wonder,' Newman said with a cynical smile, 'how Drew obtained all this information, including photos Paula took.'

'I really have no idea,' said Tweed as he gazed at the ceiling.

'You know,' Newman went on, 'when you're

telling a whopping great lie you always gaze up at the ceiling.'

'I was watching a spider.' Tweed looked at Paula. 'How is Coral now?'

After the shooting of Nelson, Paula had taken Coral back to her flat. There she had called Professor Saafeld who, after examining the body of Nelson Macomber, had rushed to the flat.

After checking Coral carefully he had suggested moving her to a private clinic where she could stay until she had recovered.

'Bloody hell! No clinic, thank you,' Coral had burst out.

'She could stay here with me,' Paula suggested firmly. 'I can watch over her.'

'Might be a much better idea,' Saafeld had agreed. 'She is only in a mild state of shock. The young can recover quickly from almost anything. I leave her in your safe hands, Paula.'

As if on cue, as Paula recalled this scene, Coral walked into the office with a springy step. She wore a new close-fitting white jumper and a white skirt. The outfit emphasized her blaze of red hair. She was smiling nervously as she looked at Tweed.

'Is it all right if I go on a short holiday with Pete Nield? He's such a nice man and wants to take me to a fabulous hotel by the sea in Dorset.'

'He's practically been living at my flat,' Paula said rily.

'He can take a fortnight off,' Tweed told her.

Coral rushed across the room, talking as she 1oved, threw her arms round Paula. 'You've been a eal brick, looking after me. I do want us to keep in ouch.'

'A long dinner, then, when you get back. My bet is 'ete is waiting downstairs for you in the visitors' oom.'

'Yes, he is. But before I do . . .'

She rushed at Tweed, hugged him so hard he was lmost out of breath. She then administered the same reatment to Newman, waved a hand and was gone.

'I did work it out eventually,' Tweed said to Paula, nking his hands behind his neck. 'The newspaper on 2oral's desk announcing Nelson's promotion, Coral .ancing with delight. That killer had charm and she'd allen for him, so she was the next victim, not the 'arrot.'

'Which I'd worked out earlier.' Paula frowned. You took your time getting to me.'

'I know. I was wrong, you were right. I'm so sorry. n future you tell me when I slip up. Don't forget.'

'I won't. You'll get sick of me reminding you.'

Don't miss these other

Colin Forbes titles!

**POCKET
BOOKS**

The Cell

COLIN FORBES

Is Al-Qa'eda about to attack London? Tweed,
reverting to his one-time role as shrewd detective,
is convinced of this. Aided by Paula Grey and Bob
Newman, he skillfully eludes Government security
services who believe that he is wrong.

The village of Carpford, hidden high in the North
Downs, catches Tweed's attention. With its strange
assortment of inhabitants – Victor Warner,
arrogant Minister of Security; fascinating but
duplicitous Eva Brand; fanatical preacher – could it
be a staging post for the terrorists? Key informants
start to disappear overnight.

Time has run out. This Tweed does know. But
what is the target and when will the attack be
launched? And *where*?

Could it happen here as it did in America?

ISBN 0 7434 6138 X
PRICE £6.99

POCKET
BOOKS

The Vorpal Blade
COLIN FORBES

*An investigation into a number of horrific and
apparently disconnected murders sweeps Tweed
across the world.*

The Vorpal Blade advances into gripping new
territory. Tweed has reverted to his one-time role
of Homicide Superintendent at the Yard. He also
retains his position as Deputy Director of the SIS.
Paula Grey and Bob Newman still assist him.

Tweed has suspicions about the strange Arbogast
banking family. Roman, the bank's owner; his
niece, the brilliant Marienetta; his daughter, the
volatile Sophie. Wherever they go, the American
Vice President follows. Why?

Tweed realizes enormous power lies behind the
five murders. But it is shrewd, stubborn Paula
Grey, risking her life, who eventually tracks down
the wielder of the blade. By herself, underground
in a remote mountainous zone.

ISBN 0 7434 4035 8
PRICE £6.99

**POCKET
BOOKS**

No Mercy
COLIN FORBES

A man is found by Chief Superintendent Buchanan
sitting on the steps of Whitehall. The man has apparently lost his memory. He utters only three words:
I witnessed murder . . . Buchanan calls him Michael,
hands him over to a reluctant Tweed, ex-Scotland Yard
star detective, now Deputy Director of the SIS. Events
lead Tweed with his assistant, Paula Grey, to desolate
Dartmoor, accompanied by Michael. There they
discover two skeletons. Later, two more – one in
London, the fourth on a Sussex canal boat.

The wealthy Volkanian family, from Armenia, have a
mansion on Dartmoor. Are they involved? Key
characters are Lucinda Voyles and Anne Barton. There is
a new development. A strange freighter, cargo holds
empty, is spotted heading from the Mediterranean
towards the Cornish coast. Tweed suspects the vessel is
linked to the four horrific murders.

The relentless pace of Tweed's investigation accelerates.
Can he break the case before a sinister deadline? He
fights ruthlessly to do so – in a riveting double climax.

ISBN 0-7434-9001-0
PRICE £6.99

**POCKET
BOOKS**

This book and other **Pocket** titles are available from your local bookshop
or can be ordered direct from the publisher.

Please send cheque or postal order for the value
of the book, **free postage and packing within
the UK**, to: SIMON & SCHUSTER CASH SALES
PO Box 29, Douglas, Isle of Man, IM99 1BQ
Tel: 01624 677237, Fax 01624 670923
bookshop@enterprise.net
www.bookpost.co.uk

Please allow 14 days for delivery. Prices and availability subject
to change without notice.